ML RODRIGUEZ

Leap of Faith

Book One - La Flor Series

Leap of Faith © Copyright 2015 by ML Rodriguez
First ebook edition: 26 May 2015

ISBN-13: 978-1511957656
ISBN-10: 1511957654

For mature readers (18 and older).

Cover Design by: Pink Inks Designs
https://www.facebook.com/PinkInkDesignsbyCassy
Edited by: Champagne Book Editing
www.champagne-editing.com
Formatted by: Integrity Formatting
https://www.facebook.com/IntegrityFormatting

Dedication

To my little monsters
Your patience and support made this dream a reality.
I love you always and forever with all my heart.

Prologue

A Fortune Told

Jake (March 2004)

I can't believe I let myself get talked into this. If any of my buddies find out I'm getting my "fortune" told, they'll have a field day giving me shit. But, really, what am I to say when my wife gives me her big, beautiful, chocolate puppy eyes and her pouty lips?

She gets me every time, but when have I ever denied her anything? She makes my world whole—she and Rylee are the most important and precious people in my life and I'll do anything they ask, even something as stupid as sitting my ass in this hard-as-hell chair in this creepy tent. *This* is what happens when you bring your family to a carnival and your girls see a fortune-telling tent—your ass goes inside and you wait for a charlatan to give you the typical "you'll find love, money, and live forever" fortune.

Shit, everyone knows these things are fake. But whatever Faith wants, my baby gets.

So here I am, sitting across from a "psychic" woman dressed to the nines in gypsy clothes, including a red bandana and a crapload of bangle-thingies on her wrists that make noise every time she moves. Her face has so much make-up caked on, she looks scary but yet so real.

Gitana, she tells me is her name, circles her ring-loaded fingers around her crystal ball, making humming sounds. I sit back and wait for her to spout her bullshit.

Suddenly, she stops and her eyes go wide. She looks up at me and swallows.

My smirk is wiped off when her eyes start glistening.

What the fuck?

"You are a good man, a father, and a husband," Gitana says. "You will know much joy but you will also know much sadness. Unfortunately, you will find death."

At this, my back goes straight. Is she for real?

"What the hell?! Aren't you supposed to tell me some crappy happy-ending fortune?" I ask her chuckling nervously.

"With many I do but you—with you I cannot. The spirits show me your future," she tells me seriously. "A future that cannot be ignored. Do you wish for me to continue?" I nod reluctantly and she continues. "You will face death and win only once. A ghost will help you, a ghost with purple eyes, who's disillusioned with a broken trust. When you meet him, your time on this Earth will be numbered, and you must prepare for the sadness that is to come. You will trust him with your life, your dreams, and your treasures; they will become his to watch over and love. You will die but your spirit will remain on this Earth to help your loved ones—you will become a guardian."

She tells me all of this with tears running down her face, smearing her make-up, and a trembling voice.

"What the fuck?!" I yell at her. "Are you telling me I'm gonna die? That I'm gonna leave my wife and my child alone?"

I want to choke the life out of this fake bitch. What the fuck is she trying to pull?

"I am telling you your fortune," she says with pity in her eyes. "You are a good man and are needed for a higher power than here. You are to be a guardian, a protector of man. It is an honor that comes with much sacrifice."

"No! This is fuckin' bullshit!" I yell at her and rise, knocking my chair over and not caring. I want to see my so-called future, so I reach for the crystal ball.

"No!" She yells but is too slow to stop me.

As my hands touch the crystal ball, a bright light explodes and I feel a shock go through my body. A flood of images runs through my mind, taking my breath away, and I fall to my knees.

I'm on the ground for several minutes before I shake my head to clear it and look up at Gitana, but I don't see her. She's gone and I'm alone. I stand and scan the small tent. She's just disappeared . . . into thin air. As I turn in a slow circle, I see the crystal ball shattered, pieces scattered throughout the tent.

What the hell just happened? What were those images? Were they really my future? But, they can't be, I tell myself as I right my chair and sit with my head in my hands. Those images can't be my future—it has to be all this mystical crap that's fucking with my head.

After several minutes, I get to my feet and turn to walk out, spooked out of my ever-loving mind. Before leaving, I feel a gust of wind against my face and I hear the word, "Guardian," eerily whispered, sending chills down my spine. I make a dash to the exit and try to forget the creepy-as-fuck things I saw and heard in there. As I step outside I look around and find one of my treasures.

"Hey, baby," I hear Faith say, as she comes and gives me a kiss. "Everything okay, love?"

I nod. I bring her body flush with mine and I kiss her like my life depends on it. "I love you always and forever, *mi tesoro*. You and Rylee are my world," I tell her, looking into her eyes. "Let's get out of here." I put my arm around her and take Rylee's hand in mine. Together we walk away from the tent.

When Rylee asks, I tell her the Gypsy woman said I'd live a long life filled with riches and love. I laugh and tell her I didn't expect to hear otherwise.

Except, that's not what the old lady told me.

That day, my life changed—the old Gypsy was right. Like she predicted, years later I met a ghost with purple eyes. The one I was to give my world and treasures to, to watch over and love, to be there because, like that old woman said, I would face death once and win, but the second time . . .

The second time, I would face death.

I would die.

Part One

the Memories

Chapter 1

Faith (2 May 2008)

"Why, Lord? Why would you do this to us? How could you let this happen?" I silently scream to God.

How can this be real? I need to wake up. If I pinch myself, maybe I'll awaken and see this is just a dream, a horrible nightmare, I think to myself as silent tears stream down my face. I know I shouldn't cry. Crying is showing a weakness that I can't afford to show now; everyone's eyes are on me.

Everything has changed. In the blink of an eye, my world unraveled and my dreams shattered. Now, I have to change, learn how to live my life without him. I have to be strong, but how can I when I'm standing here in front of my husband? My husband, the man I swore to love with all my heart through good times and bad times, through sickness and in health, forever.

He was supposed to be my forever.

But now he's gone, and I'm laying him here to rest.

As I stand here surrounded by family and friends, I look back at our time together. The day I met him, I was home from college on winter break and my parents were hosting a Christmas party for my father's squadron. That's when I saw him. He was one of my Daddy's soldiers.

❦

Christmas 2000

I notice him the moment I come down the stairs. He's standing with a group of guys, they're laughing and enjoying their beer. I don't know what they're talking about, but I see him making all sorts of wild gestures and funny faces.

In that moment, I feel an undeniable pull to him, like my heart is reaching out to him. It must be the way the others treat him—with respect, admiration, and friendship. In our world, I know those aren't easily given or earned and that alone makes him special. Yet, there's something else about him that calls me. Unable to look away, I continue to watch him and I smile.

He's not afraid of being silly and doesn't seem worried of what others might think of him—he knows how to have fun. I'm fascinated by him and can't turn away, so I look my fill. He must feel the weight of my stare because he starts looking around the room. Then, his eyes land on me and they widen in shock.

Everything disappears except the two of us.

As our eyes meet, I feel a jolt of electricity, like lightning striking my body, going right through me. He's the handsomest man I've ever seen. I know he's the one for me from that instant—he's my Prince Charming. It's inexplicable and crazy, but I know he's supposed to be mine. Before it was a feeling, now it's a certainty. I've never believed in the so called "love at first sight," until now.

At seventeen, I've found my soul mate.

My eyes are only for him, and then I see her. A little girl, about four or five, appear from behind him and takes his hand. He looks down at her and smiles. He picks her up, kisses her, and hugs her. The resemblance is uncanny—she's his daughter. I feel a huge disappointment. My eyes close and I feel my heart break. He's married. My eyes fill with tears and I reluctantly force myself to turn and walk away.

Hours later, I help my mother cut the cake. His precious little girl comes to the table and asks for a slice. I look at her and she looks back at me, studying me curiously. Her eyes are serious and beautiful. Oh my . . . she looks like a porcelain doll, her hair curled and cascading down her back. She's in a pretty pink dress with tights and cowboy boots. She's a perfect little princess with vivid green eyes. With her beautiful light tan skin and caramel-colored hair, I can tell she's going to be a beauty when she grows up.

Wow!

She smiles and my heart skips. Her smile is beautiful and I feel *myself melting for her.*

"Hi, my name is Rylee. What's your name?" she asks me. "You look like a princess and my daddy can't stop looking at you. He thinks you're beautiful. That's what I heard him tell his friends."

I gasp. Why would he say that in front of his daughter? I refuse to be rude to her, so I answer her question.

"My name's Faith and I think you're the cutest little girl I've ever laid eyes on," I tell her as I hand her a slice.

"Can you give me another piece but make that the biggest piece possible, please?" she asks.

I smile and cut another piece—making it "the biggest piece possible" and hand it to her. Her smiles gets even bigger and she thanks me, turns, and carefully walks back to her father.

When I glance up from watching her, a smile on my face, and look across the room, I see him again. His eyes are on me and he's smiling. All I can think is—why does he have to be married? Sometimes, life really stinks.

No matter how hard I try, I can't leave it alone. Since he's married, I know there can't be anything between us, but I can't stop thinking about him. I need to know more. I'm curious and I feel horrible for wanting him, but something in me just won't let it go.

So, I go where almost every woman goes for information—to my mother. I casually ask her about him, using the pretext that his daughter is adorable, which she truly is. My mother sees nothing amiss, so she tells me everything she knows—knowing I'm not one for gossip and won't go around repeating.

Rylee, his daughter, is about five years old, going on thirty. She's mature for her age and she loves soccer. "Maybe you can volunteer to coach her for a bit this winter during your break," my mother suggests, since I live and breathe soccer. I intend to play professionally after college. Well, I dream of playing in the Women's World Cup one day and am thinking of trying out for the 2003 team. Over the years, I convinced my parents to send me to every soccer camp available and I played club soccer for many years. I currently play college ball, and I've given up weekends and time with family and friends in order to practice and better my skills. I've been tired, sore, and I've bled and sweated for my love of the game. I understand the importance of starting young, so I agree and tell her I'll speak to Daddy and have him pass on the offer.

She continues on about Rylee and her father.

He's about five years and a few months older than me, putting him at twenty-three. He commissioned through Officer Candidate School after graduating college and putting himself through school and providing for his daughter by being in the Reserves. He's worked hard to be both mother and father, a soldier, and full-time student. It was difficult at times, but he did it with the help of his family. Now, he's completing Infantry Basic Officer Leadership Course (IBOLC) before heading out to his next duty station.

Rylee's mother left them, telling him she wasn't ready to be a mother at eighteen, and hasn't had anything to do with them since then. She left him to raise Rylee alone. He joined the military to make sure his daughter was protected and make his own way. He's a single father doing his best to raise his little girl.

It was a heartbreaking and inspiring story, but the only thing I could think was, "He's not married!"

Feeling empowered by this information, I decide to introduce myself. I take a deep breath and approach him. He's standing by the food table, facing away from me. I go up to him, thanking God he's by himself.

I reach him, tap his shoulder to get his attention, and inform him, "You're gonna think I'm crazy but I just want to let you know that I plan to marry you one day. We have to get to know each other, but I know you and me, we're meant to be together—forever."

I see his shock. He doesn't even know my name and here I am claiming him. He stands there looking at me, but I don't waver. He's going to be mine. Then, he smiles. His eyes turn tender and I want to throw myself at him and kiss him. That look he gives me and his smile make me feel all gooey inside.

"You know your father's gonna go crazy, right? I'm one of his soldiers and his princess is claiming me. I'm older than you and a single father," he tells me. "Are you willing to take that on?"

I meet his eyes, hoping he sees my determination.

"You're the handsomest man I've ever seen. You've taken it upon yourself to raise your little girl. She adores you, and she informed me you said I was beautiful. Those men over there," I point to the group of guys he was speaking to earlier, *"offer you their friendship and at the same time, they look at you for leadership and they respect you. Knowing the world we live in, I know that isn't easily given or offered, it has to be earned and it speaks highly of the person you are. When I first saw you, I felt a jolt go through my body. I know you're meant to be mine and I'm meant to be yours. I may be young, but I know what I feel for you is strong and I can't go against that. It's crazy and impossible but I know it's real and meant to be. I want to be with you forever."*

❧

We spent the rest of that day and the following weeks getting to know each other. I helped Rylee with soccer, running easy drills with her and sometimes pushing her a bit more than normal for a five-year-old, but she was that good and loved it.

But, I kept a secret.

I didn't tell him my age that night, nor did I tell him the times I met him and Rylee for breakfast, lunch, or soccer practice. It wasn't until my parents' New Year's celebration that he discovered the truth. To say he was pissed is putting it mildly. He was livid.

I smile at the memory.

I don't think I ever remembered Jake being so angry before.

It was my parents' New Year's celebration and Daddy had just bragged to his friends that all I needed was one more semester and I'd be a college graduate at eighteen.

Unfortunately, Jake happened to overhear this before I could tell him, and he was not happy. I don't know how, but he somehow managed to get me out of the house without my parents or friends noticing.

❧

Leap of Faith

New Year's 2001

*H*ow the hell could you keep this from me, Faith? You're in college at seventeen, for God's sake. Seventeen! How's that even possible? Your father's gonna fuckin' kill me," he mutters as he paces back and forth on my parents' balcony.

He finally stops and looks at me. He sees me calm and collected. I don't know how, but I know everything is going to be okay, so I'm not worried. I just want him to listen to me. He closes his eyes, counts to ten, and then opens them and waits for me to say something.

I calmly start talking to him.

"My birthday is in one month, and I'll be eighteen. I didn't tell you because I knew you'd turn away from me, no matter the feelings between us. You would've shut the door on our relationship—we never would've started. You thought I was older and I let you. I may be seventeen, but I don't act like it. I know what I want to do with my life and I have plans. Meeting you has changed some of those plans, but I wouldn't have it any other way." I pause to take a breath and continue. "I'm sorry. I'm sorry for not telling you, but I'm not sorry we started us. I love you and I know you love me. What we have is true and I'm willing to stand with you. And, I love your daughter, Jake. I know the two of you come together as a deal. I'm willing to brave my father's wrath, my family to be with you. Is that not telling you enough?"

He looks at me for a long while.

"I love you too, Faith. I've fallen for you hard. You're here for me and for Rylee—you show us you care, and that means the world to us." He takes me into his arms. "When I first saw you, you captivated me. You looked like one of Rylee's Disney princesses—so beautiful, so untouchable. When you came to me and claimed me, you blew my fuckin' mind out of the water because I never thought I had a chance with you. This beautiful creature wants to be mine, I thought to myself. I'm one lucky bastard."

❧

A few days later, I returned to school to finish my last semester of college. We kept in touch through Facebook and Skype at every opportunity. The distance was hard. His schedule was crazy busy and mine wasn't any better, but somehow we made it work.

I flew back to my parents' home for spring break. I was finally eighteen. Jake told me he was going to speak to my father and there was nothing I could say to stop him. He hated having to hide our relationship, with only Julia, my best friend and roommate, knowing.

The day Jake decided to speak with my father, I was a nervous wreck. My father was going to *explode*. We hadn't done anything wrong—all we did was get to know each other. However, my father wasn't going to care about that. All he would see would be Jake, a single father and one of his soldiers, a person who would constantly have to put his life on the line to protect our country. A person like my father, always gone and in danger, the kind of person my father never wanted me to marry. The military is a hard life; you're constantly moving, you go months without seeing each other, and it's stressful and sometimes lonely.

My father always said I'd graduate college, accomplish my dreams, and marry an ordinary man when I turned thirty. Ha, there was no way the last one would happen now. Daddy was going to Flip. The. Freak. Out.

When he got Jake's call requesting a meeting, my father was under the impression Jake needed to speak with him about work. He didn't have a clue about our feelings for each other. He was going to be blindsided.

Jake finally arrived to my parents' home and greeted my mother. Then, he bravely walked into my father's office. The door closed and moments later, we could clearly hear my father through the door.

~∞~

Spring Break 2001

"WHAT THE FUCK DID YOU JUST SAY TO ME, LIEUTENANT?! Are you fuckin' kidding me?" he yells. "Do you seriously expect me to give you my blessing to date my daughter? MY BABY GIRL. You're out of your goddamn mind if you think I will. She's barely eighteen years old and you're a twenty-

three year old single father! She has her whole life ahead of her and you expect me to allow her to be with you. I'll fuckin' ruin your career if you don't leave her alone. You fuckin' hear me!"

I can't hear Jake's response. Different scenarios are running through my mind; mainly, my father beating the crap out of Jake. Daddy may be older but he's fit and can fight with the best of them.

I'm terrified.

For a moment, I'm afraid Jake will leave me. He does have a daughter to raise and provide for, and he's only known me a short time. I shake my head. I can't allow myself to think like that; I need to have faith in our feelings and our connection. I think of our time together and I know he won't let me go.

My mother runs toward the office to see why my father is yelling. She finds me outside the door.

"Oh, honey, what have you done?" she asks me in a voice only a mother can use with her child.

"I love him, Momma. I know I'm young and this isn't what you and Daddy wanted for me, but I love him. I won't give him up," I vow to her.

She closes her eyes and takes a deep breath. Then, she hugs me saying, "I'd hoped the look you two shared during the Christmas party was a passing thing." She notices the surprise on my face. "You didn't think I saw that, huh? I see everything, darlin'. When will you and your brothers realize that? It's my mommy magic— when I had you children, I gained mommy superpowers. I just didn't expect you to fall in love. Come, darlin', let's go make sure your father doesn't kill my future son-in-law."

She turns me toward the door and takes us inside. Daddy and Jake are standing facing each other, like in those old Western movies. My father's face is red and he's breathing hard, his nostrils flared. Jake is holding his own, refusing to be intimidated by my father, his commander.

"I won't let her go, sir. I love her and I promise to take care of her," I hear Jake tell Daddy.

My mother goes to my father's side like she always does, standing with him. She touches his shoulder and tells him to calm down. I go to Jake and stand next to him. My father notices and doesn't like it one bit; this is the first time I don't go to him first. I go to Jake, just like my Momma goes to my father. As soon as he sees this and realizes the significance, he takes a long, defeated breath.

"Is this what you want, Faith?" he asks. "Are you willing to give us up to go with him? To put your dreams on hold so you can follow him around? You know this life isn't easy. The only reason we survived as a family is because your mother held us together. She made sure you kids were raised right and she put me in my place when I got out of hand. Are you willing to take that on at your age? To raise another woman's child as your own?"

My father is right, do I want to take on the responsibility of a child at such a young age, am I ready? Am I ready to put all my plans aside to follow Jake and build a home together? Can I do all this at my age?

In a matter of seconds, I make a decision that will affect the rest of my life.

Yes. The answer is yes, because I love him and I love Rylee. There is a reason everything is falling in place the way it is—everything is happening at a whirlwind and it's inexplicable, but I can't go against my feelings and my instincts. I need them and they need me. Things might not always be easy, but for them, I'm willing to take everything on and make us a strong and happy family because they deserve it.

I take a deep breath and nod. "I love him, Daddy. He's a wonderful man and he makes me happy. I know Rylee and Jake come as a package, and I'll do everything in my power to make us a family. I love him and I love that little girl. Things aren't always going to be perfect and my plans will have to change, but I'm not giving up, Daddy. I know we're supposed to be together."

He closes his eyes, turns to my mother, and hugs her.

"You know this isn't what I wanted for you, right? I never wanted you to live this life—going days, weeks, and months without seeing your husband, practically being a single parent, and carrying everything on your shoulders. I wanted you to marry a man with a nine to five job, a man who could be at home at reasonable hours so you could have your career without stressing about who'd watch the *kids or pick them up. This life we live isn't easy, Pumpkin," he tells me swallowing hard, as if holding back tears. "I felt I put your mother through enough, I didn't want that for you."*

"I know Daddy, but I love him. I can't turn away from him and Rylee because our life might be hard. I learned from you and Momma—I know I can do this."

He takes a deep breath and then he says to me in his commander's voice, "You'll finish your degree first—that's an order. Jake, you hurt my little girl and I'll fuckin' kill you—I'll kill you, you hear?"

At his words I feel a huge weight lifted from my shoulders. Jake and I turn to each other and hug. We've surpassed our first obstacle; we have my father's blessing.

～✕✕◞

Four months later, Jake gets orders to Germany. Refusing to leave me behind, we marry a week later at the Justice of the Peace. It wasn't my dream wedding, but we couldn't bear to be parted. We wanted to belong to each other legally and it was the only way the military would allow me to join him.

That day, we promised to love each other through good times and bad, in sickness and in health, until death do us part.

On 21 July 2001, I become the happiest woman in the world—I become Mrs. Jacob Hunter Duval II.

We had forever to live as husband and wife. From then on, it was Jake, Rylee, and me against the world.

The years passed. Things weren't always easy; between finishing my degree, deployments and his demanding work schedule, Rylee's schedule, and my career, time was precious for us. Yes, I accomplished my dream of playing in the World Cup—it wasn't easy and at times, I wanted to give up, but with hard work, determination, and Jake's undying support it happened. I played on the 2003 and 2007 team and represented my country from 2002–2008. I was on top of the world—I had the career I always dreamed of. Even now, I'll never forget the first time I stepped onto that field.

～✕✕◞

21 September 2003

I take deep steady breaths. In and out. In and out.

This is it. This is what I've been working for all my life.

Finally, I've made it here. Last year, I made my first appearance at the North American Cup but now . . . this is the World Cup.

My dream.

I bring my cleated right foot up to the bench—the ritual begins. I'm careful not to spill my bag of skittles, my good luck charm for as long as I can remember, and I tie my cleat nice and tight. Then, the other, and I go through my routine of finishing my bag of skittles, pulling my socks up tight, and then folding them over just right— first the right and then the left. I stand up, do the Sign of the Cross, and send a prayer up above. Finally, I tighten my ponytail and make sure my headband is secure. Everything has to be done in a precise order—always. I go through all of our plays in my mind and try to calm myself. I have butterflies in my stomach, I'm nervous and excited, but in a good way.

Finally, I'm here.

All the time away from Jake and Rylee—the exhaustion, sweat, blood, and the sore muscles—everything has been worth it because today, my family gets to see me out there on the field. Today, they get to see me make my World Cup debut on my home soil.

"You ready, chica*?" I hear from my right. I turn and see Julia.*

"Heck, yeah!" I reply excitedly. "I'm more than ready. It's almost time, Julia. Pretty soon, we'll be out on that field playing the game we love so much. We've done it."

"Damn right we have, Faith. This is our time, babe. It's our time to shine."

We follow our teammates and make our way through the tunnel leading into the stadium, we do this together like we've done so many things over the years. Jake is my happily-ever-after, but Julia is my best friend—she's taken care of me and I've held her hand when she's needed me.

We hear the cheering of the crowd and revere in the feeling it invokes. The adrenaline starts pumping through our veins as we step out onto the field and we look around. The stadium is full of fans, most are dressed in red, white, and blue but there are other colors mixed in. Coach has us warm up for several minutes and then we're called to the sidelines.

It's game time.

We line up, place our right hand over our hearts, and the other on our teammate's left shoulder. As the singer starts to sing the National Anthem and I proudly sing along with her giving it my all, I look up into the crowd and I find Jake. He looks at me and he smiles proudly.

I'm here on the field with Julia but he's supported me the whole way here. We made it.

∽∝∾

Life was perfect for us. Our family was beautiful, happy, prospering, and we were considering expanding the Duval family by one more. Our dreams were coming true and we had forever.

But life always has a way of changing even the best-laid plans. Life decided she had other plans for us, and in the blink of an eye, our perfect world unraveled.

Tragedy struck.

Our "forever" lasted six years, nine months, and five days. On 26 April 2008, I got that dreaded knock on my door that changed my life and shattered my dreams. That day, I lost Jake and a piece of my heart.

At age twenty-five, I was left a widow with a daughter to raise.

A week later, we flew across the ocean to bury my husband in Texas.

Two weeks later, I started vomiting.

About a week after that, I discovered I was pregnant.

Chapter 2

Fall 2012-Grangersville, Texas

"**R**ylee! Hurry up or you'll be late for your first day of school!" I yell to my daughter. "If you don't get down here in the next five minutes, I'm hauling your butt myself. How will you like having your Momma takin' you to school on your first day?"

Having a teenage daughter is hard work. I don't know how I made it to adulthood without my momma killing me. Rylee—that girl is just like me. She may not be my daughter by blood, but she's my daughter in every other sense. Like now, she's taking her sweet ol' time getting dressed. Everything has to coordinate from the top of her pretty head to her toes.

I guess my momma and I are to blame. Momma taught me to always be presentable and never leave the house looking a disaster. When we dress nicely, we feel good about ourselves, and the way we look reflects on our husbands. I followed that mentality into my marriage with Jake and I made sure to never embarrass my husband with my appearance. Don't get me wrong—Jake thought I was the most beautiful woman in the world, even when I looked like crap and was sick as a dog. But, appearances do count in the world and my momma wanted me to be prepared.

Even now, I still keep in shape. Partly for work but even then, I enjoy a long run and a weight session every now and then. Rylee and even Skylar are the same way—I guess the tradition continues with my girls.

"I'm coming, Momma. It's my first day and I'm the new girl. Like you say, perfection takes time and effort. I can't go to school looking like a dork. The horror it'd be if my outfit doesn't match," I hear coming from Rylee's room upstairs.

Yup, she's my daughter alright.

"*I'm* ready, Momma," Skylar says from the breakfast table where she's munching down on a bowl of Apple Jacks. How that little girl prefers Apple Jacks to Lucky Charms, or any of the other more sugar-infused cereals, still baffles me, but at least she's happy and semi-healthy. "Rylee takes *forever* to get ready, Momma. *I* never take that long."

I laugh to myself as I hear these words from my little princess's mouth. This little darlin' is well on her way to emulating her big sister and her momma. At the age of two, she started dressing herself and refused to wear clothes she didn't pick out; she has her own sense of style. Skylar manages to mix polka-dots and stripes, layers her clothes, loves her sparkle and always wears pink in some form or another. She's my mini-fashionista who's constantly going through Rylee's and my closets, and she loves wearing our shoes. Ha! The only reason she's ready on time today is because I made her pick out her clothes last night.

It's moments like these that I miss Jake the most; moments that are sweeter shared with your other half—your partner, your lover. Today, both of our girls are heading to their first day of school.

Rylee's starting her senior year at a new school; it surprised me she didn't throw a fit when she discovered we were moving to be closer to my work, and because that's what Jake always wished. Knowing college scouts would find her might've played a huge part in evading an epic melt-down. Julia was also offered a teaching and coaching position at this new school, and Rylee wasn't losing one of her long-time coaches. But most of all, I think she needed a change. There were too many memories at the old place for her—she's lost enough and I think she really needed to get away. Whatever the reason, I'm grateful I didn't have a fight on my hands and a massive dose of teenage drama.

Skylar, our precious little girl whom Jake never got to meet, is headed to her first day of Pre-Kindergarten. Oh my goodness, Pre-K! Where has the time gone? I still remember the weeks following Jake's funeral. I thought I'd caught the flu in the middle of spring; not only was I grieving the loss of my husband and helping Rylee through her loss, but I was also puking my guts out. Sounds gross, but it's true. I was miserable and couldn't hold anything down. My mother finally convinced me to see a doctor. Let's just say that doctor's visit was one for the record book.

∽⬡⬡

22 May 2008

I'm sitting in the examination room after briefly speaking with the nurse and doctor about my symptoms. I had to pee in a cup even though I told them I wasn't pregnant because my husband wasn't here, but they told me it was "just in case." I'm praying I don't have some mutated strain of the flu when Dr. Brown steps into the room.

"Well, Mrs. Duval, I have some good news for you," she says smiling. "You don't have the flu or anything contagious. On the contrary—congratulations, you're pregnant."

My heart stops and I just look at her for several moments, before recovering my voice.

"That's not possible," I reply. "It can't be true. My husband's gone. He's dead."

She stands there completely speechless. That happens a lot when people find out; they don't know how to behave or what to say.

"I'm sorry for your loss," she responds, finally composing herself. "With all due respect, how long has your husband been gone?"

"Jake has been gone almost a month," I answer, still struggling with the reality that I'll never see my husband again. Sometimes it's easier to tell myself he's on deployment instead of facing the harsh truth.

"It's still possible. You're about six weeks pregnant according to your last menstrual cycle," she says.

We conceived right before his death—I do the math as tears begin to fall.

∽⬡⬡

Coming back to the present, I remember how shocked Rylee, our parents, and all of our friends were. I was so angry that Jake would never get to meet our baby, but I was also grateful that God was blessing me with a miracle that Jake and I created. I was going to have another piece of Jake in my life.

Rylee and I managed to make it through our move back to Texas, my pregnancy, and helping Gunner keep The Phoenix Corporation—his and Jake's recently started company—afloat. I took over Jake's dream and made sure it didn't die. I wanted his company to succeed as an honor to him. As a result, I had to change and put aside my career, but it was worth it. I went back to school to earn my MBA so that I could help run the company, and I acquired some other skills along the way.

Today, Phoenix has made a name for itself and is well respected. All of our sacrifices haven't been in vain. It hasn't been easy, we've had some tough times, but we're blessed to have a wonderful support system in our family and friends. Our kids have turned out pretty normal; they know they're loved, they're happy, involved in extracurricular activities, and well provided for. Overall, I think I've done a good job. I only wish that Jake could be here to share these precious and unforgettable moments with me. I think about him every day and miss him so much. I've learned to live without him, but I've never stopped loving him.

I finally hear Rylee run down the stairs, bringing me out of my thoughts.

"Do we have any granola bars?" she asks hurriedly. "I'm gonna be late if I sit and eat breakfast."

"Yes, there're some in the pantry. Hurry, unless you want Mommy to take you to school," I tease.

She gives me a horrified look, grabs a granola bar, throws me a goodbye kiss, and runs out the door. But not before yelling over her shoulder at us. "Good luck, Peanut! I love y'all always and forever."

I watch her climb into the used midnight-blue Jeep Wrangler I bought for her sixteenth birthday and drive away. I turn to Skylar. "Alright, kiddo, let's get you to school."

Chapter 3

Arriving to the elementary school is easy, but finding a parking spot, not so much. Everyone, and I mean *everyone,* decided to bring their kid to school on the first day, causing a massive traffic jam and a shortage of parking spots. I drive around for a few minutes until I see a spot come available and rush to beat all the other parents.

I won't give this parking spot up! Especially since it's located in the parking lot of the school and I don't have to walk a mile to take Skylar to class. With some amazing driving skills, I make it and slide right in.

Yes—I got it! I do a small victory dance in my seat.

"You're so silly, Momma," I hear from Skylar.

"I know, Peanut. Don't ever be afraid to dance and be silly," I tell her. "But you still love me, right?"

"I do, Momma," she assures me. "Very much."

I park and walk around to Skylar's side to open the child-proof locked door and get my little girl out. She takes a deep breath and looks up at me. She looks so adorable in her little white tank top with a pink sparkly flower in the center, her color-block pink and purple flared skort, and her pink-sequined Sperry's. Her long brown hair is divided into two pigtails with matching pink bows. She's my little princess—the fashionista.

"I'm nervous, Momma," she tells me. "I'm a little bit scared. Do you think my teacher is gonna be nice?"

"It's okay to be nervous and scared, Skylar, this is a whole new experience. Just don't let those feelings overtake you. Take a couple more deep breaths and let's go start your new adventure," I reply.

I really hope her teacher is nice.

She grabs her brand-new Tangled backpack from the Jeep, steps aside so I can close the door, and waits for me. As I'm closing the door, I hear her squeal.

"Rylee! You're here!"

I turn and see my eldest waiting next to our black Cherokee SRT. "What's going on, Rylee? Is everything okay? What are you doing here?" I ask. Last I remember, she was rushing out of the house and heading to school.

"It's the peanut's first day of school. There's no way I'm missing that. Daddy can't be here but I can. I made this at the last minute, so don't laugh." She gives Skylar a sign. "Hold it up and get together with Momma. Smile for the camera."

She takes the picture and then switches places with me. After all the pictures are taken and we take a selfie of the three of us together, we each grab ahold of Skylar's hands and march towards the school.

We arrive to the classroom where Skylar is assigned and meet her teacher. Skylar and Rylee head toward the backpack hooks and cubbies while I speak with Skylar's new teacher, Ms. Jones. She explains the rules of the classroom and hands me several papers that need to be filled out, signed, and returned the following day, since we were unable to attend the meet-the-teacher conference held earlier in the month. I ask her about lunch and receive a menu and form to fill out so Skylar is able to eat at school when I don't send her with a school lunch. I thank the teacher and excuse myself, allowing another parent to take my place.

I walk toward my girls. Skylar is showing her big sister her desk, introducing her new desk mate, and showing Rylee how she's going to organize her supplies. I stand back and listen to my little girl adjust to her surroundings. I look at her and know that no matter how scared or nervous she is, Skylar is going to love school. A sense of peace fills me just as a small gust of wind passes through the room. I know Jake is watching over our little girls from heaven. I bend down and give my little peanut a big hug and goodbye kiss and tell her, "I love you." I step back and let Rylee have her turn.

Rylee does the same but adds, "Good luck, Peanut, and don't forget, take care of yourself in the playground. Don't let the big kids be mean to you. If you have to slip and 'accidentally' have your foot meet their shin or your fist meet their face, then do so."

Here we go.

I should probably expect a call from the principal later today. Thanks, Rylee, I say to myself, but I'm glad she said what I wanted to say. Finally, Rylee and I head out the door. As I step out of the classroom, I take a couple deep breaths and look at Rylee.

"Our little baby is growing up so fast. Thank you for being here with your little sister on her big day."

She smiles.

"We're all we have, Momma. I wouldn't miss this for the world. Daddy would've wanted me here and so here I am," she tells me.

We hug and then start walking toward our Jeeps.

"Now let's get you to school. Hopefully, the school doesn't have a problem because you're late," I say.

"Eh . . ." she says with a shrug. "I'll tell them today was my little sister's first day as well and if they have a problem, then that's on them. Family always comes first. Love you!"

Chapter 4

Instead of heading to work, I call the office to let them know I won't be coming in today, and they need to forward any urgent calls. And *only* urgent calls—I don't want to be notified unless it's an emergency and we're going to war.

Today is one of those days for me—the ones where I hurt and I get emotional.

This will be the first day I don't have Skylar with me. She'll be at school the whole day and won't be in my office coloring or trying to do flips over my chairs and couch. I'm really going to miss my baby.

This milestone makes me miss Jake more than normal. People say time heals all wounds, but mine don't seem to be healing. I've learned to live my days for my girls, but the nights—those are the hardest. They're lonely and long. I only have our memories to keep me warm and my tears to soak my pillow.

Jake and I were always cuddling, always touching in some way. He always held me after our lovemaking and would tell me he loved me more every day. Now, I don't have that—I'm alone in my bed and almost five years later, I still miss his body next to mine. I had to sell our old bed because I couldn't bring myself to lie there alone. It held so many memories—memories of our love, our antics, our fights.

Memories of our time together and what was robbed from us.

∽✖✖⤳

10 April 2008

"*I love you so much, Faith, more than you can ever imagine. I thank God every day you were brave enough to approach me, making me the luckiest man in the world. I must've done something right because I have you beside me," he says to me as we lie in our bed.*

We had just experimented with some toys I bought at a neighbor's Passion Party. Jake was extremely pleased when he came home late from work due to a lockdown. I met him at the door dressed in a sexy purple negligee and told him I had a surprise downstairs. He ran upstairs to give a sleeping Rylee a goodnight kiss, and then rushed downstairs to me. We had TONS of fun with those toys.

"I know, baby, I love you too," I reply with a satisfied sigh.

"No, Faith, you don't understand what a saving grace you are. Before you, I was a shell of a man. I've done my best from the very beginning to raise and provide for Rylee, but that was it. Rylee's biological mother hurt me when she left, and I never thought I'd be able to trust another woman after she abandoned us. She left my newborn baby girl like she was nothin' to her and she walked away from me. What did I know about raising a baby? I could barely take care of myself."

Lately, he's been acting strange—coming home early as much as possible, declaring his love more often, and doing things he normally doesn't do, like take pictures without me asking. It's almost as if he knows something . . . something he's not sharing with me.

"Faith, you've shown me what a good woman really is and you've made me into a better man. You gave up your youth to marry me—never getting the chance to go out and drink or party all night like the other people your age. Instead, you took it upon yourself to make my daughter your own and make us a family. You are the glue that keeps us together—a stronger person I've never known. I'm gone more often than not for work but you never complain, and when I come home, you meet me at the door with a kiss every time. You even help take off my boots and my uniform. It's you who keeps me in line when I become a hard man to love—when I bring the stress of work home. You encourage me to do my best and hold me when I feel like a failure. You've made this place a home and us into a strong and loving family. Thank you, for everything you do, but mainly for loving me."

After those beautiful and heartfelt words, I'm sniffling and tears are starting to fall. I've been so emotional lately and his words just push me over the edge. The sobbing starts. I push my face into his neck and really let loose. Oh man, do they come. I can barely catch my breath, and all Jake can do is hold me.

Not only have I been an emotional wreck, but I've had this pain—a heaviness in my chest. I catch myself rubbing my heart at times. I don't know what this feeling is, but I know I don't like it and hope it goes away soon. Jake is here with me and not in Afghanistan or a war zone, so I know he's safe. Thank goodness I don't have to worry about getting that knock on my door—having my friends call or text before every visit or getting scared every time I see a soldier in dress blues in the neighborhood. My husband is here with me and he's safe.

"It's okay, baby. Don't cry," he tells me as he rubs my back gently.

"How can I not cry, Jake, when you say such beautiful words to me? You always let me know how much I'm loved and you do your best to provide for us. You respect me and treat me like a queen," I reply. "I love you, my lover. You are my forever and I'm blessed to have found you. I'm the lucky one—I have you and Rylee. My world is perfect."

He moves on top of me and starts to kiss me tenderly—my lips, my cheeks, my eyes, and moves to my neck. He bites that one spot that always makes me shiver and laughs softly. He knows what it does to me and he loves it. His hands move from my face, slowly trailing to my breasts. He caresses them—playing with my nipples, making me breathe faster. He suckles one nipple and continues to play with the other. His hands leave my breasts and make their way down my body until he reaches between my legs.

He gently spreads my legs, moving his fingers back and forth along my most sensitive part. They gently massage my clit until I'm begging him for more.

"Patience, my love," he says. "We have all night . . ."

∽⌦⌐

I return to the present as I reach the stoplight. I stop and shake my head. All those memories—so haunting and beautiful. How will I ever be able to let go? When will I be able to move on? Miranda

Lambert's "Over You" plays on my stereo as I wait for the light to turn.

I listen to the lyrics and realize how true they are. He went away, leaving me alone—how dare he? I know he didn't mean to leave, but he did. He went away and now I'm here raising our daughters. Alone. God, why did you have to take him from us? Why . . .

I've gone through the stages of grief but nothing takes away the pain, the loss of him. After hearing the news, I pretended he was deployed and just couldn't call me. When I couldn't pretend anymore, I became so angry—angry at the person responsible and angry that Jake would never meet our unborn child. I was angry at everything he'd miss. I also turned my anger and blame to the job he loved and the responsibilities he held. Later, I just wanted to wake from the nightmare of reality. I prayed for the nightmare to go away and I lost myself in a sea of "what ifs" and "only ifs." The only things keeping me from going into a full and dark depression were our children: Rylee and our new little miracle. I needed to be strong for them. And then, there was Phoenix. I couldn't let Jake's dream die with him. I had to toughen up and take charge. Julia was going through her own loss, so my pregnancy not only gave me strength, but it also helped bring back my best friend.

Finally, I pulled myself together and came to accept the loss of my husband. I began to live my life for our children and his dream. I existed, but I didn't *live*. My smile never reached my eyes, but I made sure to put on a strong face for my loved ones. I lived during the days and I cried myself to sleep at night. I had to learn how to live without him—I've accepted his loss but I don't like it. At times, with everything that occurred, I wonder if there was a higher power at work—guiding us, giving us strength, and making things happen.

In the distance, I hear the roar of a motorcycle, getting louder as it nears. I hear it stop beside me. I turn to my left and see this huge, beautiful black-and-chrome motorcycle. I think to myself how much Jake would like that bike and would totally want it.

My eyes leave the bike and move up to its rider. I see the side profile of a man wearing sunglasses and one of those black helmets without a visor. He looks handsome, I think, surprising myself—I haven't looked at another man since Jake. He's dressed in black from head to boots, his shirt molded to his muscular chest and his pants covering amazing-looking thighs—a work of art. I stare at him for what seems like an eternity. I know I need to stop, but for some strange reason, I can't bring myself to look away.

He must feel my stare because he turns toward me. We stare at each other. I can't turn away and I can't see his eyes. I feel a strange force refusing to let go. His right hand slowly comes up and he removes his glasses.

I gasp.

I feel that jolt, like lightning.

Oh my . . . his eyes—can they be?

From our short distance, I'm mesmerized. I've never seen eyes that color in person. So unique and beautiful. They hold me captive—I stare and get my fill. And his face . . .

Holy freaking crap!

He looks like a model. His skin is tan, his eyebrows are perfectly arched, his cheekbones are high and defined, his nose looks slightly crooked (like it was broken at one time—so he can't be a model), his lips are full but not feminine, and he's grinning.

He knows his effect on women. He's a walking dream—all deliciousness on a stick. But it's his eyes that hold me captive. They're unique to the point of being strange, and yet amazing. I can only describe them as violet. His eyes are freaking purple!

By now, I'm almost drooling, but also uncomfortable. It's been years since I've been affected by the opposite sex, and I don't know how I feel about it.

I may be drooling and staring, but so is he. I mean, he's staring back at me. He gives me a wink and that cool-man chin raise I always thought was so sexy when Jake did it. As soon as Jake comes to mind, I feel like cold water has been thrown on me and I'm quickly pulled out of my daze.

What in the world, Faith?

I'm so engrossed, I don't notice the light has turned green until I hear a loud honk behind me. I immediately turn away and start pressing the gas to move forward. I hear him rev his engine. I take a quick glance at him one last time and notice his eyes are still on me. I think he wants me to put my window down, but I quickly look away and start moving forward. As I'm speeding away, I look into my rearview mirror and see him still in the same spot, watching my Jeep drive away.

Finally, I hear him accelerate and see him turn left. Thank goodness he went in another direction. I feel weird and unsettled. I try to shake those feelings off and keep driving. I speed away from that beautiful and electrifying man and make my way to Jake. Right now, I need to be near him and I need to share this day with him.

No matter how much I try, I just can't help but feel like my world is about to change—that it's about to be flipped upside down once again.

$\propto\!\infty$

Zane

There she is. She's even more beautiful than I remember. I've spent the last few years working to better myself—to be a man worthy of her because she deserves that and so much more.

I've waited so long and now it's time.

I'm here for her and the girls. To hold, love, protect, and treasure them.

Finally, it's time to keep my promise and make them mine.

Chapter 5

I park the Jeep and make my way to Jake's grave. I arrive at his headstone and stand for a long while looking at his resting place. Over the past years, the girls and I have visited regularly but it never gets any better. Time hasn't taken away the pain that grips me every time I stand here in front of his grave—the final reminder that I'll never see my husband and love of my life again.

Jacob Hunter Duval II

3 January 1978–26 April 2008

Beloved Father, Husband, Son & Friend

RLTW

I take a seat next to him, place a can of long-cut wintergreen Copenhagen (his favorite) by his headstone, and rest my head on my knees. After several deep breaths, I bring my head up and start talking to him, telling him about our days since we last came to visit. I tell him about the eventful shopping trip to the mall to buy our girls their new clothes for school, and I mention how excited our little peanut was about starting Pre-K, how nervous and scared she was. I continue until I have nothing else to say and I start rambling nonsense.

Since we didn't keep secrets from each other during our marriage, I tell him about that moment at the stoplight. That moment when I couldn't look away from that stranger and the invisible strong force that kept me frozen in place.

"I know you're gone, but I still feel guilty for being affected by him. I haven't noticed a man since you and now he comes along. It was so strange, Jake," I say. "I couldn't look away. I got butterflies in my stomach and that feeling of excitement and anticipation—I was mesmerized by him and wanted to memorize every one of his features. When I first saw you, I knew you were gonna be mine and I was gonna do everything in my power to make it so. I didn't have any doubts about us.

"But this—this is different," I continue. "It's unsettling and I don't like it one bit. I know you'd be happy I'm finally feeling something again. I've been so lonely and numb—a part of my heart went missing when I lost you. I feel empty. I know you'd want me to be happy and move on with my life, but I don't know if I can or if I'm ready. You'd want me to find another man that would treat me like the queen I was to you, would treasure me, and would love our daughters like his own. But is there really a man out there for me now that you're gone?"

∝∽∝

26 April 2008

"Holy shit, Faith! This water is fuckin' hot!" Jake exclaims as he joins me in the shower. Every Saturday morning after my workout, we make it a point to spend "us time" while Rylee is watching morning cartoons. We make love and then we shower together in the tiny shower stall in our master bathroom.

It's a tight fit, but we make it work.

"Stop being such a baby. The water feels just fine to me," I say laughing at my overgrown boy of a husband. He's always been this way and he complains every single time he steps in the shower with me. You'd figure after more than six years of marriage he'd get used to the fact that I love my showers, I'm a water hog, and I love my water hot. He constantly complains but I know it's all for show.

"I like when you wash me. When I shower after PT, it takes me less than a minute, but you—you take your time. I especially love when you wash my cock. Falling asleep with you in my arms and our time on Saturday mornings are the highlights of my week," he tells me. "After a long and stressful day and week, I get to be with you in my arms. I love you."

He's always saying sweet things to me and making me feel special. But now, it's more frequent and he's still acting strange.

There's something he's not telling me—I just need to wait it out and eventually he'll let me know what's on his mind. He always does.

After cleaning him, I get on my knees and give him a Saturday morning present. It never gets old and I'll never stop loving the taste of him. I feel powerful and amazing, like I can conquer the world, when I make him lose control and hear him call my name as he releases into my mouth. I, being a good wife, swallow—enjoying the salty taste of his cum.

I get to my feet and bring my mouth to his ear.

"I love you too," I whisper. "Forever, Jake. Forever, my love."

"Forever, Faith," he replies as he caresses my face and kisses me.

After dressing, we head upstairs to get Rylee ready for our family outing. We decide to go on a bike ride and have some ice cream on our way home. That evening during dinner, we talk about our future and the what-if that hangs over the head of every military family.

"Faith, if anything ever happens to me, you'll be set financially, I made sure of that. After this last deployment, I managed to take out a better life insurance policy so you and Rylee would never suffer for money in case I don't come home one day," he says.

"Don't speak like that," I reply, refusing to think about any such thing. "You're home and you're safe. Nothing's gonna happen to you."

"No, baby. But if anything ever does, I want you to continue living. Live for Rylee and live for yourself. I would want you to find another man to love, to treasure you. Another man that'll take care of you and Rylee. Go back to Texas where I used to visit my grandparents—there you'll find your place. Promise me, Faith."

"Seriously, Jake! Stop talking like that. You're here with me and nothing's gonna happen to you. Okay?"

"Promise me, Faith!" He demands. "Give me your word and I'll drop the subject."

"Okay," I tell him. "I promise to live and move on if anything happens to you. I'll keep my heart open, but I won't have to because you aren't going' anywhere. You're here and you're stuck with me.

Can we please stop talking about this now?"

He drops the subject and we go on with our day. We have a family movie night after dinner and stuff ourselves with popcorn, lots of candy, and Dr. Pepper floats. Two movies and a lot of junk food later, we take a sleeping Rylee to her room and make our way to ours.

It's "us time" now.

Later that night, his phone rings.

It's work.

One of his soldiers, the same one that's always getting in trouble, was in a car accident and Jake needs to go pick him up at the MP station, and then write and file a report at the office. He reluctantly leaves our bed and dresses himself. He makes his way to our night table on my side of the bed to grab his keys, wedding band, and college ring.

"Go back to sleep, baby," he tells me. "I love you." He kisses me and then walks out of our bedroom.

"I love you too, honey. Be careful," I call after him.

I snuggle back underneath the covers and go back to sleep, not realizing those precious moments were the last I would spend with my husband. The next morning, very early, there's a knock on my front door. Since I'm not expecting anyone this early, I call Jake's phone to check if he lost or forgot his key, but it goes straight to voicemail. There's another knock and I walk up the stairs, heart in my throat—there's only one reason I'd be getting a knock so early in the morning. I see two shadows through the glass, illuminated by the morning light.

"Mrs. Duval," one of them calls out, they must see my figure through the glass.

I stand there for several minutes, refusing to open the door. They knock again louder.

"Please open the door, ma'am."

I just stand there not moving. I feel my throat tighten and tears well up in my eyes. I'm so scared.

Can it be?

I stand there and the knocks continue. After what seems an eternity, I take a deep breath, preparing myself. I walk to the door and place my shaking hand on the door handle. Slowly, I turn it and open the door.

Standing in the doorway are two soldiers in Army Service Uniforms, dress blues.

One speaks, "Mrs. Faith Duval?"

I nod and manage to whisper, "Yes."

He takes a deep breath. "On behalf of the Secretary of the Army, I regret to inform you . . ."

With that knock, my dreams came crashing down around me.

My perfect world unraveled, and I was left a widow.

⤥⤤

Oh, the memories. Those beautiful memories and my girls kept me sane these last few years. Jake may be gone, but those sweet memories of our time together will always be with me. Never in a hundred years would I have thought our lives would be changed so drastically. I never thought my husband would survive multiple deployments and lose his life in a car accident.

Life can be cruel at times. We had so many plans, thinking we had forever. He was so young, only thirty years old with his whole future ahead when he was killed in a car crash caused by a drunk driver. Another soldier who decided to get plastered at a party and was stupid enough to attempt to drive back to the barracks. His decision cost my husband his life.

After a while, I check my watch and notice that I've been here several hours and my stomach is growling.

"I'm hungry, Jake, and you know what happens when I get hungry," I tell him. "I just wanted to share this day with you. Our babies are growing up so fast and soon I'll be sending Rylee off to college. Skylar's just starting school, but I know time is gonna fly by. I need to treasure every moment I have with our girls, my love. I'll come back next week and I'll bring the girls with me. I love you."

I feel caressed by a gust of wind that surrounds me as I get up and dust myself off. A sense of peace fills me, a feeling I lost the day

Jake died, making me feel lighter. It's time to finally accept that I'm still here and I'm alive. I place a kiss on his headstone and turn toward the Jeep. Remembering our last day together and finally understanding and accepting his wish for me to move on was liberating.

It's been four years since I received that dreaded knock on the door that changed the course of my life. Four years since I last made love. Four years since I last kissed a man or was held by someone other than family or friends.

Maybe this move, even though it was only a short distance, will mark the beginning of a new journey—a new chapter in our lives. Maybe, just maybe, I might be able to take a leap of faith and open myself up to the idea of love again. I might never fill that void in my heart. I had my "forever" with Jake, so I can't be greedy. But, I need to start moving on.

I need to show the girls that life goes on after death. These past few years I've lived for my girls; now it might just be time to start living for myself. I just need to find the power. I made Jake a promise on that last day we were together, thinking I would never have to fulfill it. Now, I have to own up to it and start moving on, start feeling and enjoying life once again.

I need to learn how to live again, for me.

I know what I have to do, so I take out my phone and call Julia—the person who has been with me through every important moment of my life since the first day we met. Aside from my parents, she has been *there* for me as I have been for her.

"Hey, *chica,*" she answers with her usual greeting. "How are you?"

"It's time, Julia," I tell her without greeting. "It's time for me to truly let Jake go. All these years, I lived in the past . . . I just couldn't let him go—he was . . . he was my other half." My voice is trembling and tears are filling my eyes. I take a deep breath to control myself and continue. "But, I have to move on. He's no longer here with me and I know he'd want me to keep going. He wouldn't want me to live the rest of my life like this. I finally understand it's not a betrayal to him for me to let go—he will always be in my heart. It's time to focus on my future because *I'm* still here. Will you help me?"

"Oh, Faith," she tells me sniffling. "You and I—we've been together through so much, you didn't let me quit when I was at my darkest. Of course, I'll be with you through this. I'm always here for you, babe."

"Thank you."

Part Two

Twice in a Lifetime

Chapter 6

January 2013

"COME ON, REF! Where's the card? She's getting hurt out there! Do something!"

Skylar's yelling at the top of her lungs—surprising everyone with her lung capacity, dedication, and support for her sister on the field. Who knew such a little bitty thing had such powerful lungs? With her tone and set of pipes, my little peanut could be a singer; however, she's currently big time into gymnastics. My heart broke when she announced she wasn't playing soccer . . . ever. Instead, she wants to be the next Aly Raisman, especially after seeing her perform and win during the London Olympics. Here, she has a retired soccer player for a mom and a future champ in her sister and Skylar wants—gymnastics. She'd rather cheer in the audience than run out on the field. "Running for so long is tiring, Momma, and it makes my legs hurt," she says.

So here we are in the stands. I'm laughing my butt off along with the rest of the audience—those that aren't in shock—as she stands on her seat yelling at the referee. It's Rylee's first soccer game of the season and that girl and her teammates are getting elbowed and kicked left and right by their opponent. The referee is letting things slide, probably because we're the visitors and this team we're playing is known for being shady, and his lack of concern is angering my little peanut. She's very protective of her big sister and feels that it's her duty as the baby to annoy and pick on her sister, but Lord help anyone else who tries to do so. She'll even take me on when she thinks I'm being a meanie to Rylee.

Sitting here, I don't know what's more entertaining—hearing Skylar cheering for her sister and yelling at the referee for making calls she disagrees with, or watching my eldest show off her skills on the soccer field. Hmmm . . . I think for a bit. It has to be Skylar.

Yup, it's watching Skylar and hearing her very creative use of non-curse words. Who knew watching ESPN with us would lead to this? At least she knows how to use the phrases she picked up from us correctly.

I laugh.

"Skylar, sit down before you end up hurting yourself," I tell her. "I'm pretty sure the referee heard you the first time, darlin'."

"But, Momma, he isn't doing *anything* about it and Rylee just got elbowed in the face! Again!" She says, upset at the injustice. "I wouldn't yell if the referee was doing his job." She plops down in her seat cross-armed and pouty.

After another chuckle, I turn to Jackie, Josilyn's mother. After the first day of school, Rylee came home and told me she met another girl, Josilyn, who loved soccer as much as she did. She was so excited she was finally going to have someone to relate to that was her age and had her passion. Since then, they've been inseparable—best friends forever, as they say. Skylar, well, that girl is my little social butterfly and has so many friends but claims Rylee is her bestest friend. Overall, the past few months have been settling in, and both Rylee and Skylar are adjusting and doing well in school.

I've been busy at the office since we expanded and we're in high demand after we finally established ourselves as the go-to guys in our specialty. I'm working more hours, but I make it my priority to be a mother first. Rylee's starting her soccer season and excelling, and Skylar is loving her new gymnastics coach. Overall, everything is going smoothly and there's no drama—something I'm very grateful for.

As for my social life, I'm finally enjoying myself more. I've gone out with Julia a few times, taking advantage of free babysitting courtesy of Rylee. The girls have noticed a change in me. Both have commented that they like the fact I'm taking time for myself and going out with my best friend. I was so focused on being both mommy and daddy for them that I forgot about myself. I forgot I was still young and I was entitled to some *me* time. I've even gone on a couple of first dates, but that was it. No second dates. There haven't been any sparks, no butterflies—nada. At least I'm trying, I tell myself.

"Our girls are looking pretty good out there," Jackie tells me. "The team has drastically improved since Julia became their coach. I think we might actually win some games this season and if we pray really hard, we might make it into the play-offs. The girls' soccer program was a joke before Julia came along, and I'm glad the school district is willing to spend the money to put our girls on the map, or at least attempt to."

"It's a rebuilding year, so don't expect too much but yes, they'll be winning some games this season. Julia will make sure those girls are whipped into shape in no time," I tell her. "Rylee's in decent shape. She even mentioned how brutal the first few practices were."

"GO. GO. GO!" I hear Skylar scream. "RYLEE!! RUN . . . RUN! GO! Come on, you can do it . . . GO . . . YES! GOOOAAALLLLLLL!!!!!!!!" Her arms are raised high in the air and she's standing, again, on her seat.

All I can hear is my little girl screaming at the top of her lungs, excited her big sister scored the first goal of the game. And it seems like everyone else is celebrating as if we'd just won the championship. I knew the team had been in bad shape, but I didn't think it was *that* bad. I guess Rylee and Julia have their work cut out for them.

I'm really thankful that Rylee was okay with our move here. This was Jake's favorite place as a kid and his prime choice for The Phoenix Corporation's headquarters. He wanted us here and I'm making sure our girls receive this part of their father.

After being honorably discharged from the Army, Gunner decided to come back to Texas and start up a company where he could put his acquired skills into use. Despite the fact he was still in, Jake provided capital and was planning on joining Gunner after his time in the military was complete. After his death, I did as much as possible to help Gunner stay afloat during the crucial first couple of years. I did some of the work from home, since I was going to school and taking care of the girls. I did the training I needed while Rylee was at school and I took Skylar with me. I needed to gain the respect of the men and that meant blood, sweat, and tears. Daddy did his best to put the company's name out here, so that helped us a lot. Now, Phoenix has gained a solid reputation and we're not hurting for money.

"Did you see that, Momma?" Skylar asks. "Did you see Rylee score?"

"Yes, Peanut, I saw her score a goal, and I think everyone from here to China heard you celebrating," I reply.

I turn back to Jackie and we discuss plans for the concession stand our booster club is working next week, which will be our first home game. Suddenly, I feel this tingly feeling in the back of my neck. You know, that feeling you get when someone is staring at you. Trying to seem inconspicuous, I carefully look around the field and finally my gaze lands on a person by the fence. My eyes widen in surprise—standing there is the delicious and incredibly handsome man I've seen several times around town—Mr. Gorgeous Eyes— and he's looking at me.

My mind goes crazy.

Holy cow, he's here!

What is he doing here?

I thought the sight of him in my rearview mirror would be the last, but I was wrong. A few days later I saw him in town and I freaked out—I ran away and made a fool of myself. Another time, I ended up in a fish store, EW! I dislike fish with a passion but that didn't matter one bit when I threw myself through the door to escape him. To be honest, I don't know why I keep running from him, and I'm not even sure he is trying to make the effort to approach me. I only know that every time I see him, I feel flustered. For that reason alone, I run. I've been lucky that the girls haven't been with me during these sightings, or I'd have some explaining to do.

Oh my!

Having a full view of him, I check him out. He's every woman's dream man: exotic eyes, rugged gorgeous face, and an amazingly fit body.

I turn back to Jackie just in time to see her stand. I start freaking out inside when she starts waving her arms like a lunatic.

"Yoo-hoo! Zane! We're over here! Zane! Over here!"

Goodness! Could she be any louder? I think unhappily.

"What are you doing?!" I hiss at her.

I really, really want to wring her neck right now. Friends aren't supposed to do this to each other. Granted, she has no idea that I'm freaking out right now, but still. Can't she see she's bringing his attention more towards me?

Oh Lord, he's coming this way.

"Jackie, please sit down," I beg her while at the same time wishing the Earth would open up and swallow me whole.

"Relax, Faith." She says, oblivious to my panic. "That's just my baby brother. He promised Josilyn he'd come watch her play."

"*What?!*" I squeak.

Yes. I. Squeaked.

"You remember?" She says off-handedly. "I've told you about Zane and how my mom's been on his case because he won't settle down, and she's itching for more grandchildren."

"Oh yeah . . ." I trail off. She's mentioned a younger brother but she never told me he looked like *that.*

Maybe, if I'm really quick, I can grab Skylar and run. Oh crap, I really need to get out of here and fast. I can't see him face to face right now. I still don't understand the feelings he makes me feel and I don't know if he's seen me during my escape attempts.

I have Skylar's hand in mine and I'm very close to escaping to the concession stand when he sits right down in front of me.

"Hey, Jackie," he says with a sexy grin. "Introduce me to your friend, will you sis?"

Goodness gracious! His voice is amazing. So smooth. Sexy. Masculine. Oh my, I even hear a slight Texas accent. You know the type of voice that'll grab you and make you want to jump his bones—that's the voice I hear.

Okay, I tell myself, relax . . . breathe. You're a grown woman, a lady, you can do this. You can talk to him and act like an adult, without showing him how much he affects you. Get your big girl pants on.

"Zane, this is Faith and this little darlin' here is Skylar, her daughter." Jackie starts the introductions. "Faith, this is Zane, my baby brother." I chuckle at her description of him.

"Hello, Faith," he says, taking my hand and bringing it to his lips. "And hello to you, little Miss Skylar," he says to my little girl, smiling at her and doing the same to her little hand.

I hear Skylar giggle. *She giggles.* Even my little girl is impressed. I bet every female from birth to eighty-five is charmed by this man. He just has that way about him.

"Uh, h-hello," I manage to stutter.

I see his grin get even bigger and realize he knows the effect he has on me. I wonder if he remembers me . . . but why would he? That afternoon was probably an everyday occurrence for him. He's gorgeous and sexy, and I bet women are constantly staring at him. I was probably one of hundreds. And the other times, well, I made a fool of myself and can only hope he didn't see or remember those times. Remembering my foolishness, I get myself together.

"My apologies," I say sounding very proper, maybe too proper. "Zane, it's a pleasure to meet you."

I hope he doesn't notice the drool that's at the corner of my mouth. Wow, this man is something else; he's just so freaking sexy—there are no other words to describe. He's the whole shebang and he knows it.

He chuckles, letting me know I didn't fool him. "How are you doing, beautiful?" He asks smoothly. "You enjoying the game?"

"I'm well," I reply, trying to keep my distance from him and coming off a tad bit rude.

"You aren't following me, are you?" He asks, catching me by surprise.

"What?!"

I'm offended. I'm not a stalker, no matter how yummy the man is. I don't chase men. I approach but I *don't* chase.

"I asked if you were following me," he repeats, knowing I heard him the first time. "I remember the last time you saw me—you couldn't stop staring at me. And then those other times, they gave me a good laugh, baby," he finishes with a smirk.

Well, of all the nerve. There's my answer—he does remember

me. Oh, but the arrogance . . . he doesn't have to rub it in my face that I've found him stare-worthy.

"How can I be following you when I was here first?" I ask him. "I should ask you, instead, if you're following me."

He gives me that sexy grin and chuckles. "I'da been here sooner if that was the case."

"I bet."

"Baby, for you, I'd go to the ends of the world—slay a dragon, climb the Himalayas, and even dance. I'd do *anything* for you." His eyes are fixed on me as he makes his declaration.

I feel myself blush and softly laugh. "You're such a flirt. I bet you say that to all the girls."

"Nah, beautiful," he tells me seriously. "Those words are just for you. And *only you.*"

"Oh," I say and receive a real smile from him.

We hear the crowd start to get loud. Zane turns to the field and watches my girl as she runs, comes face to face with another player and skillfully maintains the ball. She makes another amazing move, getting her closer to the goal. Now, it's just her and the goalie.

Come one, Rylee, you can do it, I silently cheer her on. YES!!! She makes it—GOOOOAAAALLLL!!!!!!!! I silently yell to myself. I smile proudly.

"Damn! She's good," he says in awe.

"I know," I proudly reply. "She's my daughter."

He looks at me and smiles but says nothing. His expression seems to say he knows something I don't.

"Did you see that?" Jackie asks. "That was amazing."

I turn to her. "Yes, I did. She did good," I reply and she turns back to the field, leaving me and Zane alone again.

"So she's your daughter?" He asks.

"Yup, she's my sister," Skylar tells him. "She's amazing and one day she's gonna be a champion—that's what Momma tells us. She's gonna be just like Momma."

"You don't say," is all he replies.

"Well, if you'll excuse us, I have to get down to the sideline and congratulate my daughter," I say. "Let's go, Skylar; let's go see your big sister."

I take Skylar's hand and say goodbye to Jackie, tilt my head to Zane, and start making my way to my eldest. As I get to the last step I hear him call out very loudly.

"I'll be seeing you later, beautiful."

❌

Zane

There's nothing I don't know about her—I know all about Rylee and Skylar. I'm not a stalker or any of that sick shit; I'm a man who believes in keeping his word, and I made sure they were safe over the years even if I was away from them. When I made that promise, I never thought I'd grow to want her—to fight to become a better man for her.

I've finally met her face to face and I know I affect her as much as she affects me. She's run away from me, but that ends now. Pretty soon, I'll have her in my arms and I'm never letting her go.

Damn right, I'll be seeing you later, I think to myself as I smile, watching her walk away from me for the very last time.

Chapter 7

Three crazy and busy weeks have gone by. I'm in my room getting ready for my night out with Julia. This Saturday is a bye week in the schedule. We decided to take advantage of this downtime to have a night to ourselves. Rylee and Josilyn volunteered to babysit, so I have no worries and I know Skylar will have a blast with the girls.

After much consideration, I decide on black dress shorts, a purple sequin sleeveless mesh shirt, purple bra, and purple high-heeled pumps with kickass spikes and rhinestones on the heels. My earrings are black, glittery, and long and I have a beautiful black-and-purple bracelet on. Yes, I love my purple. I finalize the ensemble with a black coach wristlet. My make-up is neutral and I put my long dark wavy hair in a low side ponytail, showing off my Aquarius tattoo on the back of my neck.

"Momma, you look beautiful," Skylar says. "I want to look just like you when I grow up."

"Oh, baby, thank you. You're gonna be more beautiful than me when you grow older," I say. "You and Rylee are gonna be strong, beautiful, and amazing women. You have your father in you as well as me. We created you and we did an amazing job."

As I'm having this conversation with my youngest, I hear a loud whistle at the door of my room. "Dang, Mrs. Faith, you look hot! *Muy caliente,*" Josilyn says and Rylee agrees.

"Thank you, girls. Aunt Julia wants to go out and I hope this is what she has in mind. I'm too old to be wearing those short dresses that show my underwear, the ones girls wear nowadays, so I decided on shorts."

"You're rocking those shorts, Momma," Rylee says. "You and Aunt Julia are gonna have so much fun. Josilyn and I have the peanut and we'll take care of everything. Just go have fun, dance, and maybe talk to a hot guy or two. And drink safely."

"Rylee!" I exclaim.

"What?" She asks. "You're still young and deserve to have fun."

Before I can say anything else, I hear the front door open.

"Honey! I'm home!" I hear Julia yell.

Julia's a hoot. She's been stuck with me from the day we met, and after everything we've been through, we're still together. I love her, craziness and all. She tries her sexy walk as she walks into my room.

"You ready, *chica?*"

She looks me up and down. I figure I pass inspection when she doesn't send me back into my closet for different clothes.

"Let's go have some fun. I'm ready to get my shake on. Woohoo!"

She starts to dance, shaking what her mama gave her and grabbing my hand in the process.

Skylar starts to laugh. "You're funny, Aunt Julia. You and Momma look beautiful."

"Thank you, Peanut," she replies as she kisses my girls on their cheeks.

I gather all my belongings, give my hair one last pat-down, and turn to my girls.

"Okay, girlies. Momma's heading out with Aunt Julia now. Be careful and have fun. Skylar, don't stay up too late and listen to your sister. Rylee, if you have any problems, call my cell phone or Aunt Julia's, and here is the club's number just in case."

I give my girls their goodbye kisses and walk out the door with Julia. We climb into the cab and head towards our night of fun, dancing, and drinking. Well, not too much drinking, I want to feel human in the morning.

✂✁

We arrive to the club about forty-five minutes later and I feel like a VIP as Julia drags me to the front of the line waiting to get past the bouncer. On the way, I hear some not-very-nice things leaving numerous mouths, and I seriously want to wash some mouths out with soap. I guess I'd be pissed as well, but it isn't my fault that Julia and I know people and so don't have to wait hours in line to get into *the* club of the year—TanZen.

We get to the door and Josh, the bouncer, lets us into the club. "Have fun and save me a dance," he says, more to Julia than me, since he's looking straight at her. Hmmm, I wonder what *that's* about.

"Well, well, well," I say to her. "Did you forget to mention something to me? Do share. You know the only action I get nowadays is living vicariously through you."

"What? Josh? He's nice a guy I went out with once. We decided to be friends after I told him there wasn't going to be a second date; I didn't have that spark with him. I can't help that I'm irresistible and guys would rather be my friends than be without me," she replies jokingly, but there's truth in her statement. She has so many guy friends that would date her in a heartbeat but she's so picky—no butterflies, no second dates. I think she's still in love with *him,* the one who broke her heart and took a piece of her with him after destroying her. But we're not going to think about him now.

"One day, Julia . . . one day, you're gonna find a man that'll make you fall in love again, and he'll cherish you beyond belief. You won't be able to wrap him around your little finger so easily," I say. "That day will come and I'm gonna enjoy watching it happen. Mark my words, babe, when that day happens I'll have front row seats and I'll even help him."

"Well, that might happen but it sure won't be today," she replies. "We're here to have fun and not talk about my love life. You're gonna have a good time even if I have to ply you with alcohol."

She takes my hand and leads me to the bar. We both order Tequila Sunrises, our poison of choice, and get to sipping; they're so yummy and there's nothing better than Tequila, orange juice, and grenadine, in my opinion. Well, maybe a frozen margarita. Plus, if made correctly, they can be strong and you barely taste the alcohol. They're my kind of drinks; I just have to be careful. And drink lots of water along the way.

As we're slowly sipping on our drinks and checking out the club, we hear "Timber" by Pitbull and Kesha come on. We quickly finish our drinks and head out to the dance floor to get our dance on. We dance and dance, doing every dance move imaginable. We're probably getting weird looks from the other dancers, but we don't care. I forgot how much fun it is to just come out and dance. I love dancing; Jake would get a babysitter at least once a month and take me dancing when we were in Germany. The music there wasn't as modern—there was a lot of eighties music, but it was still fun nonetheless. Even now, I'll put on music at home and start a dance jam with the girls.

Julia and I are doing all those club moves you see in the YouTube videos. We're laughing and I'm having the time of my life. "Danza Kuduro" comes on and I go *wild.* This is my jam—I love this song! I'm showing off all of my dance moves and as the Tequila takes effect, I even impress myself. *Damn, I'm freaking awesome.* Suddenly, I see Julia go completely still—her eyes go wide, mouth hanging open. She's trying to tell me something, but nothing comes out.

"What?" I shout to be heard over the music. I don't know what her problem is; she probably saw a really hot guy, but I don't care, I keep on dancing like there's no tomorrow.

She just points behind me and before I can turn around, I feel a set of arms circle my waist. *What in the world!* I'm about to let loose on someone and give him a piece of my mind. You just don't go up to someone and put your hands on them. I don't care that we're at a club; you don't do that crap to anyone, much less me. I turn.

Oh my goodness!

It's Zane!

No wonder Julia's in shock. I told her about him, but it just can't do the man justice until you see him in person.

Realizing who it is and that I actually semi-know him, I calm down. I look at him and say, "You're lucky I know you. I was about to let my deadly weapons loose on you for putting your hands on me and I could've seriously hurt you, you know. Next time, let me know it's you and that you're gonna to touch me."

He softly laughs at me and then gives me his sexy grin. "Hello, beautiful. I told you I'd be seeing you again. No more running. I've got you now. Dance with me."

He doesn't ask, he tells me, and keeps his hold on me. I decide not to fight it, at least for tonight, and he's Jackie's brother so I can tell on him if he gets out of hand. In his arms, I turn to Julia to let her know why this strange man's hands are on me and I'm not kicking butt.

"It's Zane, Jackie's brother," I tell her and then lean in and whisper loudly, "Remember? Mr. Gorgeous Eyes."

Julia's still in shock and wondering why I'm not freaking out that his hands are on me. To be honest, I have no idea why I'm not freaking out. I don't know him that well aside from the first time I saw him and felt that strong pull to him. Then there are those times I made a fool of myself by running, and you can't forget the game. Holy cow, when you start to thinking, he must think I'm the biggest dork.

Nonetheless, I relax in his arms. It feels right. Yes, he makes me feel out of control, but at the same time being in his arms feels safe. I feel like I belong. It's nice and terrifying at the same time, but tonight, I'm not going to worry about it. I'm here to have fun and if he wants to dance with me, I'll dance with him. No biggie.

Julia finally comes out of shock and smiles. Then, she starts to laugh. She's laughing so hard, I think she might start rolling around on the floor or wet her pants.

"Seriously, Faith! Seriously," she says, wiping tears of laughter. "We come here to have a girls' night and you manage to pick up a man without even trying. I mean we're here dancing; you're doing your 'famous dance moves,' which are freakin' hilarious; and this hot, and I mean seriously HOT specimen of a guy just comes up to you and puts his arms around you. You're one lucky biatch, babe."

I turn towards Zane and see a smile on his face. I guess he's not weirded out by my best friend; that's good.

"Um, I don't think I've picked up a man, Julia," I say. "I mean, Zane knows me already and he knows I have two girls, plus he's seen me do some really dorky things. I really don't think he wants to pick me up . . . you know, that way."

"Faith, for being so smart, you can be so clueless at times. He's looking at you like you're a big fat juicy steak and he's a starving man. You have the best luck in men; first Jake and now this yummilicious man. If I didn't love you so much, I'd be jealous and hate you."

"You're wrong. He doesn't want me that way," I say and turn to Zane to get his agreement. I see him chuckling and his next words leave me speechless.

"She's right," he whispers in my ear sending chills down my spine. "I do want you. I've caught you now and I ain't letting go."

Chapter 8

Oh, dear Lord!

I stop dancing and stand there. I'm in the middle of the dance floor in Zane's arms, and I'm stunned speechless. Finally, they take pity on me.

"Take her and go talk some sense into her," Julia tells him. "I'll be fine."

"You sure?" he asks.

"I'll be fine. Go explain the situation to my bestie," she tells him when she sees he's reluctant to leave her alone on the floor. "Don't worry about me. Look, here comes Josh—I'll be fine with him until y'all come back."

Zane quickly but calmly guides me off the dance floor. He takes me to a booth located in the back but still within sight of the dance floor in case he has to go back for Julia. He sits me down and climbs in next to me, keeping me on the inside so I don't make a run for it. He's not taking any chances tonight.

Finally I get some sense back into me and I start talking. "Um . . . I think I might've misheard you earlier. What do you mean, Julia's right and 'now you've caught me'?"

"What part don't you understand, beautiful? Do I have to spell it out for you?" he asks.

"Apparently," I inform him. "Zane, you can't want me. How . . . I mean, look at you and look at *me*. You're single, attractive, and I know you don't lack for female attention. I'm . . . well . . . me. At the soccer game, you let me walk away and I haven't heard from you in three weeks. *Three whole weeks,* Zane! Please, help me understand because I just don't see why you would even care to try."

"This is all wrong," he says with a trace of frustration in his voice. "I asked Jackie for your number, since you have the habit of running away before I can ask for it. I was going take you out. I wasn't planning on talking to you in a club. My plan was to take you out on a proper date and tell you I want you and I want to be with you."

"Well, *why* are you here if you weren't planning on talking to me at a club?" I'm starting to sound a bit bitchy, but I just can't help it. I'm confused and don't like it—that just makes me testy.

"I'm here because you're here," he says as if it's obvious. "I'm not about to let some random guy put his fuckin' hands on you. Shit, I about flipped the fuck out when Jackie showed me your picture earlier at dinner. You look fuckin' hot and you're here alone with Julia. You know the shit that can happen to two lone women? Most of these guys are dicks and can't understand the meaning of 'no.' No way in hell was I gonna to let that happen. No fuckin' way."

"First, how did Jackie get a picture of me? And second, what I do is none of your concern," I tell him, refusing to let his high-handedness slide.

"First, Josilyn was at your house and she knows how I feel. I've been at their house almost every fuckin' day hoping you'd show up. I ask lots of questions about you, and they're not fools. Second, you're my concern. Everything you do is my concern after today. Faith, I want you and I always get what I want. I've worked too damn hard and waited too long." That last part baffles me, but I continue on since I'm already all worked up.

"So, just because you say you want me, you're gonna have me?" This just pisses me off even more. I take a deep breath before going on. "What the hell, Zane? That crap doesn't fly with me. I'm not a piece of property you can just take and conquer at will. You barely know me and I barely know you. What if I couldn't stand to look at you, huh? What then?"

"Faith, don't lie to yourself and *don't* lie to me," he says through gritted teeth. "You want me. You've wanted me since the moment you first saw me that afternoon—you couldn't look away from me. I know you felt it because I felt it too. You ran away from me then and you ran away from me every time after. I let you go to give you time, but that stops now. No more running, babe," he tells me.

"For your information, *babe*, I'm not one of those bimbos you're used to having. The ones that come to you every time you crook your finger. I won't be used and tossed aside like yesterday's trash. I have two girls to think about, I have to set an example, and I will *not* bring someone into their lives who's not dependable," I inform him. At this point, I'm steaming hot and ready to take him on. Our faces are so close, our noses are almost touching.

"You're right, I'm used to bimbos, as you call them," he fires back. "I haven't been a saint, and yes, I've fucked around a lot. So much that I know what I want and what I don't want. I'm done with that shit. I don't want easy. I want classy, beautiful, and a body that can bring me to my knees and I can worship for hours. I see the way you are with your girls. I see how much my sister and niece respect you. And, I've also seen you make a fool of yourself and you just laugh, not letting it get to you. I like that and I want it. I. Want. *You.*"

Oh my . . . what can I say?

He's completely right. I do want him. I want him so much it scares me, but it's not just me; I have my girls and I have to set a good example for them. I can't have one-night stands; I have too much respect for myself, my girls, and for Jake's memory to lose myself in that. And Zane looks like the type of man that doesn't do relationships, that doesn't do *permanent*—even his own mother is worried he won't settle down. I want him, but I can't just indulge for one night. I wouldn't want my girls to do that and I would be ashamed if they ever found out that I had . . . I just can't.

"Those three weeks you didn't hear from me, I was thinking real nice and hard—did I want to take that responsibility on? I knew I wanted you from the very first moment I saw you, but you came with more than just yourself. I had to get my head on straight. I understand there's more to this than just you and me, there's the girls," he tells me. "Yes, I want to fuck you; I want you any way I can get you. But, I also want to spend time with you. I want to own you, possess you. I want only my hands and my lips on your body. Just the thought of someone else with you makes me want to commit murder." His hand gently caresses my cheek as he looks me in the eye. "I've never felt that before with anyone. And I wanted you to get used to the idea of me."

Hearing his words sends a thrill down my body, but I need to stand strong. I have the girls to think about and I'm also scared—

what if I come to care about him so much and then I lose him? Or worse.

"The first time at the stoplight, I just wanted to drag you out of your Jeep and bend you over my bike and fuck you raw. I wanted to own you from the very first moment," he tells me passionately. "Then, I saw more of you and your personality. I know you're more than just an easy lay. My sister would have my balls if I messed around with you and then high-tailed it. And, I have more respect for you than that. That's why I had to think long and hard, and I realized that you are worth so much, and I need to be a better man to deserve you. I'm going to give it to you straight. I want you—I want to know you in every possible way. I want to meet your girls and get to know them. Things won't be easy, I'm warning you now; I like things my way and I can be an asshole. There'll be times when you want to slap me and leave, but I won't let you leave, never. I'm gonna say and maybe do shit that will piss you off. But, I will never intentionally hurt you. I have a past and I haven't been a choir boy, but that stops now. I've pissed off a shit-ton of people and fucked around a lot, but I've never made an effort to be a better man until now. Until you."

I don't know what to say, so I just sit there taking it all in. I do want him and I want to get to know him. He fascinates me, but he also scares me—not a bad scare where I'm afraid he'll physically hurt me, but scared that he can hurt me emotionally, and where would that leave me. I'm scared of the feelings he evokes, the feelings he's awakened in me. I've loved with all my heart and I've lost that love, leaving me in a pit of despair that I never want to experience again. What if he just leaves? I'm normally not insecure, but my situation is different. I come with responsibility; I won't say baggage, because my girls will never be a burden, but most men aren't ready for a ready-made family. Shit, most of them run away at the first sign of responsibility; the ones who've never had relationships, the ones that usually just fuck around. The fuck-em-and-leave-em type. Men like Zane.

"I can almost hear that brain working overtime, baby." He gives me a gentle kiss on my forehead. "Let's go dance. Enjoy your night, but I'm gonna be here the entire time taking care of you; dancing with you, anything and everything. Tomorrow, we'll talk. Tonight, I want you to have fun and I'm gonna have my hands on you, holding you. Look at me, Faith." He takes my face and looks me in the eyes. "Tomorrow we'll be us; tonight is for you to have fun."

Just as he brought me to the booth, he takes my hand and leads me out. I'm still digesting everything he's told me so I let him lead me without a fight and I miss that sneaky "we'll be us" part of the conversation. He takes me to the bar and gets me a drink. The whole time we're at the bar waiting, he doesn't let go of me. He doesn't leave my side.

The bartender brings my drink and Zane hands it to me. I take a sip and start to relax. I can do this, I tell myself. I can let this go for tonight and have fun. Tonight is supposed to be my night to put all my worries aside and just drink, dance, and have an amazing girls' night with my best friend. And that's what I'm going to do. If Zane wants to stay here and watch over me, then so be it; I'm not going to stop him. I'm going to go back out there on the dance floor and dance my heart out.

With that decision made I turn to him. "You're right, Zane, I do want you, but you know what? Right now I'm not gonna think about that or how much it scares me. I'm gonna go back out there and dance my heart out with Julia. If you want to stay, stay. I'm not gonna stop you or make a big deal out of it. I'm here to have fun." He smiles his sexy smile and my heart skips.

I quickly finish my drink and head back to the dance floor and Julia, leaving a smiling Zane at the bar. What I didn't realize was I shouldn't have told him I was scared; now he was going to do everything in his power to make that fear disappear and with it, my resistance. This time around, I'm the one that needs convincing to take a chance. I'm the one that needs to take a leap of faith—that needs to believe. It isn't just me that could get hurt because now, I have my girls.

⌒⌒⌒

Zane

She said it—she wants me. That's half the battle: getting her to admit it. She went on and on about her fears and reasons why we shouldn't be together, why I shouldn't want her, but I'm a guy. We only hear what we want to hear and for me it was, "Stay. I'm not gonna stop you."

And that's what I'm going to do. I'm going to stay beside her, keeping her in my arms and never letting go.

Because this is my time now.

Chapter 9

After making my way across the dance floor, I finally reach Julia, who's now dancing with some random guy. I manage to get her attention and she sends him on his way. She grabs my hand and then *she* leads me to a booth—the same booth Zane and I used. She sits me down and slides in next to me. Once again, I'm stuck on the inside and have nowhere to go. So I decide to take the offense.

"What happened to Josh?" I ask her.

"He still has to work. He just came to collect his dance and then headed back. I didn't want to interrupt y'all's conversation so I decided to grab a dance partner and dance with him till you came back. Now enough about me. Spill. What did he say to you?"

"What did he say about what?" I try to play dumb.

"Don't fuckin' mess with me, Faith. I'll get rough with ya if I have to. Now talk, and don't leave anything out," she growls and for a few seconds, I fear for my life.

I softly chuckle at my friend. Man, I love it! The suspense is killing her and I'm tempted to drag it out, but I know she'll throat punch me and then wait for me to stop choking for me to talk. Nope, don't want to be punched, so I better spill the beans. I take a deep breath and start telling her what he said to me, leaving nothing out. Not my fear, not the fact that he wants me, nor the fact that he wants to meet Rylee and Skylar.

"Holy shit! He said all that?"

"Yeah, he did. I'm really scared, Julia. I'm not one that can sleep with someone and not become invested. I loved Jake with all of my being and I haven't had anyone after him—I haven't felt the need and I also have the girls—but Zane's different. He makes me want him. I don't know if I'm ready for this. I'm attracted to him, but I'm scared of the feelings he's awakened in me. I deal with attractive men on a daily basis and he takes the prize, but it's not just his looks, there's something else. Something I can't explain."

"It's okay to be scared, Faith. No one expects you to jump in without having some fear. Talk to him and explain what's going on in your head. He wants you, *chica*. He wants you bad and he seems to be the type of person that gets what he wants. Let him know that he'll have to work for you—your trust, and for you to trust him with the girls. Let him know that the girls are the main priority here. Regardless, babe, I think he'll be good for y'all. Right now, though, don't think about anything and just have fun. We came here to dance, so start getting your groove back on." She gives me a hug. "I love you, Faith, and I'll always be here for you."

"I love you too, Julia," I say, getting all teary-eyed. "I'm so lucky I have such an awesome and amazing best friend, and I'll always be here for you too." She grabs my hand and pulls me out of the booth and onto the dance floor.

I do what Julia tells me and I start dancing with her. We get our groove back on, oblivious to the looks from the men and the jealous glares from the women. As we're dancing, Zane returns with another Tequila Sunrise for both Julia and me. I take it, thank him, and continue dancing as I'm sipping my drink. "Vivir Mi Vida Remix" comes on, reenergizing the whole club. I grab Julia and really start getting into it. This song is just what I need; I need to laugh, I need to dance. I'm going to live, and I'm going enjoy my life. Look to the future and not the past. I have to let go and really move on. I have to be brave and take a chance. Take that leap and not let the fear control me.

As I'm thinking about my life and dancing, I feel Zane put his arms around me and pull me back towards him. I allow him to and lean back, moving my hips in a seductive figure eight. As dance, I lift my right arm backwards and place it behind his head. I pull him closer to me and continue dancing; our bodies so close together, every bit of them touching and moving in sync.

Since Jake, I've danced with other men at family gatherings and weddings, but none have felt this natural or seductive. It's been years since I really enjoyed dancing with another man; years since it's felt so right.

One song leads to another and another, and it's just Zane holding me and not letting go. Out of the corner of my eye, I see Julia switching partners every other song. She's here to have fun and not get laid. She doesn't want to lead anyone on, so she switches out. I see no problem with that, so I just keep an eye on her in case she needs help.

As for me, I don't know where this is leading but it feels wonderfully. Being here with him, feeling every bit of his body against mine feels so good. It's amazing; calming yet exciting, and feels so right. Everything else disappears and it's just the two of us. If only life could be so simple without worries of whether I'm doing the right thing or not. I push that thought out of my mind and go back to just the two of us.

"You having fun, baby?" He whispers in my ear and I feel chills go down my body. His normal voice is so smooth, so manly, so *him*. His whisper is all that and so much more, almost taking me over the edge. Oh, God!

"Mmmm hmmm," I softly reply, turning and leaning my head back so he can hear me.

"That's good. I just want you to relax and stay here in my arms. Keep dancing with me until you're so tired you want to fall from exhaustion. I'll be here to hold you and catch you, Faith. I'll always be here for you, love." He softly kisses my neck.

Oh, that feels so good.

He kisses me again and then takes my chin and gently turns my head to him. He brings his lips closer to me and kisses me. One soft kiss, then another, followed by more until I'm almost begging.

"Please . . ."

I somehow manage to turn my body to face him and we kiss. His lips take mine, I let him in and he explores my mouth. We get closer to each other, my arms around his neck, and his arms around me pulling me closer, like we want to become one.

We stop dancing and just kiss. This is the first time in so long that I have felt a man's lips on mine. It feels different and yet so natural, so right.

We finally separate, both breathing hard. We look at each other and he places his forehead to mine. We remain like this, just taking each other in and breathing. We don't separate. I don't want to let him go and I don't want him to let me go.

"This is what I'm talking about. This here . . . it needs to be explored. That one kiss was fuckin' amazing and mind blowing. I've never felt that before. I like it and I want more of it. I knew it would be like this with you from the beginning; I felt a pull towards you. If we feel like this after one kiss, Faith, imagine how good it will feel when I have you in my bed. When I'm exploring every part of your body with my hands and my mouth. Imagine my fingers trailing down your body, my fingers playing with your nipples; teasing them, pulling them gently, rolling them between my fingers, driving you crazy. My lips on them, taking 'em in my mouth and sucking 'em, then biting 'em."

His words are making me squirm and he notices. "You like that, huh? My hands going lower and lower until I reach between your legs. I play with you, asking for entrance, and you let me in. Think how good it will feel when my fingers slide inside of you. My fingers going in and out, like my cock will after I make you cum the first time. As I'm going in and out, my thumb will be playing with your clit; tickling, teasing, and gently pinching it, making you crazy with pleasure. Imagine how good it will feel to just let go, going over the edge while I fuck you with my hand. Then, my mouth replacing that hand and I'm eating you up. Making you cum with my tongue. Mmmm . . . how good you will taste. After you cum a second time, I'll slide my cock inside of you. Imagine how good it'll feel, that sensation of fullness. I'll bring you so much pleasure, love. You'll cum for me again and I'll make you mine. Mine, Faith. That's how amazing it'll be between us." He finishes his monologue with a kiss and then turns me around.

I . . . oh . . . I almost climaxed with his words. I want him. No, I *need* him. I need him so freaking much.

"Zane, I need more. Give me your mouth one more time, I need you." I try turning back, but he doesn't let me. He holds me in place and starts to dance.

"No, Faith. That's all you're getting until after our talk tomorrow. I want you to want me, to desire me, to crave me. I want you to be mine. So, tomorrow, baby—after tomorrow, I'll give you anything you want."

Zane

Well, fuck! Now I'm hard as a fucking rock and I'll find no release until I take care of myself at my place, after I make sure Faith is safely in her house. Regardless, it's all worth it. She wants me as much as I want her. I just have to make sure she agrees to be mine before I break down and give her the physical release she desires.

When I finally take her completely, it'll be because she's truly mine at last.

Chapter 10

I was definitely not a happy camper last night after Zane had me all hot and bothered with his kisses and his sensually descriptive talk. Man, does he know how to talk to me. How to make me crave his touch.

Following our mind-blowing kiss, he bought me a couple more drinks and we danced until the club closed for the night. The entire time, I was in his arms and I loved how safe I felt there—I knew no harm would come to me while I was there with him.

After leaving the club, he drove us back home and made sure Julia and I got inside in one piece. Both of us had had a little too much to drink so we needed help stumbling into my house without waking the girls. I really should've taken some Aleve and a whole bottle of water before falling face down in my bed. Now, it's morning and I'm paying for my night of fun.

"Momma! Momma! Mooommmmaaa!" Skylar shrieks as she comes running down the hall to my room.

"Ggggmmmmmm," I hear beside me. "Oh, God . . . please. Stop yelling."

I turn and see Julia next to me. Guess she was too tired to get to the guest room. Damn, we must both look a fright this morning. I see she fell asleep with her make-up on and now it's all over her face. I don't remember taking mine off, either; hopefully Skylar doesn't think a monster is sleeping in Momma's bed.

"Momma! Wake up!" She hollers, storming into my room and jumping onto the bed. Good thing I know her different yells—I can decipher that the house isn't burning down. This is her "I'm excited" yell.

"I'm up, sweetie," I half say, half groan. I'm getting too old for late nights like this.

"Please go back to sleep, darlin'," Julia begs Skylar. "It's too early in the morning for this. Let Aunty Julia get a little more rest, please, baby. Have mercy on me. Why don't you drag your momma outta here and let me go back nighty-night?"

That witch. I'll remember this and one day I'll get my revenge, I silently vow.

"Don't be silly, Aunty Julia. "It's not early; the clock's little hand is on the nine and the big hand is on the six. And, the clock on the stove says nine-three-zero. That's late."

"Oh, God . . ." I hear Julia moan.

"Momma, there's a man in our house. He wants to see you. Can we keep him, Momma?" She asks excitedly. "He looks like one of my Disney princes, only way bigger. Can we keep him? Please, Momma. Please . . ." she says with her hands clasped together underneath her chin, begging.

"What?" I'm suddenly wide awake and jumping out of bed. "What man in our house? Where is he?" All kinds of crazy scenarios are running through my head as I quickly throw some clothes on.

"Relax, Momma," Rylee says as she comes into my room. "It's just Josilyn's uncle, you little peanut, and I told you that too. Don't be scaring Momma like that, you little bugger. And you can't keep people. It's just not done."

"Don't call me bugger!" Skylar cries at her sister and then turns back to me, making those cute puppy eyes that I find irresistible. "But he's so handsome and I really want to keep him."

"Momma, he's here to see you," Rylee says, turning to me. "I wonder what he wants. Hmmm, might be why he's been asking questions . . ."

Oh, crap. He seriously wants to talk *now?* Doesn't that man realize that it's too early in the morning for our "talk"? I've made my decision but I wanted to tell him when I didn't look like a clown with a bad paint job.

"Tell him I'll be there in a few minutes. Let me jump into the shower first real quick."

"Okay. By the way, he's in the kitchen. He brought breakfast tacos and I wasn't turning those away—they're my favorite. He's pulling out all the stops and I'll take full advantage," she says, laughing at my predicament.

"Okay, okay. I'll hurry." I'm too freaked out to get onto Rylee for letting him in our house without my permission.

Well, there goes my long hot shower to work the kinks out of my body. Instead of my long and leisurely Saturday morning, I am going to have to do everything in less than ten minutes. He owes me for this. Big time.

Twelve minutes later, I'm walking into my delicious-smelling kitchen. Oh, yeah . . . nice greasy breakfast tacos after a night of drinking and dancing. Best breakfast *ever.*

I walk in to find everyone. Even Julia is up, sitting at the table eating. I have to keep my laughter in when I see Zane eating his taco off a pink Disney princess plate, a purple place mat, and drinking from a pink cup. I can guess who gave him the dining set. I wish I had my phone on me for a picture. He looks so darn cute, poor man.

"Did y'all save me one?" I ask.

"Of course, Momma," my girls say at the same time.

"There's one in the bag for you, baby," Zane informs me.

At the word "baby," Rylee and Julia just stop and stare. Oh man, how do I explain this? And, Skylar—well, she is too busy eating her breakfast to notice anything. That girl was blessed with her father's stomach and fondness for food.

Rylee looks between Zane and me. She slowly starts to smile and then resumes eating. She quickly finishes and asks to be excused, then rushes out of the kitchen. I'm sure it's to phone Josilyn. Great! Now, I should expect a call from Jackie. Well, there's no keeping it a secret now. Damn it. I'm sure he did this on purpose.

Julia keeps staring until, I imagine, she starts remembering the events of last night because she perks up, like a light bulb went off in her head. I'm sure she saw us kissing and remembers that Zane and I danced the whole night until he brought us home and led us to the door. Now, *she* starts smiling. She scarfs down the rest of her taco, grabs Skylar and her unfinished breakfast, and high-tails it out the kitchen, leaving me and Zane alone. Thanks a lot, Julia.

"Morning, baby." Zane greets me like it's the most normal thing in the world and he's not barging into my world and turning it upside down.

"Seriously, Zane. You couldn't let me talk to the girls first before having you over?" I'm pretty upset. "I remember we agreed to talk today and that's all."

"Faith, I remember saying 'tomorrow we'll be us,' and now it's time. You're damn lucky I wasn't at your door earlier. I told you we're talking today and we are . . . about *us*. If I let you pick the time, you'll put it off until God knows when. I want this handled so I can grab you and kiss the hell out of you. I want to be able to hold your hand in front of your girls without worry. I'm taking this out of your hands and we're getting this talking over and done with, so eat up." He pauses to continue eating off the Disney princess plate. He looks seriously *adorable,* not that I would tell him just yet. "And, I want to tell the girls together, like we'll be from now on."

"Zane, you know that Rylee is currently on her phone telling Josilyn about breakfast. We're probably gonna be getting calls from Jackie pretty soon."

"Good. News will travel faster than the speed of light once my sister is informed. I'm not gonna hide that I want to be with you. The girls saw me here and didn't get upset. I want to talk to them together. I want to let them know I plan to get to know their momma and them, that I'll respect them and that I'm here if y'all need me. My cards are on the table. I'm being honest with you. I want to be with you and I know that they come with you. I'll never make you choose between us. I need their permission to date you. For me to ask those girls for permission should tell you how serious I'm about you. I don't want to just fuck you, Faith, I want to be your man and I want to call you my woman."

Beautiful.

Last night, I loved being in his arms and his kisses—well, those put me on fire and something else. He took care of Julia and me and made sure we made it home safely. The notion of this bigger-than-life man asking my two girls for anything is surreal. How can I say no to him? Do I really want to let this opportunity pass?

No, I don't.

He's right; we need to talk to the girls. I can't let my fears keep me from experiencing something that might be great. If this doesn't work out, at least both girls will know that their momma wasn't afraid to take a risk. We've been through much worse and made it through.

Taking a deep breath, I look at him.

"You're right, Zane. We need to speak with the girls and inform them about us. I do want you and I'm not gonna let my fears keep me from being with you. We need to tell the girls they'll always come first; they're my first priority. Always. Just don't hurt me, please." I pause for a second. "Um . . . I don't think you'll have a problem with Skylar. She thinks you look like one of her Disney princes; she wants to keep you and was pretty upset when Rylee told her we couldn't keep people."

As soon as I finish speaking, Zane scoops me into his arms and claims my mouth.

Mmmm.

Delicious.

The kiss is even better than I remember from last night.

"Thank you," he says. "I thought I was gonna have to do battle with you again to get you to see things my way. You enjoyed being in my arms last night, but I didn't know if you were gonna blame the alcohol or agree that it's the strong pull between us that led to the incredible night we had." He places our foreheads together, not giving me a chance to be anywhere but in his arms.

I can see now I wasn't the only one that was afraid. I was afraid to take a chance on him and he was afraid that I was going to reject him. I never thought this big strong man would be afraid of anything, but I was wrong. We all have fears.

I just pray that I'm not making a mistake in bringing him to the girls too soon. Things are moving incredibly fast between us, as if an unknown force is pushing us together—pushing me to be with him—but it just feels so right, like it was meant to be. I feel like I belong with him. I pray he decides to stay with us after he finds out my tiny little secret. Right now is just not the time to bring it up.

From that first moment I saw him, I knew he was going to change my world. I wasn't ready for him then and that's why I ran; I was scared of the feelings he awakened in me. Back then, I still hadn't let go of the past. I wasn't ready to move on. Now, moving on doesn't mean that my love for Jake is ending, because I will always love him. He was my husband and he gave me the most wonderful gifts a man can give a woman—he gave me his love, his devotion, his last name, and he gave me two beautiful daughters. I thought he was my forever. When we married, we believed we had a future together. We couldn't have known life had other plans for us. I'll always be grateful for the years we shared, and I'll always treasure our time together. But now, I have to close that chapter in my life and begin a new one.

Zane will be a new chapter in my life that I'm going to enjoy wholeheartedly. We're going to be "us" and we'll see what life has planned for us.

⤝⤞

Zane

T hank you, God.

She's not going to fight me. This morning, I thought I was going to have a fight on my hands, but I was wrong. I feel a huge weight lifted from my shoulders and everything is starting to fall into place.

She's going to take a chance on me—on us.

Thank you.

Chapter 11

After our conversation, we called the girls into the living room and we spoke to them about our newfound relationship. I told them I really liked Zane and Zane really liked me. I had to speak in simple terms so Skylar could understand. Zane spoke to them about his desire to get to know not only me but them as well, and how he was going to do his very best to make us happy. We told them we would be going out on dates both as a couple and all together. After several dates, we were going to introduce each other to our families, meaning their grandparents and his parents. It was a new adventure for all of us, but we were doing it together.

I was worried Rylee would be upset since she remembers our time with Jake and she was his little princess, but I was wrong. She was happy I was going to date again and that the person was Josilyn's uncle, someone we knew.

"I'm glad you're gonna go out with Mr. Zane, Momma," she tells me. "I'll never be upset because I know how much you loved Daddy and how you did everything possible to make our lives run smoothly and us into a strong and happy family. Your love story was one for the fairy books, but he's not here anymore. I also remember your struggle after he died to keep us together and to make sure his dream lived on. You deserve this and so much more. Daddy would want you to be happy and *I* want to you to be happy. If Mr. Zane makes you smile again, I'm not going to stand in your way. I love you always and forever, no matter what. Plus, he's really hot for an old guy," she adds, grinning. "You've done good, Momma." Before I can reply, she runs away laughing. That girl thinks she's so funny. I pray my baby girl finds her prince again someday and he loves her like her daddy did me.

As for Skylar, that girl was ecstatic. *Ecstatic.*

"So does this mean I get to keep him?" she asks, all excited.

Before I can reply, Zane answers. "Yes, princess, y'all get to keep me."

Well, there it is. We get to keep him. Please, God, let that be true. I really, *really* like him. Please . . . I send a prayer up above.

⌖

16 February 2013

When you're happy, time just flies by. Before we know it, four "us" dates, four family dates, and numerous dinners together at my house have passed and we've managed to meet during the day for lunch during our busy work schedules. I've managed to keep him away from the office until I work up the bravery to let him know what I do and who I work with.

And now, we're at the point where we get to meet his family. I don't remember being this nervous when I first met Jake's parents; maybe I was too young to know the significance back then, or in my pretty little mind, I just knew nothing could go wrong. That attitude is totally different now. Oh boy. I pray that this goes well.

I just can't help all the different thoughts running through my head. What is his family going to think of me? Most importantly, what is his *mother* going to think of me? After a very excited Jackie phoned me with questions and then congratulations, she told me that Zane's a really big mommy's boy. He's the baby of the family and the only boy out of five children; therefore, the apple of his momma's eye. It's just peachy for me.

After giving myself pep talks all week, the day finally arrives. It's Josilyn's birthday party. Of course, all of us going is a must; Rylee is Josilyn's BFF and I'm Zane's woman. Yes, woman. I called myself his girlfriend once and he quickly corrected me.

"Babe, I'm your man and you're my woman. What we have isn't high-school shit, it's real. So none of this boyfriend/girlfriend crap. Understand?"

So now, I find myself decked out in Miss Me black shorts with bling on the back pockets, a mint-green mesh three-quarter sleeve shirt with a same-color tank underneath, and black wedges. My hair is in a side braid, my jewelry matches my shirt, and my make-up is neutral. I look at myself in the mirror and give myself a thumbs up on this Bar-B-Q get together-worthy outfit. I'm right in the middle between dressy and casual—perfect.

Rylee's in Miss Me blue jean shorts, a sparkling loose sleeveless cream blouse, and gold gladiator sandals. Her make-up is so light, you can't even tell she has any on. And Skylar, well, that girl is a mixture of pink and purple with a bit of turquoise thrown in for accent. Like I said before, mini-fashionista and she manages to pull it off beautifully.

We gather in my room and check each other over and agree we look beautiful like always. I've made it my mission to instill in my girls that we're always beautiful. I don't want either of my babies to be self-conscious about their bodies; if our clothes start fitting us a bit tightly, we'll go exercise or we'll just buy new clothes that fit our bodies better. My girls are beautiful, no matter what shape or form they take.

Deciding that we're ready to go, we head to the kitchen to wait for Zane and have some sweet tea.

"Did you find the present you wanted to buy Josilyn?" I ask Rylee.

"Yes, I did and Skylar decided that Josilyn just *needed* some purple and pink slap bracelets," she tells me. "So aside from my present, she's also getting slap bracelets and a princess card."

She tries to sound put out by her little sister's antics, but I know she enjoys them and loves her very much. For years, it's just been the three of us and Julia. Yes, we've had Gunner and the guys, but when it came down to it, it's been us girls against the world. As a result, we're extremely close and I'm very grateful the girls welcomed Zane into our little mix.

Five minutes later, the doorbell rings and Skylar runs to answer. She asks who it is and when Zane answers, she throws open the door and launches herself at him. Having gone through this numerous times before, Zane is ready for Skylar and catches her. He picks her up, holds her like she's the most precious thing in the world, gives her a kiss on the forehead and turns to us. He heads to Rylee and gives her a hug before making his way to me.

"Hey, baby. You ready?" He asks and gives me my hello kiss.

Every time I see him with my girls or hear him speak to me, my heart melts. Whenever we're together, he always takes the time to show us he cares for us and no matter how much my girls chatter and fight with each other, he never gets annoyed. He enjoys every moment with us and tells me they're precious memories for the later years.

"We're just waiting on you, honey. Do you want to take your truck or the Jeep?" I ask.

"We'll take the Jeep, since the car seat is in there already and if we decide to both drink, Rylee can drive the Jeep home. The truck's too big for her."

His truck is an awesome Dodge Laramie Longhorn 3500 black with chrome, the color just like his bike. It's big. It's beautiful. It's *badass!*

"Anytime, Zane. Anytime," Rylee eagerly agrees.

She's allowed to drive my Jeep only when I need a ride home, which is hardly ever when I have the girls with me and I just recently started going out again. So, anytime she gets to drive it, she's more than willing. I'd be too if I was her age; my Jeep is freaking *awesome!*

Rylee and I head to the kitchen to grab the food we made for the party: cupcakes, cookies, buffalo chicken dip, and rice (all Josilyn's favorites), while Zane buckles Skylar into her seat. We head out the door, load everything up, climb in, buckle, and set out to meet Zane's family.

The whole way there I'm giving myself pep talks. I seriously hope his mother doesn't have anything against me or against my girls. Regardless of what she thinks, Zane and I are together, but it makes it so much easier if I have her approval. And his sisters . . . oh crap, please let them be agreeable and nice. The only one I know is Jackie.

Zane grabs my hand and brings it to his lips. I sigh. I really love when he does that.

"They're gonna love you. They're gonna love you and the girls and if they don't and give you a hard time, well, that's their problem. I won't take shit and regardless of their feelings, they'll respect you or answer to me. You and I are together and no one is gonna come between us. I've found y'all and I'm keeping y'all. Fuck anyone else." He holds my hand tighter while running his thumb over my knuckles, not letting my hand go.

"I know we're together, honey, but I still want their approval. I don't want them to give you a hard time."

"Why would someone not like you, Momma?" I hear Skylar ask from the back seat. "You're an awesome mommy and we love you. Just do what you tell me when I'm nervous or scared: 'It's an adventure; take deep breaths, just have fun and hold your head up high.'"

"I know, Peanut. This is the first time I'm meeting Zane's mom and I want her to be nice."

"It's gonna be okay. If you feel uncomfortable, just tell me or Jackie, and we'll handle it. If it's too bad, we'll leave. I promise," Zane tries to reassure me.

Jackie let it slip accidentally that this family gathering is more to meet me than for Josilyn's birthday. Josilyn had her birthday party with her friends last week and this week it's for family. So all the sisters, cousins, aunts and uncles, parents and grandparents will be gathered. Shoot, I even think some family friends are invited as well. Jackie told me that everyone was curious to meet the girl that turned Zane's head. He was an "I'm-never-gonna-settle-down" kinda man for years before meeting me.

Can't say I blame him. I'd be too, if my girlfriend at the time was sleeping with my best friend while I was away on deployments and training. And then had the audacity to tell Zane he would accept the baby since it was his best friend's. Don't even get me started on that bitch (because she is one). If I ever meet her, I'm liable to smack her good. I'm not fond of women that can't keep their legs closed when their men are away. It's not that hard: be a lady, don't mess around or have sex with someone that isn't your boyfriend, fiancé, or husband. Respect yourself and respect your man, and, I hold men to the same standard—respect your women. Simple.

A short while later, we arrive at Jackie's house.

Lord, have mercy.

There are vehicles parked everywhere. Every. Where. I imagine the only person not here is the president.

Oh God, I pray, please give me strength.

Zane, with his badass alpha male magic, finds a parking spot close to the house and we unload. Before grabbing Skylar and the food, he takes me against him and lays a good one on me.

"You're mine, Faith. Remember that," he says. "You're amazing, strong, smart, beautiful, and you've done well raising the girls. My family is gonna love you because I do. If they have a problem, I have no problem settling it and protecting my girls. Got it?"

Did he just say what I thought he said? It can't be. He's just giving me encouragement . . . right? Yes, that's it, I tell myself; it's encouragement. There's no way this wonderful man is in love with me or would say it first. He's too much of a man's man to put himself out like that. Even with Jake, I said it first.

"I do, honey. I got it. I'm with you and no one is gonna change that. You're mine and I'm yours," I reply. I give him a kiss, squeeze him tight, and turn to get the food with Rylee's help.

"Momma, it's gonna be okay. We got this. Just like everything else life's thrown at us—we got this," Rylee tells me.

Here goes . . . there's no turning back now.

We turn from the Jeep and the four of us together as a unit walk toward Jackie's front door. Whatever opinions that may lay ahead, we're facing them together, as it should be. I take a deep breath and walk forward with my head held high.

✁

Zane

I've fallen hard for this woman and her daughters. I just sneakily told her I loved her—something I never thought I'd do first, but I don't regret it.

She didn't run for the hills. Faith's here and about to face a family gathering just for me. She and the girls are scared, but like the strong and amazing women they are, they straighten their backs and walk forward with me.

They're willing to face the unknown and risk rejection—for me.

I'm one lucky man.

Chapter 12

I allow myself one last second of panic when I notice that instead of letting himself in like he normally does, Zane rings the doorbell. A few moments later, the door is opened and a late-middle aged woman stands there. She's Hispanic, about five-one, full-figured, and very beautiful. By the way she greets Zane, I can guess who she is.

"¡Mijo! ¿Cómo estás, mi papi-lindo?"

She reaches for his head and he bends down, allowing his mother to kiss his forehead like he was still a child. He's definitely a momma's boy.

She's takes us in with her eyes, noting that Skylar is in his arms.

"Who do we have here, mijo?" She asks with a huge smile.

"Mamá, this beautiful little girl in my arms is Skylar, and this is her sister, Rylee." He introduces them proudly. "This amazing woman beside me is my Faith. I've found my one and I'm keeping her." He emphasizes by taking my hand and pulling me as close as possibly allowed by the food, and giving me a kiss on my forehead.

"Faith, Rylee, and Skylar, this is my mother, Angélica."

"Hi, Mrs. Knight," the girls say.

"It's a pleasure to meet you, Mrs. Knight," I tell her in Spanish.

"It's Angélica or Mamá for you, bella Faith, and Abuelita to you, niñas," she says to my girls. "Mrs. Knight is my mother-in-law."

She gives us each a hug and a kiss on the cheek and allows us in the door. I swear I hear her mumble, "Well, that girl's not going to be happy," but it's so soft I think I might have imagined it. She walks us to the kitchen, passing by the living room, which is filled with family members watching a soccer game. If only I could escape to there, I wish to myself.

We say hi to everyone in passing and finally make it to the

kitchen, where I see Jackie and Josilyn. Finally, some familiar faces.

"Did y'all bring the food?" Josilyn asks eagerly without a greeting.

"Josilyn! Where are your manners, *niña?* That's not how we treat guests," Angélica scolds her.

"But, *Abuelita,* they're not guests. It's Mrs. Faith, Rylee, Skylar and of course, Uncle Zane. I'm always at their house and they know how I am," Josilyn replies and turns to us eagerly.

"Of course we brought the food," Rylee tells her. "Momma made you your favorite cupcakes: vanilla with Oreo cookie at the bottom and whipped chocolate icing on top. We also brought you M&M cookies, buffalo chicken dip, and *arroz con pollo*—everything that you love from our house." She turns to Jackie. "Where do I put these, Mrs. Jackie?"

"Put them on the counter over there," she says. "Grab y'all some drinks and head out the back and meet the rest of the family. Faith, we have wine and margaritas, and if you really need them, I think we can find ourselves making some Tequila Sunrises."

We put the food down and I give Jackie a hug.

"Pray for me," I beg her.

She softly chuckles. "It's not that bad. Everyone is just dying to meet the girl that changed Zane's mind."

"Come on. Let's go meet everyone else so we can eat. I'm starving. I didn't get to eat breakfast at your place, since I had to work last night at the firehouse." Zane grabs my hand and leads me outside. "It'll be fine, baby, I'm with you."

We make it out the door into the backyard. It's full—I mean really *full*—of family members. Aunts, uncles, cousins, sisters with husbands, little kids running around, and an older couple are all scattered throughout the yard. We make the rounds and we're introduced to so many people, I don't know how I'll remember everyone. I may have an awesome memory, but it's just too many people.

We finally make it to the grill where Jonathan, Jackie's husband, is speaking with a gentleman. His back is to us. When he turns around, I gasp. Now I know where Zane gets his looks and his eyes. My goodness! This man is handsome and his eyes . . . his eyes are just like the ones that look at me with such tenderness when I look at Zane. Yes, Mr. Knight has aged very well. Zane is a lucky man; he'll still be extremely handsome when he gets older.

"Dad," Zane says to the older version of himself, "I want you to meet my girls and my woman. Rylee, Skylar, and Faith, this is my father, Julian Knight."

"Dad, this little girl in my arms is Skylar and this young lady is Rylee. And here on my side is my "one," my Faith. I've been lucky to find her and I'm not letting her or the girls go," Zane proudly announces.

Did he just announce that to his whole family?

"Hi, Mr. Knight," the girls greet him in chorus.

"Oh my, now I know where Zane gets his god-like looks," I blurt before realizing what I'm saying. "I mean—it's a pleasure, Mr. Knight; you have a wonderful family."

Everyone chuckles as I blush. Leave it to me to say something ridiculous.

"I know, little lady," he replies. "His mother is a lucky lady and I'm a lucky man to be blessed with such a beautiful family. Please call me Julian. Girls," he says to my daughters, "y'all can call me Grandpa, if your mother allows." I'm surprised at their quick acceptance.

"It's a pleasure, Julian," I say as he takes me in his arms and gives me a small hug. After looking at Zane and nodding, I say, "Julian, it would be an honor for the girls to call you Grandpa. Thank you."

"Well, now that y'all have met Zane's woman and we can see she's not an imaginary person, let's get everyone fed," Jackie says.

With the introductions over, we move to get the food set out so everyone has an opportunity to serve themselves. I go inside and grab the plates, cups, and plastic-ware. The girls follow to help and grab the food we brought over to take outside with Zane's help. He's proudly showing us off to his family. I figure out that there are a couple people that don't like the idea of us dating. For example, there's an older woman I think might be a friend of Angélica, and a younger woman who I'd guess is her daughter, both are giving me the stink-eye.

I see Zane in line with Skylar, helping her fill her plate. He takes her to a seat next to Josilyn and Rylee, who are sitting at the "young adult" table. He sits her down and heads back to me.

"She's set, babe. Now it's our turn," he says to me as he meets me in line and gives me a kiss.

As we're filling our plates, I hear someone ask, "Who made the rice?"

"My sister did," Skylar tells the young man. I think his name is Colton; a cousin.

He gives Rylee a look of disbelief. "*You* made it?"

"Yes," Rylee replies with a blush.

"You can cook?" he asks and at her nod he dramatically cries, "Marry me!"

His demand makes everyone laugh and Zane leans into me. "He's addicted to food. Swears when he finds the first woman that can cook as good as his mother, he's gonna marry her. Don't worry, he's a sophomore in college so Rylee won't see much of him."

I chuckle and begin to fill my plate. When I reach the end of the buffet table, I wait for Zane and see his plate *loaded* with food. Guess it runs in the family, I chuckle to myself.

We head to the table where his parents and Jackie are sitting and find room for ourselves. Everyone starts asking questions about me and we answer them all.

A voice pipes up, "How can you be Rylee's mother? Were you, like, fourteen when you had her? And where is the girls' father—or fathers?"

These rudely asked questions came from the younger woman who had been giving me the stink-eye. Since her mother and Angélica are friends, it figures that she's at our table. I'm astonished at her rudeness nonetheless, and Zane tenses.

"She's a bitch and pissed Zane found you," Jackie whispers to me. "For years, her mother has been claiming that she"—here she points at the young lady (and I use the term loosely)—"and Zane will marry and make my mother and her related through marriage. Don't worry, Zane never went there with her. He only tolerates her for our mother."

"Yes, I'm Rylee's mother and no, I wasn't fourteen when I had her. I was eighteen when I *adopted* her and *their* father passed away years ago," I inform her politely.

I hear a soft intake of breaths at the straightforwardness of my answer.

Lisa—that's her name—gives me the stink-eye again. "That must've been hard," she simpers. "I guess now that you found Zane, you expect him to take care of you. That's not very fair to him."

"Lisa, shut the hell up," Zane growls. He's pissed and ready to explode, but I'm going to handle this. Not him.

"No, Lisa, I don't expect Zane to take care of us. I can provide very well for my family. I may be young, but I do have a steady job and money. That car we came in"—I point to the Jeep—"is mine. That baby there is a Jeep SRT, custom ordered and terribly expensive. *I* paid for that. My clothes are designer and so are Rylee's. *I* paid for those. With my own money that *I* earn working. And, before his death, my husband made sure we were taken care of. He made sure that we would never suffer for money." I jerk my thumb at myself. "I help run the company he started with his friend, The Phoenix Corporation . . . you might've heard of it. If not, please look it up. But, most importantly, *I* raised my daughters to know right from wrong, to be respectful, and to love and accept themselves. I've tried to be the best mother and we made it through a situation that could've torn my family apart. I'm gonna tell you this only once—you can say whatever you want about me but *never* bring my daughters into a conversation where you're being hurtful and rude because you will *not* like the way I react. So, you see, I can take care of my girls and myself. Now, please tell me what you do. I'm very interested to hear about *your* job."

I smile sweetly, but I really want to drag her across the backyard by her hair extensions after slapping her silly.

She's shocked at my reply and opens her mouth to respond, but nothing comes out. She looks like a gulping fish. Serves her right. I don't want to sink to her level, since my momma taught me to be a lady, but if she continues to be rude to my daughters, she'll see the mama bear I can turn into. For my girls, I'll do anything to protect them—I'm not afraid to get my hands dirty.

"I'm really sorry," I say quietly, turning to Angélica and Julian. "I do hate to be rude but I don't want y'all to think that I need Zane to take care of us financially. I'm pretty well off and I'm not looking for a hand-out. In reality, I didn't want to start seeing Zane. I'm not a typical woman of my age; I am a mother first and foremost. I was pretty clear with him that I came with my girls; that we were a package deal. If y'all have a problem, please let us know and we'll leave."

"If anyone has a problem with my woman, speak up NOW!" Zane announces in a commanding voice. "This is the last time she will be disrespected. Next time, I won't let her handle it—I will. No one messes with my woman or my girls. If anyone needs to leave, it's Lisa."

"How dare you . . ." Lisa's mother gasps. "How dare you treat her like that?!"

She turns to Angélica for support, but Angélica is looking at Zane with big shining eyes. I imagine she's planning our wedding right this second in her mind, and picking out baby names for her future grandchildren.

"No, Mrs. Angelo, y'all listen here," snaps Zane, pointing at both her and Lisa. "Faith is my woman. She's the woman I spend all my time with and the woman that I'm not letting go. I've found the one that I want to spend the rest of my life with. And that person sure as hell isn't Lisa. So get it out of your head that you and my mother are gonna be related by marriage. I. Will. Not. Marry. Lisa. I've been cordial to y'all because you're my mother's friend, but that's gonna stop if y'all continue to be rude to Faith. If this family has to choose between y'all or Faith, I can tell you hands down that Faith is gonna win. She's my woman and will be respected as such." He looks around at the rest of the family. "Anyone else have a problem?"

No one says anything and I don't blame them. Zane has gone into protective mode and you don't want to mess with him. Having Zane stand up for me—us—like that is freaking awesome. If we weren't surrounded by his family, I would drag him into a secluded corner and show him my appreciation.

"Well, that's settled," Julian announces. "Congratulations, son."

Angélica is looking at us with tears in her eyes and smiling from ear to ear.

"So, Lisa, you leaving?" Jackie asks gleefully. Yup, my friend is more than happy to finally have that girl put in her place.

"Hurumpf." Lisa settles down with a pout.

After that, we all resume eating and making small talk. People stop to chat with us and congratulate us on our relationship. Everyone is happy that Zane is ready to settle down. His male cousins say it's because they'll get to sweep up all the broken-hearted women that will finally realize they have no chance with him now. Before, Zane was the unattainable, the one every woman wanted to change, but no more. He's with me now. He's mine and he's happy. I look at my girls and see Rylee laughing at something Colton is saying. Skylar's too busy munching down on her food to make conversation.

Life is good.

We've been accepted into Zane's family and I can breathe easier. I was afraid they would disapprove of me and my girls, and I'm glad to see that those fears were for nothing. They accept us because we make Zane happy and that's all they want.

The rest of the day is spent mingling and getting to know the rest of the family. There are so many of them that I know I won't be able to remember everyone's name. We cut Josilyn's beautiful cake, a five-tier chocolate fondant cake splashed with a variety of colors (turquoise, purple, pink, yellow, and orange). Each tier is wrapped in a different color edible ribbon, and each layer is a different flavor. Amazing, beautiful, and so delicious.

Of course, after the cake cutting, we all gather around to cheer the young'uns on while they break the soccer ball piñata. Yes, a piñata. Josilyn says she's still a kid at heart and she'll have a piñata until the day she is no more. The piñata is a big hit, especially since Zane's in charge of handling the rope that takes the piñata up and down, and he's having a blast messing with the kids that are trying to hit it.

Everyone is having a good time and Lisa's rudeness from earlier is forgotten. Rylee is hanging out and getting to know Josilyn's cousins, and Skylar is having the time of her life playing with the other kids her age. I . . . well, I find myself in Zane's arms. He keeps me close and tells me how much he loves having us here with his family.

"If I didn't know that it would freak you out, I'd ask you to marry me right this instant," he tells me, catching me by surprise. He chuckles at my expression. "Relax, I won't ask because I know you're not ready, and I don't have a ring yet." He laughs at my gasp. "You were worried my family wasn't going to like you, but they love you and the girls. They just want me to be happy and they realize that y'all are my happiness. I knew the first time I saw you that you were gonna change my life. I'm glad that you're changing it by bringing laughter to me and showing me that there are some women, besides the ones in my family that take care of their men and are there to take their back when needed. Thank you, baby."

"No, Zane, thank you. You barged into my life and made me take a risk. Thank you for showing me that there's more to life than what I was living. When I lost Jake, I lost a part of myself, and my dreams and future changed. I don't regret my decisions, but I lost the sexy and fun part when I took over being mother and father to my daughters. Thank you for showing me that I'm still sexy and young. Your alpha-male, chest-beating, you're-mine attitude may piss me off, but I wouldn't change it for the world."

I can tell that he's happy with my reply because he grabs me and kisses me. I think he's going to plant a hot and sexy, drop-your-panties kisses, but I'm wrong. His kiss is so tender and full of emotion, I want to cry from the strong feelings it evokes. I forget we're surrounded by his family, and I and lose myself in our kiss. That kiss relays an emotion I'm not ready to verbally admit to, but I can show him. I'm afraid to lose what we've found. I pray that life decides to let me keep Zane. He's come to mean so much to me and the girls. He wants to show us that he'll be here for us, and is constantly showing his affection and dedication for us. The "I'm never going to settle down" man is reformed and not afraid to shout it to the world. I send a prayer up above: Please, *please* let us keep him.

We finally separate when the whole family starts cheering. He keeps his arm around me and we head back to sit with his parents. Instead of letting me have my own seat, he settles me on his lap. I try to get up, but his hold on me tightens.

"It's okay, Faith. Here's where you belong. You belong with me, so start getting used to having my arms around you and being in my lap whenever possible, even in public. I wasn't one for PDA until I met you," he tells me and gives me a quick peck on the lips.

I decide to throw caution to the wind and enjoy our closeness. If anyone is bothered by it, they don't make a peep and everything continues as normal. Both Jackie and Angélica are smiling these big, huge smiles and have faraway looks in their eyes; Angélica is probably dreaming of wedding colors and grandbabies, and Jackie is probably thinking of ways to tease her baby brother later on. Me, well I'm just happy in Zane's arms.

Moments later, I hear a ruckus going on behind us and I turn to see what's going on. The younger generation of Knight males, the ones around Rylee's age, have a soccer ball and are going around rounding up other males. I'm confused about what's going on until Jackie fills me in.

"Every family gathering, we play a game of *fútbol*. Sometimes the girls play, but it's mostly the boys and men. Regardless, we all head to the park to cheer them on," she tells me.

"Ah," I say with intrigue, getting my thinking face on.

I turn to Zane. "Do you play, honey?"

"Ha, do I play?" He replies. "Baby, I'm the shit." He puffs out his chest, trying to look all macho.

I laugh at my man's humble reply. Hmmm . . . I wonder if they'll let me play. I could use a game of soccer to relax and have a bit of fun.

"So can anyone play, or is it only y'all men?" I ask.

He looks at me and chuckles. "You wanna play?"

"Of course. It looks fun," I reply tongue-in-cheek. "I think Rylee and Josilyn will want to join as well."

"These games are serious. We're a competitive lot. I don't want you to get hurt, but if you wanna play . . . I'll let you be on my team since you're my woman and all," he tells me with a grin on his face.

"Oh! You'll let me be on your team. Thanks," I say with a bit of attitude.

He probably thinks I'm doing it to get brownie points, but he doesn't know that I love to play. This is something that hasn't come up in conversation and it might come as a surprise.

"Baby, I'm good. I'll be humble like you and just say that I'm pretty good so you won't have to worry about me."

He looks at me with a big smile from ear to ear, which baffles me because I figured he'd be surprised. He just smiles and doesn't contradict me. Smart man. "Okay, babe," he says. "You and the girls wanna play, y'all will play."

"Hey y'all," he yells out to the rest of the guys. "Faith, Rylee, and Josilyn want to play."

The guys laugh and there's some grumbling, but it quickly dies when they see that we're serious.

"They're gonna to be on my team," Zane announces and some of the males on his team don't look happy.

"We'll take it easy on y'all then," one of his cousins replies.

Colton, the sweetie, says, "I'm on Uncle Zane's team."

Bless that boy, I think he has a crush on Rylee. He's going to be disappointed, since she's currently dating a boy from her school. I don't think he's good enough for my baby girl, but I support her and don't make a big deal out of it. It's not serious, since she's only been out with him a couple of times due to all her practices and schoolwork, but apparently they're "going out" as the school-vine says.

"Alright, everyone. Go change and then we'll make our way over to the field," Zane announces.

The girls come over to me, and Colton is right behind them.

"Mrs. Faith, you really going to play?" Josilyn asks in disbelief. Even though she's Rylee's best friend, I don't think Rylee has told her that I used to play back in my day.

Rylee and I share a look and smile. "Yes, darlin', I'm gonna play today. It's been a while since I played and I want to have some fun and a little challenge."

Jackie, who knows my little secret, and Rylee start laughing. The guys look at them as if they're out of their minds. I just tell the guys, "Relax, I know how to play." I turn to Zane. "Honey, trust me, we're going to kick ass."

At that, Rylee and I head to the Jeep to get our gear, which I keep in my vehicle in case I get a craving to play when I have some free time. I may not be playing ball professionally anymore, but I still like to keep my skills sharp. Not only was I a hell of a student, I was also a hell of a ballplayer.

We head out to change, leaving everyone else behind in disbelief. I hear Jackie say, "This is going to be *so* fun. Ma, we need the popcorn and chairs." She chuckles all the way to the house.

⟡

Zane

She thinks I don't know about her talent, but she's wrong. I can't wait to see my Faith play. I've heard of her skills and seen some YouTube videos showcasing them, but I never had the pleasure of seeing her play in person.

To get to actually play on a team with her, even if it's just a friendly and very competitive family game, is going to be an honor that I'll treasure always.

Chapter 13

W hen everyone's finished changing, we make our way to the park. There are twenty people playing, so nine will be on the field for each team and the other two on goalie for their respective teams. Our team is comprised of Zane, Rylee, Josilyn, Colton, Julian, myself, and four other family members. The other team is comprised of more uncles and cousins, whose names I've yet to remember.

"Josilyn, you're goalie," Zane, our team captain, orders. "You play the position in school and are probably the best qualified out of all of us. Rylee, Colton, and you (he points to a cousin) are midfielders. Dad, you and y'all (he points to his two uncles) are defenders. Y'all stay in front of the goal, so y'all won't have to run much. Faith, you'll have to be a forward along with my cousin and me."

If I didn't know any better, I would say he knows I know how to play; otherwise, he'd put me on defense. But how can he, since I haven't told him about that part of my past? Unless he seriously follows soccer. It's been a few years but my name still goes around and I still make rare appearances. Nah, I tell myself. He's doesn't know. He probably just assumes I have more endurance than the older gentlemen. That must be it. Poor man must be worried we're going to get our butts kicked.

"Honey, it's okay," I reassure him. "I know how to play. Who do you think practices with Rylee at home and taught Skylar about the game?"

"I'm not worried. I know you can play," he tells me, taking me by surprise. "These family games are different than the regular games y'all are used to playing and I don't want y'all girls getting hurt. The cousins and uncles tend to get competitive and a little pushy. They turn into asses. Just be careful."

"Relax. We'll just push back, I promise," I tell him, trying to be reassuring.

After handing out positions, we make our way towards Angélica and I hear someone say, "Look at her. She thinks she can play. Psshh. I hope Zane sees her make a fool of herself."

As expected, it's Lisa speaking, but at least the other ladies are smart enough to quiet her down and remind her of my place in Zane's world. Since Zane made my position clear with the family, and they now realize that my girls and I just want Zane to be happy, the rest of the aunts and cousins have taken an even better liking to me. Thank goodness, because I was about to head over there and slap the crap out of that woman. There are just some women that rub you the wrong way and Lisa is one of those for me.

I see Zane's jaw tighten and I lean in to give him a kiss. I want him to have fun and not worry about Lisa's jealousy. That kiss on the jaw leads to a kiss on the lips, which leads to Zane wrapping his arms around me.

"A kiss for good luck, baby," he says.

My smile turns into a laugh when I hear Lisa's "harrumph," but she still doesn't leave. She's like an annoying buzzing mosquito that doesn't go away.

Skylar is sitting next to Angélica, ready to cheer her momma and sister on.

"Yay, Momma, Josilyn, and Rylee! Kick some tushy!" She exclaims excitedly.

"What about me, my lil' princess?" Zane asks, trying to sound offended. He picks up Skylar and starts tickling her.

Between bouts of laughter, she cries, "You too, Zane! I'll cheer for you too. Momma make him stop! I'm gonna pee in my pants!"

We all laugh at the two of them and Zane finally puts her down and gives her a loud smacking kiss on her forehead. Throughout all of this, Angélica is smiling fondly and sharing looks with Julian.

"Ready for some *fútbol*," yells the opposing team.

"Alright everyone," Zane calls. "Let's get on the field. I want to have bragging rights, so don't allow them to score! One, two, three, GO!"

We run out onto the field and take our positions.

The game starts out pretty mild. The other men try to take it easy on us girls, but after Zane scores the first goal and our defense is pretty solid, they start getting more aggressive. I get pushed around, which annoys the heck out of me but I deal with it like a big girl. When I finally get pushed down and it's not accidental, that's when I've had enough. It's time to show these boys what I'm made of—no more nice Faith. It's time to get my game on.

"What the fuck, Juan!" Zane's pissed that my butt is on the ground and Juan did it to be an ass. Juan is one of his uncles through marriage. Zane doesn't like him; he's a bit conceited and to be frank, an asshole.

"If she wants to play with the big boys, Zane, then she has to deal," Juan replies smugly.

Big mistake. Zane is now livid. He charges over, getting in Juan's face and grabbing him by his shirt. The rest of the males are trying to calm the situation with no results. Zane outweighs Juan by a good bit of muscle, is taller, and very, very pissed off. I finally get myself together and touch Zane's arm.

"It's okay, baby," I try to reassure him. "That just hurt my pride and that's all. Come on, honey." I try to lead him away and after a few tugs, I finally succeed.

As we near the sidelines I hear snide remarks coming from Lisa. That girl is really starting to piss me off. Seriously starting to get on my last nerve.

Rylee and Josilyn make their way to me. "You okay, Momma?"

"I'm fine, baby girl."

"My uncle's an ass, Mrs. Faith, and so are his sons. Sorry about that." Josilyn sounds embarrassed.

"It's okay, girly, no harm done," I tell her. It's not her fault some people don't have any manners.

I turn to Zane and the rest of the men on our team. "Alright. They wanted us to play like the 'big boys,' so we'll show them. Rylee"—I turn to my girl—"no more holding back. Give it your all and you too, Josilyn. No goals, and I mean *absolutely no goals* allowed. Got me?"

The girls nod their heads. The males are surprised at my announcement and my tone of voice, but Zane, that man is smiling from ear to ear. I'm really starting to think he knows one of my secrets. I'm talking in my "in the zone" voice, meaning it's time to play some serious ball.

"Zane, I told you I could play and I can. I'm actually pretty darn good. They want us to bring it aggressively, so we'll bring it. *Shit just got serious,*" I say, trying to sound like a badass. "Be ready, okay?"

Julian starts to chuckle. "What's your last name again, darlin'?"

"It's Duval, sir," I reply. It seems a strange time for him to ask, but I answer nonetheless.

He starts laughing and when asked why, he replies, "Y'all will see in a bit. Keep your eyes open and pay attention. Today, we'll see grown men cry." After his prediction, we run onto the field and open up a real "can of whoop ass" on them boys.

And boy did those men cry. They cried rivers of tears, so much you could drown in them. It was one of the most beautiful sights I've encountered. Juan and his sons ate their words and Zane got bragging rights. Rylee and Josilyn were able to showcase their skills and, oh my goodness, did they do it. I'm so proud of those girls. Josilyn stopped every goal attempt that came her way and Rylee, well that girl sure did surprise everyone. That last goal was *amazing.* I passed the ball to her and while covered by two defensive players, she stopped the ball with her chest, found an opening, got the ball up, and scored a bicycle goal. Like I said, *freaking amazing!* That had everyone's jaw dropping—except mine and Skylar's, of course.

That goal ended the game. Skylar was running around with her arms in the air, yelling at the top of her lungs.

"GGGGOOOOAAAALLLL!"

I had Rylee in my arms, since she jumped on me to celebrate. Like I said, *awesome!* Everyone was in awe and Julian was laughing his ass off. He finally let Angélica in on his joke and then she started laughing.

"Babe, what the hell was that?" Zane asks in awe.

"That, baby, was *fútbol* or how they say in Germany—*Fußball.*"

"Okay . . ." he trails off, waiting for an explanation.

"Well," I say, biting my lower lip. I'm not sure how to get my words out, but I try anyway. "Rylee played soccer in Germany for six years and, let me tell you, they really take that sport seriously. Football is a religion here in Texas, but in Germany, *Fußball* is life. And I, well . . ." I trail off, not knowing how to put it into words and have them not look at me differently.

A few years ago, soccer was a huge part of my life. I ate and breathed soccer. I was blessed with the ability to soccer and play it well. I spent a lot of time training and worked my behind off to make it to the USA women's team over several years, both Julia and I did. I was living my dream, both in my personal life and my career, until that dreaded knock on the door changed my plans forever.

"What's she's trying to say, son, is that she's Faith Duval," Julian tells everyone surrounding us.

"Yes, dad, I know who she is," Zane answers.

"No, boy, you ain't getting me here. She's Faith Duval. Think, boy. *The* Faith Duval. One of the youngest players to play for the United States from 2002–2008 until she retired. She played in two World Cup tournaments—2003 and 2007—and the 2004 Olympics. And she's now with you," he says proudly, and then he turns to me. "You wouldn't happen to keep in touch with Julia?" He asks me, making Rylee laugh.

Right now, I just want the ground to open up and swallow me. I'm not ashamed or embarrassed about my past accomplishments; it's just that people treat me and my girls differently after knowing all the facts.

Zane is just as quiet as everyone else. He stares at me, working something out in his mind, but strangely, he doesn't seem surprised. "Why didn't you say something to me sooner?" He asks.

"Well, people act differently after finding out my history, plus it's been a while. I'm fine when it's just me, but when it starts affecting my daughters, that's when I start getting upset. I didn't want you to look at me different. I figured I would eventually tell, especially once Rylee starts playing college soccer and when she decides to try out for the USA team."

"Babe, I wouldn't treat you differently. You're still the same person I fell in love with. This won't change anything. Am I surprised? Hell yeah, I'm surprised you didn't mention anything before now. My woman is a badass on the soccer field and it's not every day you meet a professional athlete, even a retired one. I'm surprised my father hasn't adopted you or asked for your autograph yet."

"So we're good, honey?" I ask for reassurance.

"Come here," Zane says as he takes me into his arms and hugs me. "Wild horses wouldn't keep me away, Faith. I've always thought you were amazing." That surprises me. "And now, I think you're beautiful *and* amazing; you're stuck with me."

He kisses me and turns me toward the rest of the family. "Anyone have anything to say to this discovery?" He asks.

No one answers. Thank goodness. I think it's more to do with Zane's imposing presence as he stands by me like a warrior than anything else. Whatever the case, I'm grateful things are still normal—well almost normal. Julian is looking at me like he wants to steal me away from Zane, in a nonromantic way of course.

We start gathering all of our things and packing up. Rylee gets Skylar who's dribbling the ball up and down the field and we head towards the Jeep.

That's when it hits me.

"The same person I fell in love with."

Does Zane really love me or was it just something he said in the spur of the moment?

I think about asking him, but I don't know if I'm ready to hear the answer. There are moments when I feel guilty. I'm starting to develop really strong feelings for Zane. I think maybe, just maybe I may be starting to love him. I know he calls me his woman and he's my man, but we've never said anything about love—not true love. The love that leads to marriage and dreams of a future with children and everything. Can it be?

I had my forever with Jake, even though it was cut short. Is it possible to be blessed in love again? Is it possible to find that kind of true and lasting love twice in a lifetime? If so, would life take him away just like it did Jake?

All of these thoughts are running through my head and it's starting to hurt. Zane must notice because he asks, "You okay? You're kinda quiet over there." He takes my hand as we drive back to my house.

"I'm good, honey, just thinking about the whole day and how much I loved spending time with and getting' to know your family. All but Lisa, of course. She's a witch and I wouldn't spit on her even if she were on fire."

He laughs.

"I'm serious," I say.

He continues to laugh and I love it.

Zane

I said the words but she didn't say them back. I can't be discouraged; I'm not the type of man that gives up easily, and I know she's not ready just yet. She still needs time. I still need to show her that I'm always going to be here for her and the girls. I need to prove to them that I'm here for the long haul. Even if it takes me years of dedicating myself to her and the girls, I'll never give up. I'll always love them because they deserve to be loved and protected.

Always.

Forever.

Chapter 14

March rolls around.

I've been busy with work, soccer season, and attending all the necessary functions needed for the girls' schools. Zane and I are stronger than ever. We still haven't taken the next step physically since my girls are always waiting for me after our dates, but we've had some steamy moments. Zane is very understanding and hasn't pressured me, which I appreciate. He wants our first time to be perfect and without regrets.

He continues to amaze me when it comes to dealing with Rylee and Skylar. He's been to every soccer game when he's not working; he even gets a kick out of Skylar and her seriously loud cheering. He's taken Skylar to gymnastics class a few times when I've been really busy at the office and Rylee is at practice.

The girls just plain love him. Whenever he's available, he comes to the house to bring us or make us breakfast, help with lunch or dinner, and he comes over for movie nights. He's had us over at his place several times for dinner and movie night, as his entertainment center is better than ours, but he prefers to spend the majority of our time at my house.

"It's homier and this is the girls' home," he tells me.

Unfortunately for him, he's outvoted by girls in the movie department and gets to watch a lot of Disney movies and chick flicks. He's taken us to the movies, bowling, and other family activities and enjoys himself. He's happy and we're happy. Everything is perfect. I'm grateful but at the same time, I'm waiting for the other shoe to drop. I know worrying does me no good, so I try to put those silly thoughts aside and concentrate on the goodness in my life. I just pray that everything stays as good as it's been.

With the month of March comes spring break and the girls are super-excited to visit their grandparents. They'll be staying with

Jake's parents in Dallas for the entire week. Carmen and Jacob are excited to have the girls and are ready to spoil them. I expect them to bring home a Jeep full of clothes and toys.

Carmen and Jacob met Zane at one of Rylee's away soccer games and they're happy for me. They know that I'll always love Jake and they remember how devastated I was when I received the news of his death. All my family and friends have been with me through the hard times after Jake's death, so Carmen and Jacob are happy that I'm opening myself up again to a relationship. They saw how wonderful Zane was with the girls and how he treats me like I'm a precious treasure, a queen. They approve of him and I'm very, so very happy. Carmen and Jacob will always be part of our lives; they'll always be my in-laws and a part of our family. The fact that they like Zane and he likes them is a wonderful thing.

The girls are packing up all their things for their week away from home. They'll be spoiled and enjoy the Dallas life with Papa and Nana. Rylee found a week-long soccer camp in the area and is excited to continue training while also seeing her grandparents, and the fact that Josilyn will be with her is also a big plus. Dean, her boyfriend, isn't too happy with her decision to head there instead of going on the trip to Mexico with some of the other kids, but that doesn't seem to bother her too much. I'm very lucky to have a teenager with a good head on her shoulders. She has goals and dreams and is working hard to accomplish them.

Zane is here with me and ready to help the girls pack Rylee's Jeep for the two plus-hour drive to Carmen and Jacob's home. I'm a little nervous. Wait, who am I kidding? I'm incredibly nervous about letting the girls go by themselves, but they insisted and I have GPS trackers on the Jeep and their phones. They promised to phone on every stop and as soon as they arrive. Zane looked over the car and made sure it was in pristine condition to make the drive to Dallas, and that both Rylee and Josilyn know how to change a flat tire. He also showed them how to hit with a crowbar in case they need to defend themselves. I made sure Rylee had her Ontario knife and Skylar her little Swiss pocket knife. I know I'm overprotective, but I just want my girls to be safe and sound.

The Jeep is packed and the girls are getting into the car. Music is chosen and I make sure all their phones are charged and easily accessible.

"Momma, it's only two hours and if I need to rest, Josilyn can drive. We're gonna be fine. I'll call you every time we stop and when we arrive to Nana and Papa's house. Just relax and enjoy your time with Zane," she says, wiggling her eyebrows.

That crazy girl. This is what happens when you only have about thirteen-year age difference between mother and daughter—and she *is* my daughter even if not by blood. Sometimes, there are no boundaries.

"Alright. Just be careful. Drive safely," I tell her. "Skylar, you be good for your big sister and listen to her and Josilyn. Josilyn, enjoy your time with my in-laws and good luck at soccer camp, girlies. I love you always and forever."

"Always and forever," both girls say to me. "We love you too, Zane, and take care of Momma," the girls say to Zane, surprising him. This is the first time they've said the L-word to him and I can tell he loves it by the big smile on his face, once he gets over his shock.

"I love you too, girls. Be careful and call if you need anything. I'll hop in my truck and go get y'all if I need to," he tells them. "Now get going before it gets dark and your Momma decides to join you."

Stepping away from the Jeep, we watch the girls drive away. I honestly don't know what I'm going to do when Rylee heads off to college and when my little Skylar is all grown up . . . just thinking about that brings tears to my eyes.

Zane sees how emotional I am. He takes me in his arms and turns me to face him. "Baby, we have the house all to ourselves for the next five days before we head up there to go dress shopping with the girls for prom."

"I know, honey. Why do you think I'm all teary-eyed? I'm gonna miss the girls like crazy."

"Faith . . . we'll both miss the girls, but these next five days are gonna be for us. I'll be in your bed *every single night* until the girls come home. I'll explore and taste every part of your body and I'm gonna make you scream my name when I make you climax," he tells me, making my body shiver with anticipation. "I'll make sweet love to you and I'm gonna fuck you rough and hard, baby, so fuckin' hard that you'll come undone in my arms—you'll explode. You'll become my woman in almost every way. Yes, we'll miss the girls, but I'm gonna make sure that the time flies by quickly. We'll spend our time together and then we'll go bring the girls home. Okay, baby?"

"Okay, honey," I reply breathlessly.

He's right, this week will be our week. I'll be able to devote all my attention, when I'm not at the office, to this incredible and patient man. This wonderful and amazing man that has done everything in his power to show me how much he wants me in his life. This week is ours and I'm going to rock his world.

I get on my toes and bring his head down to me. I place my lips on his and before long he takes over, putting his hands on my ass and hauling me up. I wrap my legs around his waist and he takes us back inside the house. Once inside, he kicks the door closed and takes the stairs up to my room. He carries me into the room and lays us both down on the bed. He continues to kiss me, but what I think will lead to something more, does not.

He frames my face with his hands and looks into my eyes. "I want you so bad, but our first time isn't gonna be fast, it's gonna be perfect and special. I want to take all night with you. I'm gonna take you out on a date and then I'll have my way with you. I'll make love to you like I've never done before. Our first time will be my first time making true love to a woman. You, Faith—you're that woman. Mine." He kisses my lips softly, creating sweet tingling feelings with his words. "Right now, I'm gonna get up and head back to my place to get a bag and get ready for our date tonight. You got me?"

"I got you, honey," I reply breathlessly and with a smile on my face. He gives me one more kiss before getting off the bed, bringing me up with him.

"Walk me out, baby, I want to kiss you and make sure that you lock the door after me."

His overprotectiveness makes me feel so good inside, especially after being alone for so long and being the only protector of our home. He takes my hand and we make our way to the door. Once there, he pulls me in for one last kiss before heading out. He waits for me to lock the door before walking to his truck. I see him drive off before heading to my room to start the long process of readying myself for our night together.

I need to find a dress that'll drive him crazy; one that's demure in the front and when I turn, *bam,* it's sexy and open in the back. I want to drive him crazy. The dress needs to be sexy but not slutty.

Hmmm . . . looks like I have my work cut out for me.

I decide not to go at this alone and phone Julia.

"Hey, *chica!* What's happening?" She answers on the third ring.

"Dress emergency! Zane is taking me out tonight and I need a sexy backless dress that's not too slutty," I say without greeting.

"Woohoo! Are you finally getting laid, my dear best friend?" She asks excitedly. She's so freaking crazy, but I love her anyway.

"Focus, Julia. Dress. Now. Give me some ideas."

I feel like snapping my fingers at her even though she can't see me. Holy crap, this girl sure has her mind in the gutter. I'm finally going to get me some, but right now I'm too worried about finding the perfect sexy dress to think about that.

"Okay. Geesh . . . let's see . . . sexy but not slutty . . ." After a few seconds: "Ah ha! What about that red Valentino dress? The backless one, the one with the bow. The one you just *had to have.*"

"Valentino. Valentino," I say as I'm searching my walk-in closet. "I know which one you're talking about. The one I bought when we saw it on sale a few months ago, and I haven't worn it yet. You're a freakin' genius!"

"*Chica*, you know I am. What would you do without me? By the way, did the girls leave already?"

"Yes, they left about half an hour ago. Are you on your way?" I ask.

Julia's one of the coaches at the camp the girls are attending for Spring Break. She's actually the one that gave us the information and convinced Josilyn's parents to let her go. Josilyn has a lot of potential and Julia wants to get her name out there for the college scouts. She believes Josilyn has a high chance of getting a full ride.

"Yup. I left my house about the same time the girls did. I'm going to stop to pick up snacks and get gas and then continue on my way. I'll give Carmen a call to make plans for either lunch or dinner sometime during the week. Before I forget, are we still on for dress shopping this weekend?"

"Yes. Jackie and I are heading up there Saturday morning," I tell her.

"Is Zane coming too? I don't see that man letting you out of his sight," she says laughingly. "That man loves you too damn much, Faith."

"Julia, it's too soon for him to love me," I say.

"Bullshit, *chica.* You knew Jake was the one for you after one meeting—literally, after one look. Don't tell me love isn't quick or it's too soon. Zane treats you like a queen and protects you like one. If he hasn't told you yet it's because he doesn't want to scare you away. But let me tell you something, girl—that man does love you and you love him. I haven't seen you this happy in years and I'm happy for you. He loves your girls and he loves you. Enjoy the ride, Faith. Not many people are lucky to find two wonderful and amazing alpha males that are swoon worthy in one lifetime. You, my friend, are a lucky bitch and I love you."

"You really think so?" I ask.

I'm afraid. I've already lost one wonderful man. I don't want to lose another, and I don't know if I would survive another loss like before.

"I'm scared, Julia. I'm so scared that this will all go away at the drop of a hat like before. I don't know if I can go through that again. I'm also terrified—you know I haven't told him about work yet. What if he can't handle it?"

"Faith, God has given you a second chance at happiness. Don't throw that away by being afraid. You need to tell him and the sooner the better. He won't leave, but you have to tell him soon. Don't keep it from him because that'll piss him off. You need to live your life to the fullest because you know better than most how quickly it can be gone. Be happy. Be happy for you, your girls, and Zane."

She always knows how to help me. She's been with me through everything. I pray one day she finds the "happily ever after" she deserves.

"I love you, Julia. You've always been there for me when I need you most, even when it's to find the perfect date dress." I finally find the dress. "I found it and you're right. It's sexy, classy, and backless. Thanks, darlin'.'"

"Enough, you're gonna make me cry and I'm an ugly crier. Go get dressed and wear your Louboutin nude heels—the super-expensive but bought-on-sale hooker heels you love. Have an amazing and orgasmic date with your hot and sexy man, you lucky bitch. I'll call you when I get to Dallas, and I love you too, babe." She says and then hangs up the phone.

I head to the bathroom to shower and get ready for my date with Zane.

Tonight is going to be *epic*.

Zane

Tonight, I have the perfect date planned. I've gone all out, asking my mother and Jackie for advice and I know Faith will love it. Hopefully, we'll soon be able to take our relationship to the next level, but surprisingly, that doesn't really matter to me. I've waited years and I'll continue to wait forever for her, as long as I'm with her because she's worth it.

Tonight, is going to be perfect—nothing can go wrong.

Chapter 15

Two and a half hours later, I look at myself in my full-length mirror. My hair is in a simple and elegant high ponytail that works well with my wavy hair. I put on my nude-colored pearl earrings and finish off with my pearl bracelet. My smoky brown eyes are lined with black eye liner that really showcases my eyes, and my lips are the same exact shade of red as my dress. I searched high and low for that shade and all that hard work is paying off tonight . . . my lips look amazing and hopefully irresistibly kissable.

I look pretty darn good, if I say so myself.

Satisfied, I grab my nude Hermes clutch, another sale bargain that was expensive but a good investment for my wardrobe. I look at the clock. Only a few minutes before Zane's supposed to be here to pick me up. As I'm walking down the stairs, the doorbell rings and I rush to answer, thinking Zane is early. I throw open the door.

Standing outside my door is Gunner.

"Gunner! What are you doing here?" I ask, surprised he's here at my house.

He's supposed to be overseas doing security for Gabriel, my brother-in-law and the current United States ambassador to the UAE. It's good to know people in high places and have them use our company—not because we're family but because we're one of the best in our field.

He doesn't give me an answer, but barges into the house.

"What the fuck, Faith?!" He yells in my face. He's pissed at me and I have no idea why. When I spoke to him a few days ago, everything was going well. What in the world happened between then and now?

"What?" I ask, confused at his anger. "What's going on and what are you doing here? You're supposed to be in Dubai with Gabriel."

"What's going on?" He repeats angrily. "What's going on is that I had to find out through Gabriel, who found out from you, that you have a fuckin' boyfriend! How could you? Why didn't you have the decency to tell me about this guy when we've spoken the last couple of months?"

"What do you mean why haven't I told you? Why would I tell you about my love life when we are having *work* conversations? Why does it matter to you anyway?" I snap, my own voice rising.

I'm pissed that he's attacking me in this manner and without reason. He's not my keeper.

"Why, Faith?" He asks sarcastically. "I have the right to know because I've been with you since Jake died. I've held you as you cried after my best friend died. Shit, I've known you even before you met Jake. You don't have the fuckin' courtesy to let me know you're ready to move on! Why the fuck do you think I've been by your side?"

"You're my friend. You were also Jake's best friend and you told me you promised you would watch over Rylee and me if anything happened to him, and you have. I apologize for not telling you—I didn't mean to hurt your feelings. But, I see no reason for this behavior. Why are you angry and attacking me in this manner? You come into my home and yell at me. You don't even have the decency to say hello. No. The problem is you, not me."

I'm very upset and angry now. My evening was going so well and now this. I admit I was in the wrong for not telling my friend about Zane, but I don't deserve this treatment.

"You're so fuckin' blind, Faith," he tells me, and pulls me to him.

His lips are on mine!

What the hell is going on here?

I try to push him off me, but he's so darn big. He's almost as big as Zane, and I can't get him to budge.

Why is he doing this?

One second I'm struggling against him and the next I hear a furious roar and Gunner is across the room. Standing in front of me is Zane. He's furious.

"What the fuck is going on here?" He yells.

He turns to me, quickly making sure I'm okay, and then before I can stop him, he's on Gunner, punching him first in the face and then moving on to his body. Gunner gets himself together and returns hit for hit. Both are equally matched and out for blood.

"Stop!" I yell, but neither listens to me; they just go on beating each other, crashing into furniture.

Not wanting to hurt them by taking a bat to their heads, I go into the kitchen, fill two pitchers of cold water, and head back to my already half-destroyed living room. Angrily, I throw water on both men, surprising them enough to interrupt their fighting. I take advantage of this and place myself between them, knowing they'd never hurt me physically.

"Look at what you've done," I yell, lighting into them. "What the hell are y'all thinking beating each other like Neanderthals? Look at my living room. Y'all are lucky that the girls aren't home or I'd be throwing your asses out. Next time, take it outside."

I push Gunner onto one of the couches and he lets me. I take Zane's hand and sit us down on the other. This lasts about ten seconds before both men stand up and face each other.

"I have every fuckin' right to beat the shit outta this motherfucker," Zane growls. "I show up to pick my woman up for our date and find this fucker with his hands and mouth on you. You would be fuckin' pissed if you saw another woman with her hands and mouth on me, wouldn't you?"

Knowing damn well I'd beat the bitch, I say to him, "Yes, honey, you're right. I would beat the ever-living tar out of any woman stupid enough to put her hands on you, and then I'd turn around and beat *you* for letting her. You're big enough to get her hands and mouth off you. But, honey, next time you want to beat the crap out of someone in my house, please take it outside. My living room is in shambles and you know I despise messes. Both of you are gonna pick up every single broken item and put everything in order and *you*"—I turn to Gunner—"are gonna replace it. You hear me?"

Gunner is glaring at Zane with something pretty close to hatred in his eyes.

"I want to know who this fucker is and why he's in your home, and I want to know now," Zane demands.

"I'm Gunner," Gunner beats me to answering. "And I'm in her house because she is supposed to be *mine.*"

What in the world is that supposed to mean? I ask myself, bewildered at his answer.

His answer only angers Zane more and knowing he's about to launch himself at Gunner again, I wrap myself around him, stopping him.

"What the fuck is he talking about?" Zane asks me.

"I don't know what he means," I answer and turn to Gunner. "What are you talking about? You're my friend but that doesn't make me yours. You're my friend and business partner—that's all. You've been a big part of our lives since Jake's death with your support, but that doesn't give you ownership of me or the girls. You need to explain yourself and now, Gunner. One doesn't come into my home, verbally attack me, and force a kiss on me. That's not your right and I need an explanation. Now! Before I lose my temper and show you what's it's like to piss off a Texas woman."

"What am I talking about, Faith? I'm talking about the fact that I love you," he tells me angrily. "I wanted you from the first moment I laid eyes on you, but you never looked at me the same way. Then, you met Jake and I wasn't even a blip on your radar. I watched you and my best friend marry and build a life together. That fuckin' tore me up. I hated him because he had you and your love. You looked at him with such love and devotion—he was your hero and your world. I wanted that for myself. But at the same time, I was happy because he deserved to smile after what that bitch did to him and Rylee. Then, I watched you fall apart after his death and that fuckin' hurt me. I was there for you to lean on and cry on my shoulder. I held you as your world collapsed.

"I promised Jake I'd help take care of you and Rylee if anything happened to him. He knew I would keep my promise because he had an inkling that I loved you. He knew I would move Heaven and Earth for you. All these years . . . stupid me . . . I didn't make a move on you because I knew you weren't over him and I wanted you to only think of me when I told you how I felt. A few months ago, you told me you were ready to start dating again, you were ready to move on and I was so fuckin' happy. Finally, you were finally gonna be mine, I thought. Then Gabriel called needing our assistance and I was sent. That was good for business because it moved us to the big leagues, but it fucked with my plan to finally show you how I felt for you. FUUUCCCKKK!"

He puts his head in his hands and clenches his hair in desperation.

Throughout Gunner's speech, Zane is tense and ready. I'm afraid he thinks that Gunner will lose control and try to hurt me. Honestly, I don't know what to think . . . I've never seen Gunner like this, but I know he won't hit me. How could I have not seen this?

"You know the worst part?" Gunner asks. "The last couple of times I spoke with you on Skype, you sounded so happy. I'm a fuckin' idiot. I thought I was the one putting that smile there with my voice. All this time it was him, wasn't it?"

I hate seeing his tortured face. I hate that I've hurt him this badly.

"Gunner . . ." I say with an anguished voice. "Yes, it was Zane. He came into my life and wouldn't let me hide . . . I . . ." How do I tell him? "I never knew you felt this way for me. I thought you were being a good friend. Did I ever give you the wrong impression? How . . ." I trail off, wondering if I ever did something to lead him on.

"No . . . yes . . . no, damn it. You didn't. It was all me. The first time I saw you, you didn't even notice me. That should've clued me in—it was a week before your parents' Christmas party. You came to your father's office to meet him for lunch. You were wearing a maroon long-sleeved shirt with a puff vest, jeans, and UGG boots. Shit. I even remember what you wore that day and I'm a guy. I'm fuckin' pathetic."

My eyes close in pain and I feel Zane tense up even more. It's killing him, not saying anything and watching me deal with this. I appreciate that he's letting me handle this situation—that he's here for support and hasn't thrown Gunner out.

"I'm so sorry, Gunner. More than you know. I didn't, I mean . . . I never even suspected you felt anything for me more than platonic feelings. Why didn't you say something to me before? It's selfish of me to ask, but why only now? Why, Gunner?" I almost beg him for an answer.

"Because I found out that you'd moved on and it pisses me off that I wasn't here so it could be me. What does he have that I don't? I've known you for years . . ."

"I don't know how to answer that, Gunner. Like I told you before, he stampeded his way into my life, the girls' lives, and didn't let me hide behind my fears. He knows everything about me," I say, mentally crossing my fingers behind my back, "and he's still here. I care for him a lot. So much that I don't know what I'd do without him."

Hearing my words, Gunner's eyes close in pain and his face. Oh my . . . his face is full of devastation.

"As soon as Gabriel told me you had called him and Carmen and Jacob were ecstatic that you were finally in a relationship, I dropped everything and got on a plane. I probably lost our biggest client. What do I get for it? A fuckin' broken heart."

"Enough," Zane barks. "That's enough. It's not her fault you were too much of a fuckin' pussy to own up to your feelings. You had years to tell her how you felt, but you didn't. You could've given her a year and then made a move, but you were too fuckin' scared. Don't make her feel like shit for something she had no idea about and isn't even her fault."

Zane is beyond pissed now. Gunner is blaming me for this and maybe it's my fault, but he never said anything. And now, I'm going to have to do some sweet talking to make sure I iron everything out with Gabriel and make sure things are covered by Gunner's second-in-command.

"Don't come here blaming her because you were too chicken-shit to man up. You had your chance and you lost it. This is the last time you get to put your lips and hands on her. The. Last. Fuckin'. Time. You get me? I'm not gonna put up with this bullshit. You're acting like a little kid whose toy was stolen. Grow a fuckin' pair and man the fuck up," Zane orders Gunner.

"Honey, don't be so brutal," I say to Zane, wanting him to take it easy on Gunner. He's heartbroken and deserves a break. Yeah, he forced a kiss on me, but it's over and done with. But, I understand where Zane is coming from. The type of man he is, Zane isn't going to let this slide.

"No, baby. I'm not gonna stand here and let him make you feel as if all this is your fault. It's not. If he wanted you," Zane says without breaking his glare at Gunner, "He shoulda been man enough to give you time to grieve and then made himself an integral part of your lives. I knew the moment I saw you that I wanted you and I made sure you knew it. I worked my way into your lives and I'm here to stay. I'm not gonna to let him come into your house and try to take you from me. You. Are. Mine."

"Listen here, you motherfucker—" Gunner starts to say, but Zane cuts him off.

"No. You fuckin' listen and listen good. Faith and the girls are *mine*. They are mine and I take care of what's mine. I protect them with my life and if I have to beat the shit outta dumbass motherfuckers like yourself, then I will. I'm not gonna let you barge into *my* woman's house and put your hands on her. I'll give you this one time because she stopped me and only this *one* time. Never again are you to put your hands or mouth on her. You try this crazy shit again, and I will fuckin' *kill* you. You got me?"

Gunner looks at him and then at me. He recognizes the type of man Zane is and the seriousness of our relationship. With a defeated sigh he says, "Yeah, I got it. I don't like it but I got it." He looks at me. "I'm sorry, Faith. I'm just upset because I feel like I lost you all over again. First to Jake and now to him. And it's not your fault, it's mine. I should've told you sooner. But now that I see you together, I see that it probably wouldn't have mattered. Even if you would've been mine, it would've been for a short while until you met him." He gives me a sad look and continues, "I'm sorry I hurt you, but I'm not sorry I kissed you. I had to taste your lips at least once and the beating was worth it." He tries to smile but fails.

My heart is breaking for my friend and I know that our friendship is going to suffer. I try to pull away from Zane to go to Gunner, but Zane doesn't loosen his hold. I pinch him, taking him by surprise. I use this opportunity to make my way to Gunner, leaving a not-so-happy Zane standing behind. I look at Gunner, asking for permission, and he slightly nods his head. I put my arms around him and he holds me tight.

"I never had a chance, did I?" He asks.

"I'm sorry, Gunner," I tell him.

I step back out of our embrace. I hate hurting him, but I need to be completely honest with him.

"You and Julia were there with me during the hardest times of my life. I will never forget that and I will always be grateful. Y'all held me together when I wanted to give up and y'all helped me take care of my babies. I love both of you as family. What I felt for Jake was strong and true, and even death will never make that go away. What I feel for Zane is just as strong. I'm scared to admit it, but I need to stop living in fear and take a leap of faith. I don't know what life has in store for us, but I want to find out. I'm sorry that I couldn't love you that way."

I pause, looking into his eyes. One day," I tell him. "One day you will meet the woman that's meant for you. Then, you'll understand that you have no control over who you love. You love me now, but one day you'll find this woman and she'll be magnificent. You and I were never meant to be, but you and her will live a lifetime of love."

I reach to give him a kiss on his cheek. This is me ending all discussion on this matter, and I'm glad he understands and seems to be following my lead.

"Now, the two of you better start straightening up my living room before I get seriously pissed off. You"—I point at Gunner and try to look fierce—"will be paying for everything that was broken during your little spat. *Capisce?*"

Gunner gives a small chuckle at my slang usage. "Yeah, babe, I got it."

"You better take good care of her," he says to Zane. "You hurt her and I'll fuckin' castrate you and feed you your dick and balls. I'll always be here for her and I won't hesitate to end you."

Hearing this speech, I know all danger of the two of them beating each other senseless is gone, so I go into the kitchen to order take-out and make the necessary calls to straighten out the situation so we don't lose a client. I'm not in the mood to cook and I'm definitely not going to make Zane cook. There goes my date night with Zane.

I hope he's not too upset and is okay with eating here at home with me. I order plenty of food and head back to the living room with a glass of sweet wine in my hand. This definitely calls for wine and I deserve it. I find the guys cleaning up my living room and being civil to each other—thank goodness.

After they finish, Gunner turns to me. "I'm gonna head out. I'm sorry for ruining y'all's evening. I don't know what I was thinking. I was desperate and I'm sorry. Let me know how much I owe you for all the broken items." He heads for the door. "I'll talk to you at work. Bye, Faith."

I say goodbye and watch him head towards his truck. He gets in, giving me one last sad look before starting the engine and driving off.

I turn to Zane and before I can say or do anything, he's on me. His lips are on mine hard—not brutal, but more aggressive than normal.

"I want every trace of his lips gone from yours," he growls. "Mine are the only lips that will ever touch yours again, you hear me? When I saw him on you, I wanted to *kill* him. I wanted to tear him limb from limb. I never want to see that again."

"I'm sorry, honey. I'm sorry he ruined our night."

"Don't apologize. It's not your fault and I saw you trying to push him off. And, our night isn't ruined. As long as I'm with you, everything is perfect in my world. Next time, knee him in the balls so hard they come up his throat. *No one* has the right to put their hands or lips on you but me. You. Are. Mine. Only mine, Faith."

"If I'm yours, then you're mine. Got me?" I give him my most serious and fierce face. "I don't share well with others, honey."

"Yeah, baby, I'm yours," he says, laughing softly. "And I wouldn't have it any other way, love."

He gives me a light kiss on the lips before letting me go. I head into the kitchen to get plates and glasses while we wait for dinner to be delivered.

After a few minutes, he walks into the kitchen, puts his hands on my hips and kisses me on the back of the neck. He trails his fingers down my open back.

"Faith, this dress is fuckin' hot."

I shiver as his lips nibble and bite. A tingling sensation starts between my legs. I'm very sensitive and what he's doing feels so good.

"Go change into something more comfortable," he says as he nibbles on my neck. "I love this dress and those shoes, but I want to be able to relax with you and you can wear it again on our next date."

"Hmmm . . . umm . . ." I can't even speak.

His lips on me feel so good and it's been a long time since I've had this. Sure, we've been a little hot with each other, but it's been pretty limited. I don't want to set a bad example for the girls, especially Rylee, since she's at that age.

"I want to eat dinner and then move to the living room. I want to hold you as we watch television together. The girls aren't here so I'm definitely gonna take advantage of that," he whispers into my ear before biting it.

I lean my head to the side, giving him better access, and he moves to my neck. He bites it and then uses his tongue. *Oh my!* I feel like I'm going to explode right here and now. I need him. With one last little bite, he steps back and I let out a sound in protest.

"Faith, our first time isn't going to be in this kitchen. I want to take my time with you and I don't want to be interrupted by dinner arriving," he tells me. "I'm gonna head out to my truck to get my bag. You go to your room and change."

"Fine," I grumble, upset at being left in need. "But, don't touch me. I'm mad at you." I give him a pouty face and make my way up to my room. I hear him chuckle and head out the door.

I change into black capri leggings, a white tank top with a lilac three-quarter sleeve loose shirt, and comfy fluffy purple socks. I take my jewelry off and remove my make-up. He told me to relax and I am definitely doing that. I head back down and hear Zane speaking with the delivery guy as he pays for our dinner. He closes the door, looks at me and gives me one of his sexy grins, and then heads to the kitchen.

"Food's here. You still mad at me?" The big meanie is still laughing at me.

"I won't be if you feed me," I tell him.

"Come here, baby."

I pretend to reluctantly walk to him. He wraps his arm around my waist and hauls me up, slamming our bodies together, and kisses my pretend anger away.

"Let's get our food, your wine, and my beer and head to the living room. We'll put something on the TV and relax. I just want to hold you," he tells me before kissing me softly and letting me go.

"Alright, honey," I say. "I'm sorry about earlier."

"We're done talking about that. It wasn't your fault and that's it. I settled it with him and if he pulls another stunt like that, his ass is mine and you won't be able to stop me."

I drop the subject and follow him into the living room. We set everything on the coffee table and look through my DVR list for something to watch. We settle on *Game of Thrones,* deciding to get ourselves ready for the new season by watching the old episodes I have recorded.

A couple episodes in and all of the food is consumed, mainly by Zane, and I'm almost finished with my bottle of wine. That stuff is delicious, but the bottle is so small I can finish a bottle in three glasses.

Zane takes the dirty dishes into the kitchen, comes back, settles himself comfortably in the couch and then pulls me to him. He puts his arms around me and I cuddle next to him. He's playing with my hair with one hand, kissing my forehead, and holding my hand with his other hand. It feels wonderful just being here with him. I love the feeling of being cherished and protected in his arms.

I turn my head and kiss him on the lips. I turn my attention back to the television and . . .

Whoa!

I don't remember the sex scenes being this hot the last time I saw the show. Holy crap—is that even possible? I ask myself.

I normally don't get hot and bothered by sex scenes, but since Zane's little tease in the kitchen and now just being here with him, I'm getting worked up. It doesn't help that he's holding me and kissing me, regardless of how innocent those kisses are. I know he won't make a move on me until I'm ready; he'll never pressure me. Being alone with him, plus the wine I just consumed, is making me brave. How much will he take before he breaks down and takes me?

I turn again and bring our lips together. I nibble on his lips and then move on to his neck. I can tell he likes this because his pulse is getting faster. He's sitting still, just letting me take the lead. I continue to kiss and taste his lips and neck. My hand slowly moves to his groin area and I feel his hard cock just wanting to escape the confinement of his pants.

I hear him inhale sharply.

"You're playing with fire. We don't have to do anything tonight; I just want to hold you in bed."

I ignore him and continue to trace my hand up and down. I tease him with my nails and I moan just thinking how good he's going to feel inside of me.

"Baby," he moans before taking my mouth. He grabs my hair and gently pulls my head back. I make little noises in protest and try to get my lips back on his. "No."

I ignore him. I want him and I don't want to wait any more.

"Once we do this, Faith, you'll definitely be mine. You'll be my woman in every way but name. I'll never let you go, you understand?"

I'm only half-listening as I straddle him and align us together. I grab a fistful of his hair.

"I want you, Zane. So much that I'm hurting. I know I want you and I'm not going to stop until I have you inside me. You've been patient with me and now I'm ready."

I stop talking and wrap my arms around him and start rubbing myself on his hardness.

Oh, how I wish there were no barriers between us.

He's finally had enough. He holds me tighter as he stands up, securing me around him. He gently bites my neck before making his way to my room. He stumbles onto the bed, making sure to keep his full weight off me.

"Stay still, baby—you move and I'll stop. I'm gonna kiss every one of your curves and I'm gonna taste you before making you completely mine."

He slowly takes off my shirt and pants. He unsnaps my bra and takes it off, and then he takes off my panties and comfy socks. He leans back to look at me. I start feeling self-conscious—it's been a long time since I've been with a man and after having Skylar, my body changed. I finally look into his eyes and am amazed at the look he's giving me. His eyes are full of hunger and an emotion I want to believe is true love.

He comes back to me and we start to kiss. He takes over the kiss and I let him. His lips leave mine and move to my neck and shoulders. He kisses and gently bites. I shiver and moan, letting him know I love that.

"You like that?" He asks. "You like it when I bite you?"

"Mmmm." I can't even speak, it feels so good.

He bites me harder and I get wetter. He continues kissing and biting my neck, and his hands start down my body. He reaches my breasts and starts playing with my nipples. At first it's gentle caresses, but then he takes them between his fingers and starts to roll them and pull them. The harder he does it, the louder I moan. He gets to the right amount of pressure and I feel almost at my climax.

I move to kiss him but he refuses. I manage to reach his neck and I bite him.

"So you're a biter, baby." He sounds amazed.

I bite him again, only harder, and I release a beast.

"You want it rough, huh? Well get ready, get ready to scream my name and have my marks all over you. I'm gonna give it to you hard and rough and I'll love you at the same time. You move and I stop. I want you to lie there for me while I taste you and get your juices all over my face. I want to feast on you."

He gives me one last kiss before making his way down my body with his mouth. He focuses on my breasts, sucking and biting them, just enough to get me *there,* and then moves downward. Anytime I move, he reminds me that he'll stop if I don't let him do what he wants. I whimper and try my best not to move, but the way he handles my body . . . let's just say he's had lots of practice and like he said, it was to prepare him for me.

Zane finally reaches down *there.* He leans back and make this noise in his throat.

"Damn, baby, you look so fuckin' edible. You're all wet and glistening, just ready for me to dive in and fuck you with my tongue."

I don't even respond before he starts. He kisses the inside of my thighs and gently nips them, first one side and then the other, before making his way to my center. He traces the left side, gets to my clit and only *kisses* it. I protest when he leaves it, but don't move. He moves to my right, nibbles, and traces up and down before once more getting to my center. My clit is now throbbing.

Instead of kissing, he uses his finger and rubs me almost to climax before backing off. I want to scream in frustration. Then I almost fly off the bed. His mouth is on my clit and he starts to suck it and when he bites it, I *explode.* I can feel myself pouring out and he's lapping it up. I'm screaming and calling his name. Zane continues to eat me up until I feel drained. He passes his fingers over my sensitive center and looks at me.

His lips are covered in my wetness and when he moves to kiss me, I taste myself on him and I'm amazed at how much I like it. Never before have I done this—Jake would always wipe his mouth before kissing me—but Zane, he takes my mouth and owns it. Our tongues are swirling around each other and he takes my bottom lip between his teeth and bites me before leaning back to look at me.

"You like that?" He asks me. I can't even answer so I nod my head. "That's only the beginning, love, and we have all night."

He discards his clothes and quickly rolls on a condom, before pressing his body on mine. I can feel his hardness between my legs. If I move just right, his tip will be at my opening. He takes my mouth once more. He moves onto my shoulders and neck and starts all over again. My hands are in his hair, then I move them up and down his body. I use my nails on his back and when I reach his ass, I squeeze with just enough force to get his attention.

Zane looks into my eyes. "After this, Faith, there's no turning back. You'll be mine forever and I'll never let you go. You'll belong to me, your body will belong to me, and only I will ever touch you again."

I look back into his eyes and smile. He leans down, I assume to kiss me, but he doesn't. He takes that spot right where my neck and shoulders meet, that spot that makes me shiver and almost come every time, and he bites me. As he bites me, he pushes himself into me and fills me up. My body arches up in pleasure. I call out his name . . .

"Mine," he growls.

He leaves his mark on my neck.

It's primal and I love it.

He thrusts in and out, gently at first and then faster and faster. The pressure is getting so strong that I scream at the top of my lungs when I explode around him. Soon he follows me, yelling out my name.

He collapses gently on me, making sure to keep his weight from crushing me. Without losing his hold on me he flips over, taking me with him, and places me on top. I feel a kiss on my forehead before I let my tiredness take over. I hear him murmur, "I love you, baby." Maybe wishful thinking on my part before everything goes black. . .

❧

Zane

That was fucking explosive!

I knew it would be like this from the very beginning. She's finally mine in every way but name. One day, I'll make her my wife when she's ready to accept me completely without fear and without secrets between us. I have just one little secret that I've kept from her. It's one that could break us and I can't let that happen.

Never.

I can never lose her because I love her more than life itself and I know she loves me too. She'd never have given herself to me otherwise. It's up to me to keep us together because apart is not an option. I've waited too long—she's my redemption, my reward, my treasure, my world.

My love. Always and forever.

Chapter 16

There's a loud buzzing sound and it's waking me up.
What is that annoying noise and will someone please shut it up?

Through my foggy thoughts I hear Zane answer. "'Lo?"

I guess it was the phone. I'm snuggling back into the bed to go back to sleep when—"Morning, princess, your mommy is right here . . . I can't wait to see you either . . . I love you too, honey."

When I hear this, I come wide awake. Oh my, it is early morning and Zane just answered a call from one of the girls. What are they going to think?

I'm freaking out inside when he hands me the phone.

"It's Skylar, baby."

I take the phone and watch him get out of bed and head to the bathroom. I place the phone to my ear, taking a deep breath to calm myself down and start talking to my baby.

"Hey, Peanut, how's your morning?"

"Hi, Momma! Why is Zane there with you early in the morning? Did he sleep over?" She sounds close to tears.

"Yes, sweetie, he stayed here last night but if it's gonna upset you, he won't be doing it any more, okay?" I say, trying to reassure my daughter.

"It's not fair!" She cries out.

"Oh, please don't cry!" I exclaim, close to tears.

This is how Zane finds me when he comes back. He takes me in his arms, silently asking what's wrong. I whisper, "Skylar is crying because you answered the phone." He holds me tighter. I don't want to imagine not being in his arms but my daughters come first. If they don't like him or the fact that he's here with me, then I'm going to have to let him go. Just thinking about that hurts.

"It's not fair that Zane gets to be there when I'm not there! Why can't he sleep over when I'm home? Why?!"

"Skylar, what are you saying?" I ask, silently hoping that she means what I think she means.

"Momma, I'm saying I want to be there. Zane never spends the night when we're there. I want to wake up and have him there. He gives me anything I want for breakfast and he takes me places—he takes me to get ice cream and other yummy stuff."

I let out a huge sigh of relief at her words. She's not upset because she doesn't want him here; she's upset because she wants to be here too. I send a silent prayer up above. *Thank you, Lord.*

"Okay, we'll talk about this later. How is everything, sweetie? Are you listening to Nana and Papa? I miss you bunches."

"Of course I'm listening, Momma. You know I'm a good listener. I have my room all to myself. Papa made hamburgers and cheesy fries for dinner last night. *Yummy!* Today, I'm going ice skating while Rylee is at camp. I'm having lots of fun, Momma, but I miss you and I miss Zane too."

"I can't wait till you get back, sweetie. I'm glad you're having fun; just remember not to eat too much candy because you'll get a tummy ache. I love you always and forever."

"I love you too, Momma. Give Zane a kiss for me, please," she tells me.

"Okay, I will," I say, chuckling at my little girl. "I need to speak with your sister, is she there?"

"RYLEE! MOMMA'S ON THE PHONE FOR YOU!"

I pull the phone away from my ear. Skylar's just about burst my eardrum. Zane just chuckles and kisses my forehead. I lean into him and savor his arms around me. I've missed this so much—being held first thing in the morning, feeling safe and that sense of belonging.

"Bye, Momma. Here's Rylee. Love you and Zane!" I hear her scuttle away as Rylee takes the phone.

"Hey, Momma," Rylee says. "I just heard that Zane's there. Well, with Skylar's lung capacity, everyone here knows that Zane is there *and* Josilyn's on the phone with Mrs. Jackie, so within the next hour, the whole world will know he spent the night," she says, laughing.

"Great. I'm glad my love life is amusing and entertaining everyone," I say sarcastically. "How are things going? Is Josilyn enjoying the stay? Are you nervous about camp? Is Josilyn? Tell me *everything!*"

She laughs at me but still answers.

"Things are going well. Papa made burgers and cheesy fries for the peanut because she *just had* to have some or she would *starve.* Josilyn was in awe of the house, but is getting over that and sees that Nana and Papa are normal grandparents that spoil us rotten. Am I nervous? Hmmm . . . yes and no. I have butterflies in my stomach but I'm also anxious to get going. Once I get out there, everything will become alright. As long as I'm on the field, I can do anything. Plus, Aunt Julia is gonna be there—which is nice since I'll know a coach—but at the same time, they'll all be expecting a lot from me. Josilyn is kinda freakin' out since this is her first camp."

"Well, you knew from the very beginning that those trainers were gonna be expecting a lot from you. Sometimes it stinks having me as your momma. But you've already made a name for yourself on your own, and I'm so proud of you. Soccer is your passion; don't let anything get to you. You're gonna be amazing. Show them what you got and blow their socks off with your soccer skills. Tell Josilyn she's gonna rock. She's gonna be awesome; tell her to just go out there and play her best, and everything will fall into place. Did Nana get you your purple Skittles?"

"I will, Momma. Yes, Nana got me my Skittles. A *huge* bag. I didn't know they made bags that big," she says, chuckling. "She said the bigger the bag, the better the luck."

I laugh at my mother-in-law's antics; that sounds like something she would do. I bet she had to call Mars to get a bag that big produced just for her granddaughter. She's humble, kind-hearted, amazing, and a hoot, and I wouldn't trade her for the world.

"Nana would definitely say that," I say. "Alright, baby girl, good luck today and always. Lots of kisses"—I send her some through the phone. "I love you always and forever."

"Always and forever, Momma. Bye, Zane! Love you! Keep my Momma happy," she yells through the phone, making sure that Zane hears her.

"I will," he answers, laughing. "Take care, girl. If you need anything call, you hear me?"

"I will," she answers. "Here's Nana. *Tschüss!*"

Those six years in Germany stuck with her. She's kept up with the language, through tutoring, that Jake and I feared she'd lose once coming back stateside, and she started teaching Skylar the language. My poor baby is probably confused learning her third language, but her sister turned out alright, so I guess I shouldn't worry. I just tell myself that knowing multiple languages makes them more employable in the future.

"So I hear there's a certain young man there with you," she says without greeting.

"Well, hello to you too," I say. "Yes, Zane's here. Are you okay?" I ask, fearing that I've upset her.

"Oh, *mija.* Why would you think otherwise? Of course I'm okay. I'm ecstatic for you, actually."

"I was worried you'd be upset. I don't want you to think that I'm replacing Jake."

"Faith. I'd never think that. My son has been gone for a very long time. He'd want you to be happy and if Zane makes you happy, then we're happy," she tells me. "I was starting to get worried about you; not one single young man had turned your head in all these years. I'm glad that Zane came into your life. You are still young and deserve to be truly happy. You're an amazing and wonderful mother and you've done so much for the girls. You've pulled yourself through a personal hell. I'm proud of you and so is Jacob. Jake would be so proud and happy for you, Faith. I know you loved my son more than life itself. You stood by him through thick and thin and you put him in his place when he needed it. You stood by his side always. God took him too soon, but you're still here and deserve to live a full life. I love you, Faith. Don't ever think I'm upset over Zane. I know you wouldn't bring him into the girls' lives if you weren't serious about him—if you didn't care for him deeply."

"Thank you, Carmen," I say gratefully. "I was so scared I was doing something wrong. I like him *a lot*. I don't want you to think that I dumped the girls on you so I could spend time with him."

"Psshh, *mija*. We both know that you'd rather have the girls there with you right now and you hate to be separated from them. Thank you for letting them come visit. Jacob and I are so happy to have them here with us. We're going to spoil them rotten and then send them home at the end of the week. We miss them so much when they're gone. This house needs to have some happy noise every now and then. Use this time to spend time with your beau. Have some fun, if you know what I mean." I can just imagine her wagging her eyebrows at me.

"Carmen, you're a hoot," I say, laughing. "Only you'd tell me to go have sex with my boyfriend." Zane perks up and pokes me when I say the word *boyfriend*—he mouths, "I'm your *man*."

"*Niña,* I may be old but Jacob and I still have a *very* healthy marriage."

"Oh my God! TMI!" I semi-yell, laughing at my mother-in-law. "I'm gonna hang up on that. My daughters better not be scarred for life after visiting your home!"

"Don't worry, we'll lock the door," she says, laughing at me. "Good-bye, *mija* and have fun."

"Bye, Carmen. Give my best to Jacob, and a hug and kiss. I miss y'all," I say and hang up the phone.

"So . . . what's this about having sex?" Zane asks.

"Oh my, *really,* Zane," I say, laughing.

"Well I was fine until I heard 'sex'; how am I not supposed to ask?"

"Carmen is a very open mother-in-law. She would always tell me to dress sexy when picking up Jake after he arrived from his deployments or when I'd Skype with him to show him what was waiting at home for him," I tell him. "Now, with you, she's telling me to have *fun* with you, if you know what I mean." I giggle at the end of my explanation.

"Well, that's a bit weird, but if she's telling you to have 'fun' with me, who am I to argue?" He asks me and then pounces on me. I let out a surprise squeal as I go down on the bed and then there's a very sexy man pressing his very naked body against mine. He proceeds to show me how much he loves my curves and my taste. He takes his time stroking me and worshiping my body before making me see heaven.

Afterwards, all I can think is how blessed I am to have such a wonderful man come into my life. I've been given a second chance at happiness and I'm going to take full advantage. I'll enjoy it, however long it lasts.

Chapter 17

The rest of the week flies by. Whenever Zane and I aren't at work, we're spending time together. I'm finally going to meet the rest of the guys, his buddies from the firehouse, at O'Bannon's tonight after work. Zane even invited Gunner along as a sign of good faith and Gunner accepted the invitation, surprising us both.

∽⌖∾

When we first arrive it's a bit awkward, but after a few drinks, Gunner relaxes and gets used to seeing Zane's arm around me. The past days have been full of tension between us, but Gunner is starting to see the change in my demeanor. He's noticed my smile is different and that I'm *happy*. He's starting to accept that Zane is the man for me.

I've told him continuously how much he means to me, and that I love him only as a friend. I think he's finally realizing that we were never meant for each other. Gunner looks at Zane and me every now and then, but instead of being angry, he's assessing the situation. He's assuring himself that Zane is good to me. Tonight is the first time he is seeing us together and he's realizing how good the two of us are together. I know he accepts it when he nods in our direction and gives me the first smile in days. I smile at him and lean into Zane. He turns back to the conversation, leaving me to Zane.

Zane's buddies are hilarious and I get along just fine with all of them. It's the barflies that give me the evil eye and annoy the hell out of me when they approach Zane. At first it bothers me, but soon I just brush those looks off and pity their useless efforts to get Zane's attention. It's their problem if they don't like the fact that he's with me. Throughout the whole night, Zane never leaves my side and not once does he glance at them. A couple of them try to get his attention, but he soon puts an end to that when he introduces me as his woman. He lets them know he's serious about me and they are wasting their efforts with him, and they should focus on the rest of the single guys at our table or around the bar.

Most listen to him and leave him alone, but there are a couple that refuse to listen. What surprises me and embarrasses me is that they ignore Zane's words. That's when he gets rude.

"You don't seem to understand, so let me put this in a manner that you will." Zane points at me. "Look at her," he tells a bleach-blonde, fake-breasted bimbo wearing too-tight clothes. "Now, look at you," and he points at the clueless woman. "She's what I want and *not* you. Why would I want someone that's had almost every dick in this bar inside of them when I have *her* in my life? She's class while you're not *and* she gives amazing head. Not only that, but she's fuckin' incredible in bed and keeps me satisfied. So satisfied that I can't even move after she has her way with me. Now, get gone and go try to pick up someone else or I'll have you banned from here." He was *very* harsh and rude but they were just not listening.

They finally clue in and leave. I'm red in the face. "Did you just really announce to everyone that I give great head?" I ask him, mortified.

"Babe, not great head—amazing head, fuckin' awesome, incredible. There's a difference, and you leave me so fuckin' worn out that I can't move afterwards."

"Zane! You don't say that in public. What's everyone gonna think now?" This is one of those times you want the earth to open up and swallow you whole.

"Faith, they're thinking I'm a lucky bastard and that you're fuckin' hot. You're like that song says, 'A lady on the street and a freak in the bed.' They wish they were in my shoes and had you in their beds, but too fuckin' bad for them—you're mine and only I will ever get to taste you, fuck you, and love you. No one else. And, I couldn't let them disrespect you, Faith. I had to say something and put them in their place."

I don't even bother to respond to this. It's a losing battle, especially when all the guys are laughing their asses off and teasing Zane about being pussy-whipped and "man-down." I just order another Tequila Sunrise and enjoy the rest of the evening with my man.

Later that night, when we get home, he shows me how much we belong together and makes love to me "where I can see how fuckin' incredible and hot I am,"—in front of the mirrors.

Before I know it, it's time to meet the girls. Zane, Jackie, and I head to Dallas for prom dress shopping and to bring them home.

Before heading out to the mall, I inform Zane that this is serious business and he should stay with Jacob. He laughs when I tell him he wouldn't last all day with us.

"Faith, if I can lay in wait *days* for a target, I can definitely handle dress shopping with my girls for a day."

And like any man who thinks he knows best, he decides to prove me wrong.

Ha, he should've listened to me. When will he learn?

Hour one, he's into the shopping. He decides to help and picks out all these . . . um . . . *horrendous* dresses—dresses even my grandmother wouldn't wear. They're more like potato sacks or muumuus. And of course, they're all rejected.

Hour two. Since he was a failure with the dresses, he decides to try his hand at picking shoes. Poor man. Let's just say that man has *no* place trying to dress the opposite sex. Thank goodness I have Julia to help me coordinate outfits because he'll be absolutely no help. Again, his picks are all put back.

By hour three, he's *done* and accepts defeat. He decides to take Skylar to a movie and "do whatever the hell she wants" just as long as it's away from dresses and our crazy selves.

"Y'all are like fuckin' military generals planning a takeover by the way y'all go about looking for the *perfect* dress. Skylar will be in college before y'all are satisfied," he grumbles. "Let's go, princess. Save me."

"I told you so," I tell him, laughing.

Skylar decides to take pity on him. They head out to have fun "away from this nightmare" as Zane puts it. And our day continues.

Several hours later, Rylee and Josilyn have each found the perfect dress. Successful in our mission, we head back to Carmen and

Jacob's house. We pack up the girls' belongings and load the vehicles. We relent and let the girls head back alone in Rylee's Jeep. Even Skylar begs. Zane, Jackie and I get into Zane's truck. It's filled not only with the girls' dresses, but also a closetful of other clothes that we *just had* to have. It's a good thing we brought the truck and the bed is covered; our loot wouldn't have fit in the Jeep.

Two hours later, we arrive at our house. Josilyn and Jackie head home, and the rest of us decide on take-out. I'm worried about how this is going to work. How am I going to sleep without Zane in my bed holding me tight? I feel guilty—I'm excited my daughters are home but at the same time, I'm dreading my lonely night.

I don't expect the girls to take matters into their own hands.

"Zane, you're staying the night, right?" Rylee asks, making us choke on our food.

Surprised, we look at each other. How do we answer that question? We want to be together, but we fear it might set a bad example or upset the girls' routine.

But before either one of us can answer "no," Skylar pipes up.

"Of course he is, silly," she answers. "Tomorrow morning, he's gonna make me French toast with strawberries on top, eggs, and bacon—my favoritest breakfast."

"Baby," I say softly to my youngest, "Zane can't spend the night with us. He has to go home to his house."

"Well, why can't he stay here?" Skylar asks, blinking her eyes slowly. Oh, boy.

Rylee looks at me and Zane and I look at each other.

"Princess," he answers, "I can't spend the night " Before he can finish, Skylar surprises us.

"But I want you to stay," she says, close to tears. "You make my mommy happy. I don't want her to cry at night. She used to cry at night and I don't want her to cry anymore. You make her smile like the princesses in my movies do. I don't like it when she cries. Please stay, Zane," she pleads.

My heart breaks.

I didn't realize my girls knew about my lonely nights.

"Oh, baby," I say with a voice full of emotion. "Why didn't you say anything before?"

I've worked hard to hide my tears from them—to always put up a strong front in their presence. During the day I was strong, but when night came—I could let myself go. I never thought anyone could hear me, especially Skylar.

"I told Rylee the first time I heard you," she replies, and I look at my eldest daughter. She looks back at me with glistening eyes. "She told me not to say anything to you that it would only make you sadder. She said that sometimes grown-ups cry when they are sad, and that you were sad because Daddy was gone and you missed him very, very much. With Zane, you smile a happy smile, Momma. I don't want you to cry anymore. Zane makes you happy."

I can't hold it in any longer; I turn and walk out of the kitchen. As I'm walking out, I hear my Skylar ask, "Is Momma okay?"

"Yes, princess, your Momma is okay. Just give her a minute and she'll be back," Zane reassures her.

I get to the living room when I feel a hand on me. I turn and I find Rylee. She has tears running down her face.

"I'm sorry, Momma," she says.

"No, Rylee," I cry. "I'm the one that's sorry. Y'all should never have heard me cry. I've tried so hard to be strong for all of us. Your daddy—he was the love of my life. I was so sure we would spend the rest of our lives together. When I lost him, it hurt so much. The days were about my two babies, but the nights—those were so hard for me. Silly me, thinking I could close the door to keep y'all from hearing."

"The peanut is right, Momma. Let Zane stay, at least for tonight. Since you've been with him, you actually smile a real smile. You're better with him. He's good with Skylar and with me—he's even offered to beat the crap outta any guy that makes me cry. He's trying so hard, Momma, to be here for us—to make things easier and to be part of our family. All we want is for you to be happy and to find love again. I could be selfish and make things harder for y'all, but I'm not because you accepted me all those years ago as your daughter and have loved and raised me. Now, it's my turn to accept the man that wants to love *you.*"

She comes to me and I hold her tight.

We cry.

We cry for each other, for the man we both lost too soon, and for Skylar because she never got to meet the incredible man that her father was. We hold each other for what seems forever, but is really mere seconds, before letting go. I give Rylee a kiss, wipe my face, and we both head back to the kitchen. As we walk in, we see Zane holding a crying Skylar. Her face turned into him, tears and snot drenching his tee shirt. Zane doesn't seem to notice, and he holds my baby tight. He's murmuring words into her ear and we see him kiss the top of her head. My heart melts at the sight.

They hear us enter and Skylar lifts her head.

"I'm sorry, Momma. I didn't mean to make you cry."

"No, sweetie," I say reassuringly. "I was just surprised and I had to get myself together. Why are you crying, my little peanut?"

"I just want you to be okay, Momma. Don't make Zane leave, please. He makes you happy and he makes us happy."

"Okay," I say, looking at Zane. "Zane can stay the night. If things feel weird to y'all or y'all feel uncomfortable, please let me know. The two of you will always come first and Zane knows this. We love y'all and want what is best for y'all."

At these words, Skylar jumps out of Zane's lap and runs to me. She hugs Rylee and me. It's the three of us like it's been for years. Then, both girls turn and look at Zane.

"Zane, it's a family hug," Rylee tells him.

"Get over here, silly. We need you with us," Skylar finishes.

At first Zane is shocked but quickly snaps out of it and joins the three Duval girls. As we hold each other, I see Zane look up to the heavens, his lips moving, and then he bows his head and holds us tighter. He's been accepted into our family by the girls. I send a silent prayer up above, thanking the Lord for first blessing me with Jake, and now giving me another chance with Zane.

Everything is perfect.

If I had known what would happen later, I would've prayed harder.

Chapter 18

That night in March, Zane became a part of our family. Since that night, he's spent every night he isn't at the station in our house and in my bed. He helps with dinner, cleaning, mowing, and taking out the trash. That's a major plus because that's the one thing I hate the most—taking out the trash. It sucks big time!

We even started sharing carpooling duties. More often than not, he picks up Skylar from school, and she even keeps CDs in his truck. It was the sweetest thing, watching the two of them jamming out to Taylor Swift. I'll never forget the image of my hot-as-hell, badass, muscular, manly man singing along to girly tunes with my youngest daughter at the top of his lungs and dancing.

It's the cutest thing *ever* and so sweet.

With Rylee, he doesn't want to overstep but he's still very protective of her. For example, any time Dean picks her up for one of their dates, Zane is always there glaring at the poor boy. One time, Zane decided to sharpen his hunting knife collection—which I didn't even know he had. Another time, he took out one of my guns and started cleaning it in front of the kid, showing him how quick he could assemble and disassemble it, and letting Dean know that he never missed his target. He was trying to intimidate the boy and was being successful. I was worried Rylee would get angry, but she took it in stride.

"It feels good having someone else worrying along with you anytime I go out, Momma. If Daddy can't be here, I'm glad Zane is here for you and for us. Plus, I think it's kinda funny," she tells me when I ask if Zane's behavior upsets her.

Her words make me realize no matter how hard I've worked to be both father and mother to my girls, they still miss and need Jake. Zane isn't their father, but he's starting to become a father figure to them. At first, I was worried wondering how the girls were going to take it if it didn't work out with the two of us, but little by little, that worry is disappearing.

After the third time with Dean, I finally ask Zane why he's so hard on the boy.

"If that boy can't take what I'm dishing out, then he doesn't deserve Rylee. She needs a man that will stand up for her and keep her safe. A man that will defend her with his life if need be. I don't want her dating a pussy and if this kid can't handle me, then he needs to stay the fuck away from our girl. I'm not her father, but I'll take care of her and Skylar as if they are my own. And I'd die for them and for you, Faith."

What could I say to that?

For this man to claim us and to tell me straight up that he would die for my girls and for me is humbling. Can it be that I'm getting another chance at forever?

"Okay, baby," is all I reply.

Nothing I say can let him know how much his words mean to me, so the only thing I can do is jump on him and show him how much I appreciate his gestures and words. To show him how much I love his body and how I love the way he makes me feel. With him I feel cherished, protected, and such a strong emotion I don't want to say it just yet, but I know it is love. I love this man.

The past years, I've had to be strong—not only for my family but also for the company that was my husband's dream. Unfortunately, Jake never got to see his dream become a reputable, respected, and feared organization. He never got the opportunity to work his ass off to make his dream come true—that fell to me.

I had to toughen up and deal with people that could eat me alive. Any weakness would be pounced upon and used against me, especially being a woman in a man's world. A woman whose only background included being a military child and spouse, mother, student, and athlete. I had no experience, and at first, everyone thought I was a joke, but I showed them and I showed them good. I put aside my career to ensure I was able to realize the legacy Jake had dreamed about beginning. To have a man that is not intimidated by my accomplishments and my job (which he still doesn't know completely about) and who wants to take care of me and protect me, is a wonderful feeling that I never want to lose.

∾✕∾

26 April 2013

Today is an emotional day for all of us.

Five years ago today, I lost the man I professed to love forever and spend the rest of my life with. Today, the girls and I are preparing ourselves to head out to Jake's grave. Since moving here, every Sunday after church we visit Jake, but today is a special day so we are visiting earlier than usual.

I called the school and let them know Rylee and Skylar wouldn't be in attendance today because it was their father's anniversary. Over the years, regardless of what's going on, we've always visited Jake on this day. Thankfully, the schools were understanding; otherwise, there would have been hell to pay.

Today is also Rylee's senior prom.

Rylee was torn, so we had a long discussion on whether or not she should attend. She was afraid it was disrespectful, but I told her Jake wouldn't want her to miss out. I explained to her that Jake will always be part of our lives and we will always love him, but our lives go on. We will always honor this day, but we can't be sad anymore—today is about remembering the great man our Jake was.

When I asked what she really wanted to do, she replied.

"I want to visit my daddy and reminisce the memories I have of us together. I want to share my memories with everyone, but I also want to go to my prom. I feel childish and selfish, but I don't want to miss out on my last prom."

"You're not selfish or childish, Rylee. Every girl dreams of her last prom and you're gonna go. We'll visit your daddy and then we'll get you all prettied up for your dance," I tell her. "Okay?"

"Yes, Momma," she replies.

Now, we're packing all his favorite snacks and drinks. Gunner, my in-laws, my parents, and Jake's old army buddies (now my co-workers)—everyone able to make the trip is waiting for us at the cemetery. Like every year before, we plan to have a small picnic with Jake. We'll eat and drink while retelling our stories of him. How he'd make us laugh, how he'd piss us off, and anything else we can remember. Many of our stories have been retold over and over through the years, but we keep retelling them so we don't forget and so Skylar can remember our memories of the man she never had the opportunity to meet.

As I'm putting everything together, I hear the front door open. It's strange because the girls are here with me, everyone else is at the cemetery waiting for us, and Zane left a while back for work. I look at the girls, but they refuse to meet my eyes so I know something's up. I go out to the living room where Zane surprises me.

"What are you doing here? I thought you were at work," I ask him.

"Do you really think I'd want to leave you on your own today?" He asks. "You didn't ask me and I didn't want to push, but deep down, I wanted to be with you and the girls. I wasn't gonna say anything and respect today, but the girls came to me yesterday. They told me that you'd never ask me to go with you because you were afraid it'd make me feel like I was being compared to Jake, but they needed me to be there for them and for you."

"Um . . . I just didn't want you to feel weird or judged by being there. A lot of Jake's old army buddies are joining us today and they've always been protective of us. I didn't want you to get upset."

"Baby," he says, taking my hand and leading me away from the girls, "I don't give a fuck what anyone thinks about me. I'm gonna be there for you and the girls even if I'm squirming in my pants. A real man doesn't give a shit about how he feels as long as he's there for his woman and his girls. Y'all are mine and I take care of what's mine. My question is, do you want me there with you?"

I look up at him and I can see a small amount of fear in his eyes. He's scared that I'm going to refuse him. He's right though—if he's going to have any place in our lives, he has to be by our sides. Jake's friends are going to have to become acquainted with him. If my in-laws think Zane is a good man for me and the girls, then Jake's buddies are going to have to become used to having him around.

"Yes, honey. I want you there with us. I want you there to hold us because today is an emotional day for us. You know I'll always love Jake. He was my first love and I thought I would be with him forever. But life had other plans for us. You're part of my world now, but he'll always have a place in my heart. Please don't be upset. I'm gonna need you today."

"Faith, I'll never be upset about Jake. I know how much the two of you loved each other. Rylee has made sure I know the story on how y'all met and how you made sure the two of you ended up together. He's your past and will always be a part of you. I want to be your present and your future, to be with you and with Rylee and Skylar, and to take care of you. I know Jake's memory will come with you and I accept that. I'll always be grateful to him because he helped make you into the woman you are today, the woman that I love, and he gave you Rylee and Skylar and in turn, gave them to me. I love y'all more than words can express, love."

"You love me?" I ask breathlessly. "You really love me?"

"Yes, Faith," he chuckles. "Out of all that, that's the only part you got? Of course I love you. Why do you think I didn't let you go when it would've been easier to do so? Why do you think I listen to Taylor Swift with Skylar and why do you think I try my damnest to scare that boy Rylee is seeing away? I do all that because I love you and I love those girls."

"Oh my . . ." I'm speechless for a moment but not for long. "I love you too, you big sweet man," I say as I jump on him and wrap my legs around his waist. I grab his face and give him a kiss on his lips. He holds me tight for a few seconds before letting me go and helping me down.

"Let's go get the girls and load everything up," he tells me and leads me back into the kitchen. That's when I notice the plastic bag he's carrying.

"What do you have in the bag, honey?" I ask. "Does it need to go in the fridge?"

"No. This is for Jake. I remember you telling me about the numerous times you had to send some to him when he was away and was unable to get his own."

He opens the bag and pulls out a can of Copenhagen Wintergreen long cut.

My eyes tear up and I hear sniffles coming from the table. The two of us turn and see Rylee wiping her eyes. Skylar is just looking at us.

"You remembered . . ." Rylee says tearfully. "You got that for my daddy?"

"Yeah, I did," Zane replies.

Rylee jumps up so fast that we barely see her move. She launches herself at Zane and hugs him like there's no tomorrow.

"Thank you," she tells him as she looks up at him through her tears. "Thank you for understanding and thank you for not trying to take over and replace him."

She goes back to hugging him and I just look at Zane through my own tears. He is holding Rylee tight and he mouths to me, "I love you."

"What about me?" Skylar asks. "I want a hug too and I want you to carry me, Zane. Please carry me out. I'm so tired and my legs hurt."

She begins to pout. Zane, of course, falls for it and picks up the little peanut. He carries her out to the Jeep, buckles her in, and gives her a kiss on the head. He opens up Rylee's door so she can jump in and does the same for me. He gets into the Jeep and turns on the ignition.

"Everyone buckled?" He asks. At our nods he backs out of the driveway. "Let's go spend the day with your father, girls. I want to get to know him through your memories." He turns to look at me. "Thank you, for letting me be here for you and thank you, girls, for accepting me into the family."

✖

Zane

I know today is hard for my girls and I'm glad I get to be there for them in case they need me. Many don't understand why I want to be part of this family, but I know this is where I belong and I honestly don't give a fuck what anyone else thinks. I'm happy and they're happy—that's all that matters.

I know Jake will always be part of us and I'm okay with it because he created this family and he was a good and honorable man. I'm not looking to replace him, I just want to love Faith and the girls. They deserve to be treasured and protected and I'm the man that's going to do so for the rest of their lives.

Years ago I met a man and I made a promise—I may never understand why I made it, but I'm glad I did because it brought me to them.

∽⟨∾⟩∾

Faith

We arrive to the cemetery and unload the Jeep. Zane grabs most of the stuff and follows us to Jake's grave. As we approach, we see everyone gathered around. I see Gunner, my in-laws, my parents, Julia, and four of Jake's army buddies—Zeke, Damon, Jax, and Duke. The guys immediately zone in on Zane and their faces go blank.

When we finally reach them, the girls and I hug and kiss everyone in greeting, and then we step back to where Zane was standing. Jacob and Carmen immediately greet him, and so do my parents. My parents flew in from Italy, where my father is stationed, so they've never met Zane face-to-face but have spoken with him by phone and Skype. Momma and Daddy are glad they finally get to meet the new man in my life.

Gunner waits until Carmen, Jacob, Momma and Daddy greet Zane before moving forward and giving him one of those man hugs—the ones where you semi-hug and slap each other on the back, followed by one of those intricate handshakes that you learn in boy school. Zeke, Damon, Jax, and Duke, seeing this, are shocked. They know about Gunner's feelings for me.

"What the hell, man . . ." I hear Jax say.

"He's good," Gunner answers just as I say, "Language!"

All the guys give each other one of those looks that communicates a whole conversation in just seconds. They turn to look at Zane, measuring him up and seeing how close the girls and I are to him. They realize he's now a part of our group because one by one they each step up to shake his hand. There are no man hugs, but at least it's a start. After the awkward first meeting, we all relax and start laying everything out.

I head to Jake's tombstone and place a kiss on it with my hand. I tell him I love him. I'm just turning back to help when I notice an almost-new can of dip. I bend down to pick it up and turn to face everyone. I know I didn't place it there, and my girls are too young to buy tobacco. We're the only weekly visitors so I'm baffled on how it got here. I get Gunner's attention and ask him if he left it, and he tells me no. The guys just arrived from their respective homes out of town, so I know it wasn't them.

For some reason I turn to Zane and ask. "You?"

"Um, yeah," he hesitantly replies.

"When? Why?" I ask. I notice that we have everyone's attention now.

"After I first met you, I asked Jackie everything about you. She told me about Jake and how much you loved him and how you've never been with anyone else since him. I was curious about the man that inspired so much devotion, especially after I kissed you at the club," he tells me. "Before going to your house the next morning, I stopped by here to tell Jake about myself and to basically ask permission to date you, as corny as that sounds. I figured if he disagreed with me, he'd let me know one way or another. Ever since you mentioned his fondness for dip, I've made it a point to drop by and leave him a can. I switch them out because every man wants fresh Copenhagen."

Hearing his explanation, I feel my eyes start to water and my nose starts feeling funny. Rylee is holding onto Skylar and my mother and Carmen have their faces in their husbands' chests, their bodies shaking.

"Oh Zane," I say, sniffling.

"I'm sorry if it upsets you, baby," he tells me. "I reckoned he'd appreciate having fresh dip every now and then. I also came to see him before spring break to talk to him about our arrangement and our plans, and I had a beer with him. Like I said, Faith, I want to be part of your life in every possible way. I figured he'd appreciate me coming and being upfront with him about my feelings for you. I'll always respect his memory and I'll always love you and the girls."

Well, that did it. My momma and mother-in-law are now bawling and Gunner has both the girls in his arms. The guys are looking at Zane with newfound respect, and I lose it. He just announced to everyone that he loves me and the girls and that he's taken the time to come see my deceased husband and reassure him that we'd be safe with him.

Who takes the time to do that?

In the midst of tears I think that only a true man would do that. And Zane is that: he's a man that will always place us first, who will make sure that we're happy and will move Heaven and Earth to keep us safe.

I sit down next to Jake's tombstone and I give thanks to God for placing such a wonderful and caring man in my life again. I know somehow Jake had something to do with this. I've always been a firm believer that everything happens for a reason. Gunner wanted to make Phoenix's headquarters elsewhere, but for some unknown reason Jake insisted on it being here. There were several arguments between the two and when I asked Jake one time why it had to be here, he told me that he didn't really know. He just had a feeling that this was the place Phoenix needed to be located because if anything ever happened to him, I would be safe here and this would be a great place to raise Rylee. Now, I wonder—could he have unknowingly placed us here for Zane?

Zane takes me in his arms.

"Don't cry," he says. His face showing panic. "Faith, stop this second," he orders.

Yeah, right. Like I'm going to stop crying just because he tells me to stop. I don't think so.

"Don't tell me to stop crying, Zane," I say, sniffling. "I'll quit crying when I'm good and ready. You can't tell me all this and expect me not to cry. To know that you'll always understand is . . . I don't know how to explain it, but it's wonderful, amazing. How did the girls and I get so lucky?"

I let out another big sob. He gives up and just holds me. Gunner has my girls and Zane is holding me tight.

Finally, after a couple of minutes, my sobs subside and I start to calm down. I lean back and look at the amazing and considerate man that I am lucky to have in my life.

"Thank you, honey. Thank you for being here with me and for getting to know Jake," I tell him. "I love you."

"I love you too, Faith. Can you please stop crying now? When you cry, I don't know what to do and I hate that shit. I hate not knowing how to make you feel better and I don't like it when you cry. I associate crying with pain and sadness and I definitely don't like it. You done now?"

"Yes, honey," I say, chuckling. "I was crying happy tears because you're so sweet and amazing."

"Babe, I'm not sweet," he growls. "I'm a badass motherfucker and we're not sweet—we protect what is ours, and you and the girls are mine to love and protect. Now, can we please get up and have the picnic. I'm pretty sure that Jake hated it when you cried. So get your cute little ass up and feed us, woman."

"You're right," I say. "He hated it anytime I cried. Okay, honey, let's go get you and the girls fed. Skylar is probably *starving.*"

This makes him laugh because the little girl that's become his princess is always *starving.* He gives me his hand and helps me up. With his arm around my waist, we turn and face the rest of the crowd. I notice everything has been set out. The food is laid out, the drinks separated with beer for the men, wine for the ladies and juice for the girls. Jax has his guitar out and is seated, ready to take requests from Rylee and Skylar. My parents draw me into a hug and Carmen and Jacob follow. Everyone is ready to spend our day remembering what a great man my Jake was.

As the day progresses, the guys tell stories of how Jake was during their deployments and at work. They have us in tears laughing at the time Jake was flipping out in his room when Duke decided to catch a camel spider—myth has it they are rather big, scary spiders—and released it in Jake and Gunner's room. In reality, it was a normal size spider that wanted to be left in peace, but Jake plain did not like spiders—from the moment we married, I became the spider exterminator in our household. That story is followed by many others from the rest of us. Skylar makes her way to Zane's lap and he holds her as he hears stories about what type of man Jake was. Skylar listens as well to the stories that will be her only way of knowing her father.

Before we know it, it's three o'clock in the afternoon, and Rylee has to leave to get ready for prom. Zane, Rylee, Skylar and I pack up all of our things and kiss everyone good-bye. My parents are staying at the Hilton and we'll be meeting at our house for prom pictures, and then a quick dinner later in the evening before their late flight back home. We make our way to the Jeep and get in. Before joining us, I see Zane look up to the sky, his lips moving, and I could swear I see something surround him.

⚡

After two long hours of getting ready, Rylee comes down the stairs looking like a Greek goddess in her ivory floor-length dress. The dress is an off-the- shoulder affair embellished with gold and diamond jewels on the top of the shoulder drape and around the waist. It fits her beautifully and she looks so grown up. She's wearing gold strappy heels that are visible through the slit, which goes up to about three inches above her knees. Her hair is down and curled in a tousled look, and her make-up is flawless. She looks beautiful and I feel tears coming on.

Rylee is growing up so fast.

Jake would be so proud of his little princess.

Zane, Jacob, and my Daddy are in the living room with Rylee's date. As she walks down the stairs, Dean turns to face her. His face freezes in amazement. We ladies have our cameras out and quickly start taking pictures. Zane jumps up, beating Dean to Rylee, and the boy quickly wipes an irritated look off his face. Zane gives Rylee a hug and whispers into her ear. She looks up at him and smiles her beautiful smile, and I capture the moment. My father follows Zane after giving him his time and then he, too, hugs and kisses our Rylee. He whispers in her ear and is rewarded with a smile. Jacob follows and gets his time with his granddaughter. He steps back, and Dean finally gets her attention. He hands her the red rose corsage—not a good choice since her favorite flowers are blue orchids, but I tell myself it's the thought that counts. Thirty minutes and hundreds of pictures later, they head out the door.

"I love you," I tell my daughter. "Always and forever." My eyes are watery. "Daddy would be so proud."

"You look like a princess," Skylar tells her sister. "Can I come with you?"

"I hope so, Momma. I know he's watching over us from Heaven. One day, we'll see him again," Rylee tells me confidently. "I love you too, Momma, always and forever."

She turns to her sister. "Sorry, Peanut, you can't come with me; it's just for big people."

"Fine," Skylar huffs and walks away with a pout.

"Be careful, Rylee. You," he glares at Dean. "Take care of our girl. You understand?"

"Yes, sir," is the only reply as Dean looks out the door.

"Rylee, you call me if you need anything. Anything. No matter the time, you hear?" Zane calls out.

"I will, Zane, thank you," she answers. "Take care of Momma and Skylar and have fun with Grandma and Grandpa. Bye, Nana, Papa, Grandma and Grandpa. Love y'all," she says as she heads out the door.

Our arms are around each other, our bodies close together. My head is on Zane's chest as I watch my beautiful daughter walk out the door. Tears are streaming down my cheeks—the five-year-old little girl I fell in love with so many years ago is now a beautiful young lady. How I wish Jake was here to see her.

I didn't know it, but that was the last time I would see *my* Rylee— my Rylee with beautiful green and innocent eyes, full of life and fearlessness. If I had known that, I never would have let her walk out that door. Five years ago, our lives were changed by tragedy, and today, Zane and I unknowingly let my daughter walk out the door and into the hands of a monster.

Zane

Today, I gained the acceptance of her family and friends. We spent the day reminiscing over memories of a damn good man— a husband, father, son, friend, and soldier. I got to hold my little princess as she heard stories of the father she never got to meet. I was there for my woman and my girls.

Jake was a good man. Knowing how much love they shared, I believe life played a shitty hand when it took him so young. We may never understand why, but we have to accept. As Faith believes, everything happens for a reason.

I'm lucky to have Faith's love. I have the amazing woman she has become in my life and I'll fight till my dying breath to keep her.

I just need to make sure that the little secret I haven't told won't tear us apart. Because, man, it could make us or break us. I just have to make her understand.

Part Three

Truths Revealed

Chapter 19

26 April 2013

That night I go to bed without a care in the world—I'm in the arms of the man I love, my daughters are safe, and Zane's been accepted by everyone.

My world is perfect.

Nothing can go wrong.

Despite busy schedules and being located all over the world, everyone managed to take a little time off to come be with us on this day, and we greatly appreciate it. The only one missing was Gabriel, but with everything going on in his neck of the woods, he couldn't get away.

Carmen and Jacob head back home because she needed to get some last-minute things ready for her show the following day. It was a rushed visit, but at least they were able to be here for us and to see Rylee head out to her senior prom. After goodbye kisses and promises of visits, they head back to Dallas.

Now, it's just us and my parents. We decide to meet at my favorite restaurant, Olive Garden, for dinner. Oh! The deliciousness of the place the breadsticks and the salad, the unlimited refills with an entrée *and* their frozen margaritas and mudslides . . . *Yummy!*

This dinner is the last one I will have with my parents before they fly back to Italy, and it's mainly for Zane and Daddy—their bonding time. During dinner, my parents get to know Zane—well, it's more Daddy interrogating him and Momma and me catching up, with Skylar coloring. They definitely notice how wonderful Zane is with Skylar. He treats her like a little princess and she has him wrapped around her little finger.

"Faith, that boy looks at you like you're his whole world. His eyes are always on you or Skylar and he makes sure that y'all have whatever y'all need. He even cut her chicken for her, darlin'! I always prayed you'd find another wonderful man and I see my prayers have been answered," she says with tears in her eyes. "He's even won your father over and you know how hard he is. He was ready to scare the boy away when you first called us to let us know about him. Now, I don't think he needs to do that or even wants to."

We both turn to look at our men and one little princess. Skylar is keeping both of them entertained with tales from her Pre-K class. She has both men captivated. My heart is filled with love. My father approves of Zane. He did put him through the ringer with his questions, but Zane held his own like a champ. Mama and I just lean back and enjoy the show that Skylar is providing while we catch up on all the family gossip—mainly, we discuss my brother, Cristian.

Much later, my father comes to my side.

"Pumpkin, you've done well. He's a good man—Special Forces and now a firefighter. Damn good man you got there, pumpkin. He treats y'all like I treat your mother and you kids. He's always watching y'all, making sure there's no danger—I like that and I can rest comfortable at home now. And, he held his own when I questioned him. Jake would've liked him. I can imagine he's sitting up there in heaven drinking a beer and watching Zane take care of his girls. I love y'all, Pumpkin. You, Skylar, and Rylee."

Despite being in the military for over three decades and living in numerous countries, neither he nor momma have lost their accent. Or their pride in their home state. As they always say, "God bless Texas!"

The night continues with drinks—for me anyway, since Zane is driving—and lots of talking. My parents and I haven't seen each other in well over a year and we want to know everything that has occurred during that time period. We share pictures and Zane tells them his side of "our story," making my parents laugh with his description of my escape attempts and the scrapes I got myself into. Everything is wonderful and good.

Then it is time for my parents to leave.

After a tearful "see you soon" to my parents, Zane helps a very tipsy me into the Jeep and straps a sleepy Skylar into her car seat. He ensures we're both buckled in before getting into the vehicle and taking us home.

"Babe, do I need to carry you inside and put you to bed too?" He asks.

"Nah, honey, I'm good." I giggle. "I'm feeling soooo good; you're gonna be a very lucky man tonight." I look at him as seductively as I can after a few drinks. "I just need you to get our little peanut to bed and then I'm gonna *Rock. Your. World.*"

"Alright," he replies chucking. "Ready. Set. Go!"

He hurries out of the Jeep and grabs Skylar, and I quickly follow him.

When the hell did these shoes get so hard to walk in? I'm only wearing four-and-a-half-inch heels, but still . . . I stumble into the house and head up the stairs to Skylar's room. I give her a goodnight kiss and make sure she has her nightlight on.

After Zane gives her his kiss, I grab him by his shirt and basically drag him to our room. I throw him on the bed and watch his body bounce. He looks at me smiling and my heart stops. He's so handsome and he's all mine. *All mine.* I'm one lucky woman.

I take a few steps back and take my clothes off, leaving only my bra, panties, and heels on. I make my way to the bed, swaying my hips like Jessica Rabbit. I unpin my hair on the way and shake it loose. I feel so sexy walking towards him—due largely in part to the alcohol, as well as the look he's giving me—like I'm the most beautiful woman in the world and the only thing that exists for him.

I reach him, climb on top, and straddle him. I grab his head and bring his lips to mine. I moan at how delicious he tastes. He takes a firm hold of my hips. Soon he takes over the kiss and I rub myself against him. I pull back and lift his shirt, shucking it off him. He takes my mouth again and I move my hands down to his belt. I undo it, unbutton his pants, and slide my hand in to cup him. He's hard and it's all for me. He lets me go and helps me get the rest of his clothes off.

Holy freakin' crap!

His body is a work of art. His panther tattoo looks wicked and dangerous—"the ghost of the rainforest," I've heard panthers are called because they're so rare and elusive. And just like the man, it stares back at me, claiming me. I love how it makes me feel, and I love Zane. He's *all mine.*

I push him back onto the bed and I look at his cock. It's beautiful—long, thick, and *hard.* Very hard. I look at him and smile. I lick my lips and tell him, "It's my turn now."

I move my lips up and down one thigh and then the other. I go over and around his cock, feeling him move. He's anxious for me to take him into my mouth, but I want to make him lose control just like he makes me. I torture him for a while longer, kissing, licking, and nipping everywhere but where he really wants me to. Finally, he begs me and I take him into my mouth. I swirl my tongue and suck him, like I do a lollypop.

Just as I'm really enjoying myself, thinking I'm going to make myself come by blowing him, he jerks me away, turns us, and pounces on me.

"No fair, honey," I say with a pout. "Tonight is my turn . . ."

"Faith, when I cum, I'm gonna cum inside of you. I want to feel your pussy stroke my juices out of me and leave me dry. I want to feel you surrounding me, love."

He tears off my lingerie and begins to stroke my body, knowing how to make me fall apart with pleasure. He takes me higher than ever before. My legs are wrapped around him and my heels are digging into his back. It's freaking hot and I love it. When we explode, I'm so exhausted that I fall asleep immediately.

My last conscious thought is Zane taking off my heels, kissing my lips, and whispering.

"I love you, Faith."

Hours later, I hear a phone ringing.

Ugh!

Thinking it's mine, I lift my hand to my nightstand.

It's not. Mine is dead—great.

It's Zane's.

I try to wake him but the man is dead to the world. Work has been exhausting lately and he hasn't been getting enough sleep.

Well, crap. I'm actually going to have to get up. This stinks big time.

I wriggle out of his hold, find his pants and search his pockets until I find his phone. I take the phone out to check and make sure it's not the station. I notice something fall out, and then I see a strange number on the screen. Missed call.

It's midnight—strange.

I use the light from his phone to pick up what fell out of his pants and notice a patch. Not just any patch—an Army patch. I'm about to put it back when I notice that a set of dog tags is attached to the patch. I think nothing of it at first until I take a closer look at the patch, and then I look at the tags.

WTF?!

DUVAL
JACOB H.
999-09-9999
AB POS
ROM CATH

These are Jake's tags!

"Zane! Zane, wake up," I yell.

He immediately wakes and looks around, searching for the unknown threat.

"Turn on the light," I say harshly.

He does as I ask and looks at me, confused.

"What the fuck is this?" I ask with deadly calm, holding the dog tags up in the air. At first he's baffled by my attitude and language, but then he sees the tags in my hand.

"Faith, I can explain—" he says, but I don't let him finish.

"Really? How could you possibly explain why you have Jake's

dog tags? Is this some sick joke?"

My voice is calm and emotionless. I feel like a knife is going through my body. I feel betrayed. I don't understand what's going on. Was everything a lie? By why . . . how?

"Those are mine," he tells me. "Jake gave me those tags."

"No!" I finally yell, losing the calmness I felt before. How dare he lie to me? "He couldn't have given you anything, Zane. HE'S DEAD. Jake is dead and he's never coming back!" My eyes fill with angry tears. "He's never gonna see our daughter grow up and marry or our grandchildren born. We're never gonna grow old together like we planned. Because he's gone forever. He's dead, Zane."

"Faith, let me explain before you go off your rocker."

"Excuse me? Are. You. Fuckin'. Serious?! Don't tell me to calm down because I'm calm—I'm just fuckin' pissed right now. And I have every right to be because I'm not the one that has Jake's tags in my pocket. Even if I did, it wouldn't be strange because he was MY husband."

At this point, I don't care if I sound irrational. Jake's tags were in Zane's pockets. Zane never mentioned meeting Jake before, and he had plenty of opportunities to inform me if they had met. He lied to me. Why would he keep it to himself?

"Calm down, Faith, and let me explain," he says, but he's interrupted by his phone ringing again.

"It's that strange number that was calling you before, and after you answer, I want you out of here," I say angrily, handing him the phone. "I need time to think."

He answers the phone.

"Yes, this is her household. This is Zane Knight . . . No, I'm not. Is she okay? . . . What hospital? Okay—we're on our way," he says and hangs up.

"Get dressed. Now. Hospital. It's Rylee. They won't tell me anything because I'm not her next of kin. Let's get moving—the sooner we get there, the sooner we find out what's going on."

My world stops.

Rylee's in the hospital.

I can't lose her. Please, God, let her be okay.

Everything else is forgotten and I start to pray.

Zane comes to me and puts his hands on my shoulders. He forces me to look at him.

"It's gonna be okay, Faith. I'm here with you. Now, I need you to go get ready to go while I get the Jeep out of the garage."

I look at him and see the sincerity in his eyes. I blink and gather myself. I take a deep breath and nod my head in understanding. Nothing matters right now but my daughter.

I move faster than I thought possible as I get dressed. I grab my purse and run out to get our little peanut, but Zane beats me to her. He picks up a sleepy Skylar, murmuring calming words, and we rush out of the house.

We get to the hospital in record time and I run to the front desk.

"My daughter was brought in. Her name is Rylee Duval. Is—is she okay? " I ask. My throat closes up.

The nurse types something into the computer and then looks up into my terrified face, then at Zane, who is holding a sleeping Skylar.

Her eyes are full of sympathy. "Just a second, ma'am, the doctor wants to see you and then we'll take you to see your daughter."

"Is she alive?" I ask in a whisper, afraid that she might say no.

"Yes, ma'am." At her words I let out a sigh of relief, and I hear Zane do the same. "The doctor needs to speak with you first. She'll be here in just a minute."

Zane and I step away from the desk and I turn to him. He takes me in one arm and I let him. Regardless of what is going on with us, Rylee comes first and I'm glad he's here with me.

"It's okay, baby. She's alive and that's all that matters. Let's wait to hear what the doctor has to say," he says to me.

"The parents of Rylee Duval?" I hear behind me. I turn and see a female doctor standing in a doorway.

"I'm her mother," I say. "How is my daughter, Doctor?"

She looks at me. "I'm Dr. Smith. Could you follow me, please? I need to speak with you."

Before I can say anything, Zane says, "You'll be speaking with me as well, Doctor."

Dr. Smith looks at me. I close my eyes and take a deep breath. It's not about him or me, it's about Rylee. I nod in confirmation. I need him with me.

"Very well. Please follow me," she says, leading us to the back.

We go into a small office and she closes the door. This scares me because she didn't take me directly to Rylee.

"Doctor, I need to see my daughter," I tell her.

"I know you do," she tells me. "There are just some things I need to let you know before you do. Your daughter was brought in about an hour ago. She was conscious, but I'm sorry to inform you that she was badly beaten. She managed to tell us that she wasn't raped before she became unconscious due to the pain. However, there were signs of a rape attempt. The police were informed about the situation, but because she's a minor and unconscious, they have to wait to begin their questioning. I'm informing you so you're prepared." Looking at Skylar, she asks, "Is there anyone you can call to help with your little one? I don't think it would be wise to have her see her sister right this moment."

I can't breathe.

"Badly beaten" and "attempted rape" were all I heard.

Rylee was hurt to the point she had to pass out to escape the pain. Oh, God! How could this happen? I feel arms come around me. I turn to him, seeing he has put Skylar down, who's still sleeping, and I let myself fall into him.

"My baby girl was hurt, Zane," I tell him, crying. "My Rylee. My baby. Oh, God . . ."

I feel his chin on my head and some wetness. I look up and see tears. Zane is crying for my daughter. My poor innocent baby girl. This just makes me cry harder.

After several minutes, he says, "Faith, do you want to call Julia to come get Skylar? The doctor is right, she shouldn't see Rylee right now." I nod and move numbly to my purse to get my phone.

"My phone is dead, Zane."

"Here's mine, baby."

I call Julia and ask her to come get Skylar. She tells me she'll be here in about ten minutes. I hang up and turn to Doctor Smith.

"Why wasn't I notified sooner?" I ask.

"As soon as she arrived to the hospital, we treated her and waited until she became conscious to gather her contact information. We tried the first number she gave us and when we received no answer, we dialed the second number."

I nod and close my eyes.

A few minutes later, Julia messages Zane to let him know she's here. We meet her in the waiting area and explain the situation. She hugs me and we both start crying. Zane separates us, after giving us some time together, and hands Skylar to her. We explain that Rylee's been given pain medication and is sleeping, but we want to get to her as soon as possible. We didn't think it was the time to let Skylar see her in her current state.

Right now, I just want to hold my little girl. Regardless of her age, she'll always be the little girl that I fell in love with so many years ago. Oh God! Just thinking of what she must have endured makes me tear up again.

Julia leaves with Skylar and Zane and I are left alone.

"Faith, regardless of what is going on with us, Rylee comes first. I love you and I love the girls. Y'all are my world and whatever I kept from you was for a reason. Please, let me take care of y'all— let me be here for you. We need to go help her and then you and I can work out our problem. Like we agreed before, the girls come first. Let me be here for you and for Rylee. She needs us now, more than ever."

"I just want to see my little girl, Zane. I want to see her and I want to hold her and let her know that I'm so sorry. I should've protected her more. While you and I were together, she was being hurt," I say, flooded with guilt. "I just want to see her, please."

"We're in this together. Forever, Faith."

He takes me in his arms and kisses my head. He holds me tight before releasing me and turning me towards the door. He takes my hand in his and together, we make our way to see Rylee.

I don't know what to expect when I walk through the door to her room, but the sight of her lying in the hospital bed almost brings me to my knees. Her face—her eyes are swollen shut, she has cuts and bruises all over her face from blows she received. Bruises cover her arms; one arm is in a cast. She has a cut above her left eye that will leave a scar after healing.

I'm suddenly filled with an anger so great, it starts to consume me. I want to hurt whoever hurt my daughter. I literally want to kill that person with my bare hands. I want that person to hurt as much as they hurt my daughter.

Beside me, I feel waves of emotion radiating from Zane's body. If his anger is anywhere close to mine, whoever did this in a lot of trouble. Knowing the type of man Zane is, he'll want to do something about this situation. It's going to be up to me to keep him out of trouble. Regardless of our problem, though, Zane is right— we're in this together.

I pull up a chair next to the bed, sit, and hold Rylee's hand. I feel Zane's hand on my shoulder. I want to lean on him for strength and after a couple of seconds, I do.

"Baby," he whispers. "I'm here for her and you. I love this girl like she was my own. I want to know what happened and find whoever did this. I want to fuckin' kill them."

I wipe my tears. "You know what's seriously wrong with this?" I ask him.

He looks at me, waiting for an answer. He still doesn't know everything I do for a living. I never got around to telling him. Not many people really know. All people know is that I work for the company my husband built. Many assume I'm a receptionist or secretary, and I let them.

"Rylee should've had at least one bodyguard on her for a while now. After the company started getting a reputation and . . . with the money that Jake left us, my daughter should've been protected. Every time I brought up the subject, she said it would cramp her style," I say with a chuckle at my daughter's words. "I didn't push the subject. I didn't think we needed it in the town we live in. The city, yes, but this town, no. *This* is on me. I know how dangerous the world can be and I didn't protect her like I should have. If I'd done what I knew needed to be done, she never would've been hurt."

"Faith, this isn't on you. It's on whoever did this to her—not you," he tells me. "Now, it's up to us to help her."

"She's going to need us, but are you going to be around?" I ask him. "You lied to me, Zane. You betrayed me by keeping something important from me. I need to know why. Was this a game to you? You never mentioned knowing Jake. You've had plenty of opportunity, but never said anything. Why?"

"Do you really want to do this now?" He asks me.

"Yes. I need to focus. Right now, I'm waiting on my daughter to wake up. My mind is all over the place and I need to focus on something other than the unknowns of Rylee's situation. I'll take care of my daughter after she wakes and tells us what happened and who did this. Right now, I want you to explain to me everything, and don't leave anything out. This will determine if you're gonna stay in our lives. After Rylee wakes, helping her will be my main priority. My daughters always come first, Zane, and if I feel you're a threat, you'll be gone."

"Okay. . . where do I start?" He asks, running his fingers through his hair.

"Start from the beginning," I tell him.

"Well . . . you might not remember, but you and I—we've seen each other twice before that fateful day at the stoplight," he tells me. He sees that I'm about to interrupt. "Yes, we have, babe; you just don't remember. Back then, I wasn't even a blip on your radar. Like Gunner said, you only had eyes for Jake. I'm gonna tell you the whole story, but wait until the end before you say anything, please."

I nod in agreement, but I'm not sure if I can keep that promise.

As we wait for our Rylee to wake, Zane begins to tell me his story. A story of two men meeting and of a special promise that was made. A story some might find strange and unexplainable.

Chapter 20

Zane (26 April 2013)

"Okay, here's how it was," I begin my story. "I met Jake in 2007 during his last deployment to Afghanistan. I was in a mentally fucked-up place—I'd found out a few days prior that Eliza was cheating on me when she called to tell me she was pregnant.

"'How the fuck did that happen?' I asked her. 'I've been away for almost a year.'

"Then it hit me. She'd been fuckin' around on me.

"'It's okay,' she tells me. 'It's Troy's'—Troy was my best friend at the time—'so you'll grow to love the baby and we can go on as before.'

"She said she'd been careful, but it had failed. She wasn't even sorry for cheating on me. She figured I'd get over it.

"Fuck. That. Shit. I threw her ass to the curb. I thought, let that motherfucker own up and claim that bitch and her poor unfortunate unborn baby because with a mother like her, I felt sorry for that child, but not enough to stay with her cheating ass.

"Anyway, so I wasn't in a good place and I thought that all women, aside from those in my family, were deceitful bitches with no sense of morals or loyalty. I'd lost faith—I was fighting for my country and here my almost-fiancée—because I thought I'd marry her one day—was fuckin' around on me.

"Then I met Jake. He sure was something else. He was well respected and admired by his men. He had plenty of confidence but he didn't come off as arrogant. There was something about him that made me want to talk to him. And, he had something I didn't think existed anymore. To tell you the truth, he didn't know what I looked like until much later."

"What do you mean?" Faith asks. "How could he not know what you looked like when you first met him?"

"Babe, you promised not to interrupt," I remind her, chuckling. I knew full well she wouldn't be able to resist—that's just how my Faith is.

"To answer your question, my job in the Army was very different than that of the traditional soldier. I was one of those soldiers that you'd read about in books, the guys that you see but you really don't. My uniform required me to be covered from head to toe. I was one of *those* soldiers—the ones many only whisper about. But like I said before, there was something about him that made me break protocol. We were in the aircraft, minutes away from jumping, when I see this soldier take out a picture and kiss it. I remember seeing him say something to the picture. You have to remember, I'd recently found out about Eliza and I was kinda messed up. So I broke protocol—I spoke to him, and I discovered the true meaning of love and loyalty."

10 May 2007, Southern Afghanistan

What the fuck is that guy doing?

"Did you just kiss that picture and speak to it?" I ask him, shocking the hell out of him and myself.

I just broke protocol.

Well, fuck.

I've never done that before, but I really need to know why the hell this shmuck did that. Was it a girlfriend's picture? I hope not because he'll be in for a fucking rude awakening when she cheats on him while he's away on missions. Shit, she's probably fucking his best friend right this second, as he's about to jump in a war zone—that's what that bitch Eliza did to me. Knowing that women are fickle bitches that can't keep their legs closed, I wouldn't put it past her.

Yeah, I'm fucking jaded, but that's what happens when your girlfriend of two years—the woman you think you might marry—calls you and lets you know that she's pregnant by your best friend.

"You talking to me?" The guy asks me. "What the hell, man? You

ain't supposed to do this shit."

"I saw you doing that and figured I'd save you a heartache by letting you know that women aren't meant to be trusted. They'll cheat on your ass and expect you to take it laying down. Your girl's probably with your best friend right this second. Your ass is here in a fuckin' war zone and she's back home doing whatever the hell she wants."

He laughs at me. "You're fuckin' delusional and paranoid. If I wasn't afraid you'd kill me with your bare hands, I'd call you a stupid fuck."

"Nah, man," I say. "That shit really does happen because it happened to me. Now, I know that the only women you can trust are your mother and your sisters—only family."

"First off," he says, "the person in the photo isn't my girlfriend." He sees my shock. "What?"

"I didn't know you rolled that way. I won't tell anyone you like guys," I assure him. "I'll keep your secret if you don't tell I spoke to you. Oh, and I'm not hitting on you or anything."

"You're fuckin' hilarious, you know that?" He says. "If you'd let me finish, I'd have told you that I just kissed my wife's picture. Yeah, I know; I look way too young to be married and a father, but I'm old enough. Trust me. Faith's my wife and the reason I love going home. She's the one that holds our family together. She took me on with a little girl and all." He laughs and continues, "She was only seventeen when I met her. She came up to me and told me I was gonna be hers. She's my everything—my queen, my treasure."

I just look at him. "You're fuckin' pussy-whipped."

"Damn straight I am, and fuckin' proud. You ever meet my wife and you'll understand. She's fuckin' beautiful and a badass on the soccer field—a damn good player. She's on the US Women's National Soccer Team," he tells me proudly. "I'm hoping to get out of here in time to see her at least play one game this World Cup, but you know how deployments are—sometimes they get extended. You know, instead of being pissed that I'll probably miss seeing her play, she understands this is my job. She says I go out and do this job so she has the freedom to play the sport she loves so much. She tells me

I'm her hero. I'm sorry that shit happened to you, but try to keep that shit away from these guys. Some of them aren't as lucky as me and it'd fuck with their minds."

"Sorry man," I say ashamed of my behavior. "I'm kinda fucked up right now. More pissed than anything, really. It just pisses me off that I've kept my dick in my pants for almost a year and that bitch so easily spread her legs. That was a dick move on my part and I apologize. Your woman sounds like a good woman—a rare breed."

"She is a good woman—the best. And in the bedroom, she's fuckin' amazing," he says. "I'm counting down the days till I get back to her. She's the best wife and the best mother. She's not my little girl's biological mother, but she's her mother in every other sense. She's the true hero."

⤫

"He was so fuckin' proud of you, Faith. You and Rylee were his whole world. His faith and love in you made me curious to meet you. I figured I never would since he'd never see my face, but days later all that changed.

"We went out on a mission. His team was to get me in and let me take care of my target, but our information was fucked. We walked into a fuckin' ambush. There were so fuckin' many of them. We were getting shot at from every direction. Instead of panicking, Jake was calm, collected, and hard. He took control of the situation as best he could and he kept his men alive. He kept me alive. I was so busy covering my front that I made a rookie mistake—I didn't guard my back. I was fuckin' lucky he was there because he saved my life. He took out the guy coming at me and we pushed forward. It was a cluster-fuck and I don't know how the hell we made it through, but we did. Even with all the shit, I managed to get my target and we made it out of there. We were bloodied as hell but we were alive. We thought we were in the clear, but we were wrong.

"We started back to the pick-up point. Out of nowhere this little girl comes out. She looked about ten years or so; didn't look dangerous but back then, kids were being used as soldiers and weapons. This kid, though, we didn't see anything on her. Jake said maybe she was walking home and we wanted to believe that. Jake stepped forward and that's when the kid shot him. She had a weapon underneath her clothes. Shocked the shit out of all of us. We'd heard of kids doing this, but this was just a little girl! Jake reacted to save his men and took her out before she could do any more harm. When we checked her, we found more guns. She was sent to take us out and Jake neutralized her before she could kill us all.

"Jake fell back and we saw he was shot in the leg and he was bleeding badly. There was so much fuckin' blood. I remember shouting that we needed a medevac and for them to hurry the fuck up. I ran to Jake and tried to stop the bleeding. It just kept coming, no matter how much pressure I put on the wound. He was starting to black out and I kept shouting at him to stay with me. I reminded him that y'all were waiting on him to come home. I reacted when I wasn't supposed to. I should've kept going but I couldn't leave him."

∾⌀∾

12 May 2007, Southern Afghanistan

"*F*uck," *groans Jake. "I should've taken her out sooner but when I looked at her, she reminded me of Rylee. She was so young. I just took out a little girl," he says through guilty tears. "I didn't want to, but she shot first. Why?"*

He looks me straight in my brown eyes, the only visible part of me to others. I look back at him, and I realize how far gone I am when it comes to taking a life. I would've taken the shot without question—man or child—but not this man who still has a conscious and feels remorse. I hope he never becomes like me.

"You're a good guy, man," he says to me, as if reading my mind and trying to make me feel better. "Shit, I haven't even seen your face but there's something about you. Don't let what that bitch did to you fuck you up. Don't give up. If I'd done that, I never would've had my Faith.

"Fuck, I'm bleeding to death—I'm bleeding out, man. I should've called her," he tells me. "I should've called my Faith one last time before coming out."

"You're not dying," I tell him. "It's a leg wound and those hurt like hell, but you ain't dying. I ain't gonna let you—I'll even show you my face if you promise to hold on. The chopper's almost here.

Just hang on."

"Okay," he says and then painstakingly starts digging in his pocket. "Here"—he puts a set of dog tags in my hand—"take these. Anything ever happens to me, I want you to look after my family. It's a strange request since we just met, but I have a feeling it's the right thing to do. I need you to promise me. Take my tags. Anything ever happens, you find your way to my girls and make sure they're taken care of. Promise me you'll take care of my girls. You protect my treasures."

"Nothing's gonna happen to you," I say to him, "but if you need me to, I promise."

I hear the sound of the chopper getting closer and landing. Soldiers rush to him. They check him out and carefully put him on a stretcher. The medics move quickly, but with enough gentleness to not jostle him. I gather my shit and jump in. I see that he's passed out. I can't ask anything because no one's supposed to acknowledge me, and this frustrated the shit outta me. I get as close as possible without hindering their work.

I stay close to him and I start praying.

I pray that he makes it because he's right . . . he's bleeding out.

"I remember praying for a man that I'd just met," I tell Faith, "a man that loved his wife more than anything, and his only regret was not calling her one last time. I prayed that he'd make it back to his wife and kid alive. He was right, he was bleeding out, but by some miracle he made it. I remember wishing I'd get to experience the kinda love he treasured more than anything in the world."

I look at her and continue.

"Once in Landstuhl, I made a point to go see him. I broke every rule in the book with that visit, but I had to see him. I couldn't let it go. I dressed in scrubs with mask and all. An unexplainable force was pulling me to visit him. I just had to see him, and I had a promise to keep."

Leap of Faith

*H*earing a voice and realizing it wasn't his, I stand in the doorway. Jake looks at me and I can see the surprise in his eyes. To my surprise, he recognizes me immediately—it must be my body build. He probably never expected to see me again, but here I am. I shake my head and eye the other guy in the room.

"Jones, can you make sure my wife gets to me as soon as she arrives? She's probably driven herself insane with worry, knowing her, and she's had plenty of time on the plane ride here from the States," he says with a chuckle.

"Yes, sir," Jones replies and gets up. He walks out the door without giving me a second glance.

"I see you're alright," I say. "Told ya you'd make it, and it's good to see you conscious."

"Yeah, it's a miracle—I'm lucky to be alive," he replies. "It hurts like a motherfucker, but I'm alive so I ain't complaining. Are you even supposed to be here, man?" He asks.

"What do you think?" I reply. "I just had to make sure you were okay. You ain't seen my face but you had faith in me, called me on my shit, and you saved my life. Not many have done that and it's something I'll never forget."

"I'm okay. Just waiting on my wife to get here. She's been stateside getting ready for the tournament coming up in September," he tells me. "I can't wait to see her. It's been months since I've held her, and I miss her." I look at him. "I know I sound like a fuckin' pussy, but I don't give a shit. I ain't ashamed to let people know I love an incredible woman, especially after what happened back there. I'll never take another moment for granted and I'll always tell her I love her before going out again. I'm never gonna have the same regret I had before."

"She sounds close to perfection, man," I say. "Are you sure she's real? I'm curious to meet this paragon of a woman."

"She has her temper and we drive each other insane sometimes, don't get me wrong, but we love each other and we're in it for the long haul," he tells me. "You still remember your promise, I hope. I *made it through this time, but there's never a guarantee. It's crazy, but I need to know you'll keep your promise. You're a good person; you've just had shitty luck in women. One day, you'll find a woman who will make your world complete, just don't lose faith. And, thank you for keeping me together when I thought I was dying. If you ever need anything, you let me know, you hear?"*

"Duly noted," I say. "And yes, I remember."

I sit in the chair Jones just left and settle myself closer to him, but at the same time I keep my way clear to the door. Just in case I need to make a quick exit.

"Good," he says and then continues, "My buddy and I are starting up a company—security and all that for the elite, and maybe some other exciting jobs on the side so we don't get bored. When you decide you've had enough of this life, you look us up. Just say my name and you got a job with us." He gives me the name and location of the company.

"Shit man, that's where I'm from!" I exclaim.

"No shit," he says, laughing. "That's where my grandparents lived and I always liked visiting them. It's probably where I'll be buried, since my dad was military as well and we moved around a lot. Gunner, my buddy, shied away from starting Phoenix there, but I finally convinced him. I had a feeling it needed to be there—strange how I've been having these weird feelings lately. Hopefully, I'll see you there after we both get tired of all this."

"I just want to make it through my job alive before thinking of the future," I tell him. "Eliza messed me up. She was fuckin' my best friend and I didn't even see it. I think it's more his betrayal that's fucked me up than her. I'm staying in a few more years before I have to sort my shit in the outside world."

"You will," he tells me confidently. "Here." He grabs a patch from his side table. "Keep this and my tags to remember me. Look me up later, even if it's years from now, and remember your promise. Some people won't understand, but as long as I do, that's all that matters."

"Alright—" but before I can go on, we hear footsteps approaching and a feminine voice.

"That's my wife," he says, smiling. I stand up and looking at him, I lift my mask and glasses, showing him my face and eyes clearly. It shocks the tar outta him. "Holy fuck, man! You could be a fuckin' model with your face, and your eyes . . ." he whispers the last part.

"A promise is a promise. I have to use colored contacts on the job. And, yeah," I say casually, as if I haven't done what could get me in deep trouble with the higher-ups, "I've been told that before." I wink at him and cover my face again before stepping out the door.

As I'm leaving, I hear him whisper sadly, "The old woman was right . . . the ghost . . ."

Instead of escaping quickly, like I should, I take my time walking down the hallway towards Jake's wife and the Jones guy. I want to see this "perfect" woman, the woman that has this man's undying love and loyalty.

As I make my way closer, I see her. A shot of electricity moves down my body, like lightning striking.

What.

The.

Fuck!

I stumble over my feet—me. I stumble over my fucking feet after seeing the woman Jake married. He's right, she's fucking beautiful.

She spares me a quick glance to see if I'm okay and then continues toward the room. For the first time in my life, I envy another man. The look on her face . . . she's determined to get to that room. She needs to see her man.

Jake is one lucky bastard, I think to myself.

He's right about everything. Eliza isn't worth my time, but that woman—if I had her in my life, I'd spend my whole life showing her my love and devotion every single fucking day.

Fuck!

I just saw the woman of my dreams, the one my body craves after just one look. The woman that's supposed to be my one. My body, heart, and soul recognize her as mine.

But that'll never happen, because . . .

She's his.

Faith is looking at me with a stunned look on her face. I laugh and congratulate myself on being able to render this beautiful and amazing woman, who never quits talking, silent for a few seconds. I look Faith in the eyes, my gaze never wavering, and continue on with my story.

"After meeting her and knowing she'd never be mine, I threw myself into mission after mission. Most were suicide missions but by the grace of God, I made it out alive. Because of my unconscious death wish, I was Uncle Sam's go-to guy and I raked in a shit-ton of money into my bank account. When I wasn't working, I was going through women like fuckin' candy. My family thought I was still torn over Eliza, but they were wrong. I was mourning the loss of *her*. To see her and know she was supposed to be mine was tearing me up inside.

"Life's funny that way, you know? She gives you a small glimpse at happiness and then takes it away. With me, I got to see my happiness for mere seconds before she disappeared into the room where her husband waited for her. Life is shit sometimes, so I went on with my shitty life. I fucked even more women and did things that would haunt me forever, but I was trying to live my life without her.

"Less than a year after meeting Jake, my life changed forever. I kept my promise to him early. I wanted to make sure she'd always be happy, so I had a buddy of mine keep tabs on Jake. I told him Jake saved my life and I wanted to make sure he was okay and that if he ever needed me, I could be there quickly. But in reality, I wanted to make sure he'd always make her happy, that she'd never hurt. I knew he'd never hurt her, but you can never be too careful. My buddy thought it was a bit much, but he kept his mouth shut and every so often he'd give me updates.

"It was late April when I got the call. I expected the usual update—Jake and his family are doing well and so forth—but this one was different."

Leap of Faith

27 April 2008, North Carolina

*"*Zane, man, I'm sorry," he starts without saying hello.
"What is it?" I say into the phone. "Can this wait till later? I got someone with me."*

That was saying it nicely. I was about to get fucked good by some woman I'd picked up at a bar. I was between missions and I needed to release some stress.

"Zane, it's Jake. You wanted to know when he wasn't okay, right?"

"Fuck! What's wrong with him?" I ask, frustrated.

I tap the woman on the hip and make a head motion towards the door, telling her to leave. She looks at me in disbelief, but I don't have time for her shit. I turn away from her.

"Talk to me," I tell him.

"Your man was in a car accident yesterday and he died on the scene." This is all I hear before my phone hits the floor.

I hear movement and turn to see the bitch is still in my hotel room.

"Didn't I tell you to leave?" I ask her.

She looks at me stupidly and it pisses me off. The bitch still doesn't fucking move.

"Get the fuck outta here!" I yell at her. "NOW!"

It finally gets though her thick head and she picks her shit up and runs to the door.

I pick up the closest thing to me, a coffee mug, and throw it at the wall. If he died in a car accident, she must've been with him. NO!

"FUCK!" I yell at the top of my lungs. "FUUUUCCCKKK! Please, God, not her!"

I sit on the bed and put my head in my hands, tears working their way into my eyes. I hear something and it catches my attention. It's my phone. He's still on.

"Yeah," I say hoarsely into the phone.

"You okay, man?" He asks.

"No, I'm not. What about his wife and kid? Did they go too?" I ask.

"His wife and kid are okay," he tells me. "From what I gathered, it happened in the late hours of the night. Records show he was called into work—one of his soldiers couldn't handle his alcohol and ended up in the hospital and then the MP station. Zane, he was on his way to get the fucker when he was hit head-on by a drunk driver—another soldier. The driver had moved over into the wrong lane and there was no way Jake could avoid him. The pictures, man . . . they're bad. He died on the scene; they both did. He's going to need a closed casket."

My eyes close.

I say a silent prayer, thankful she and his little girl are okay, but for him to die that way—because some soldier wasn't smart enough to not drink and drive—it makes you want to hit something.

Now, a good man has been lost.

✑✑✑

"A week later, I was back in my hometown. I was there to see a good man laid to rest. A man I'd known for less than a week, but those days created a bond between us that couldn't be explained—that stayed with me forever. A man who trusted me with his treasures when he thought he was dying.

"I was there to say my final good-bye to Jake . . ."

✑✑✑

2 May 2008, Jake's Funeral

I stand as far back as possible away from everyone, but still close enough to see her. This is the second time I've lain eyes on her since realizing what she means to me.

She stands there, her arm around the little girl, Rylee. I thought his girl would be younger, but damn, Jake must have had her young. The girl looks to be ten or so, maybe older.

My eyes go back to her.

"Faith," I whisper her name.

She's even more beautiful than I remember and she's standing there, sunglasses on, watching her husband being laid to rest in the ground. She stands there like the strong and beautiful woman Jake described her to be. I look at both of them, Faith and Rylee, and my heart hurts for the both of them. I can see the sadness in the little girl's eyes and the tears rolling down her face—sobbing. I look at Faith and I see the strain on her face; she's trying to keep it all in. Her tears fall, but she's silent.

I want to jump over everyone and go to her. I want to hold her until all her pain goes away. I'd even trade places with Jake just to see her smile, take this pain away. At that moment, I realize I'd do anything for her and her little girl to make sure they're safe and happy. But first, I need to change—I need to be a man who is worthy of them.

I look around her and see she's surrounded by family and friends, and I know she'll be okay—for now.

I remember my promise to Jake, but I have to get my shit together first. I need to atone for my shitty behavior over the past months and I need to leave the life I'm living now. I need to make peace with myself, and I need to make sure she heals before I go to her.

I look at Jake and make him another promise. I promise to get myself together and then I'll take care of her and his little girl like they deserve. I promise to make them mine and when I do, I'll treasure them forever and never take them for granted. I'll spend every day showing them my love and devotion. I'll do anything to keep them safe, I silently vow.

I look back at her one last time before leaving and I feel her eyes on me. She's staring at me and I look back. We both have sunglasses on so we don't make eye contact, but I can feel her eyes on me.

I take my fill of her before turning around and walking away.

✎

"That's the last time I saw you," I tell Faith. "I made sure y'all were okay, but I didn't lay eyes on you again until almost five years later—on that fateful day at the stoplight when both our eyes finally met. The day *you* finally saw me."

Chapter 21

Faith (26 April 2013)

"You see, Faith, I always knew you were the one for me," Zane tells me. "What you think happened so fast between us has been in the making for years. The first time I saw you, I knew you were supposed to be mine—I can't explain how, but I did. That's why I was so determined to follow you every time you ran, why I worked myself into your life.

"I need to be with you like I need to breathe. I'm not trying to replace Jake; I just want to be the man to love you and hold you when you hurt. I want to fight your battles and I want to make sure you never hurt again. Just like you knew Jake was the one for you when you first saw him; it was the same for me. I knew you were supposed to be for me. Even now, I'd trade places with him so he could be here with you—I love you that much. But that's not how life works, and everything happens for a reason.

"Maybe, I was supposed to meet Jake so he could lead me to you. You were supposed to be his first, so I could become a man worthy of you—a man that didn't take you for granted because for the time that you were with him, I knew you'd never be mine and that hurt. It tore my heart up and I know I never want to feel that again. I'm in it for the long haul, love. I'm sorry I didn't tell you I met Jake years ago, but things were just so hard to explain. How was I to tell you everything without you turning me away?"

I sit there silently looking at the man I now love. I'm still trying to process everything he's told me and thoughts are running through my mind. I'm angry but mostly, I'm hurt. He made a promise and what if that's all we are? What if we are just a promise? Can I trust him—can I trust that our love is real?

"You should've told me, Zane," I say to him dishearteningly. "If you keep something like this, what else will you keep from me? How can I trust that all we have is real? Rylee and I were a promise you made to a dying man. How can I believe you truly love me that you're not just keeping your word to Jake?"

"You know I love you, Faith," he tells me running his hand through his hair in desperation. "You have to trust me—in *us*. Please." He looks at me, his eyes pleading with me to believe him, but I don't know if I can.

"I . . . I need to . . . to think . . ." I tell him. "I just don't know right now." I finish the sentence and I feel the emotion start to take over.

"Faith, please don't do this," he begs me, his voice cracking. "I love you and I love the girls. Don't push me way. I'm sorry I didn't tell you but you have to understand."

"I need you to give me some time, Zane," I tell him, making myself stand firm when I really just want to throw myself in his arms. "You didn't tell me when you had plenty of opportunities and you watched us for *years* without our knowledge—I need time to process everything."

He looks at me, devastated by my request, but I need time to think everything over. I need to make sure this is *real* because it's not only me who will be hurt if what we had over the past months was only about a promise made, but also the girls, especially Skylar.

His eyes remain on me urging me to change my mind, but he sees I'm standing firm. He closes his eyes, takes a deep breath and then opens them and says, "I'll give you time, Faith, but I'm not going anywhere. I'm gonna be outside in the waiting room until Rylee goes home, and then if you haven't had enough time, I'll camp outside your house, but I'm not leaving y'all. Y'all are my girls and I'm gonna make sure y'all are taken care of. I admit I was wrong in keeping the fact I met Jake from you and the words exchanged. *That's* why I'm giving you time, not because I don't love you. You think about us, Faith, think about our time together and you'll realize that y'all mean the world to me. What we have is more than a promise that I made to a dying man—what we have is *real*."

With that, he gently places a kiss on Rylee's forehead with his hand, turns and walks out of the room. He's giving me the time I need, and I feel like my heart is getting ripped from my body.

Zane

Walking out of that door is one of the hardest things I've ever had to do in my life. I know I was wrong in keeping things from her but I had my reasons—I just hope she understands them and soon. I don't want to be without her ever again and not having her by my side is tearing me apart inside.

I'm giving her time but I'm not leaving—ever.

Faith

As soon as Zane walks out of the door, I turn back to a still sleeping Rylee. I gently take her hand, bend my head, and I pray. I pray she gets better and that everything works out the way it's supposed to. I pray for much needed guidance.

Minutes later, my eyes slowly start to close and I drift off to sleep. It seems only mere seconds pass before I feel someone gently touches my hair.

"Faith," I hear whispered. "Babe, you have to wake up. I need to speak with you."

Reluctantly, I open my eyes. I expect to see Rylee right in front of me, instead I'm met by empty white space. Realizing my daughter is missing, I jump back and quickly start looking for her, and I see nothing. *Nothing!*

"Rylee!" I cry. "Rylee!"

"Calm down," I hear. "She's safe, my love. Everything is okay."

That voice . . . can it be? No, I think, shaking my head. I must be going crazy. There's no possible way.

"Yes, Faith, it's me," he tells me, laughing at my reaction.

My throat tightens and tears fill my eyes.

"But how?" I ask, turning in circles looking for a sign of him.

"You prayed for guidance," he tells me. "I know how stubborn you can be and figured I had to tell you myself to make you understand. So, I asked for permission to come to you." He appears before me.

"Jake?" I whisper in disbelief. I see his green eyes, so much like Rylee's, and his caramel colored hair, short and wavy like the last time I laid eyes on him. "Is it really you?"

He gives me his gorgeous smile. "Yes, Faith, it's me."

I raise my left hand to cover my mouth and muffle my cry, and I slowly raise my right hand to touch him. I can't believe he's right before my eyes. For years, I wished for one more chance to see him—to let him know that I loved him, to say good-bye because that's what almost killed me. I never got to say goodbye to Jake.

My hand gently traces the face that was once so familiar. His eyes close and he inhales deeply. I see him clench his jaw and swallow.

I can no longer hold back, so I give up. I throw my arms around him, hold him tight, and I let my tears fall. His arms go around me and he buries his face in my neck. He breaths me in and I feel his body shake—he's sobbing.

"I'm so sorry, Faith," he says to me. "I'm sorry I had to go away—I never meant to leave you and Rylee alone. I tried to make sure y'all were taken care of."

I don't answer but continue to hold onto to him. To see him one more time, to speak with him, to let him know we're okay, that's something I never thought I would have the opportunity to do.

Slowly, he pulls back and gazes into my eyes.

"I love you, so much, baby," he tells me. "You and the girls—I love y'all with all my heart."

"I know, Jake," I reply. "We love you too. Rylee and I miss you every day. Skylar, she knows you through our memories and all the pictures we have. We make sure she knows what an amazing man her father was."

"Thank you." He brings his face down to mine and gently places a kiss on my lips. "I've been wanting to do that for years—I miss you."

"I miss you too, Jake," I tell him, looking at him lovingly.

"I know you do and I worried for you until he came along," he tells me, surprising me. "Zane's a good man, Faith. Don't turn him away. You haven't been completely honest with him either."

I bend my head in shame. He's right, I've kept some things about my life from Zane, nothing as important as what he kept from me, but I still wasn't completely honest.

"He loves you, Faith, and he loves our daughters. A better man for the job I couldn't have asked for. When he made that promise to me so many years ago, he'd never seen you. He kept an eye on you as a fulfillment to that promise, but he fell in love with you because of the woman you are. Because you complete him and you make him a better man."

"But, how can I trust in everything, that it was all real?" I ask him.

"Just like you came up to me and told me you were gonna marry me one day and I trusted a young girl with my heart and my daughter—I took a leap of faith," he tells me. "Nothing is guaranteed, you have to believe and you have to take a chance. The girls love him, your parents, mine, and even the guys and Julia like him—he's a good man. He would give his life for y'all. He *loves* you like I love you, Faith. The question is, do *you* love him enough?"

My eyes widen in surprise. "What do you mean?"

"Do you love him enough to accept him—the man he was, the man he is now, and the man he is to become? Are you willing to stand by his side? Or are you gonna let this little thing get in the way? You're no longer the young girl I met, Faith, you've grown up and now you have responsibilities. I'm sorry, love, but you have to start behaving like the woman I know you are—don't let this ruin everything."

"Jake!" I say offended.

"You know I'm right, Faith, you can be irrational at times, and at least now I can call you on it. Poor Zane is gonna have to put up with you now," he tries to say this jokingly but his tone and face are sad.

"He's a good man, Jake."

"I know. I rest easy now that my girls are taken care of," he tells me.

"You know I will always love you. Please, don't ever doubt my love," I tell him.

"Always and forever, Faith. I was your past, but he's your present and he's your future. Go back and put the poor man out of his misery. Be happy. Remember, I will always watch over y'all. I love you . . ." He tells me before disappearing.

"Good-bye, Jake," I call out. "I love you."

"Always and forever." He says before leaving me.

As if waking from a dream, I open my eyes. I feel something in my hand, I look, and see Rylee's hand in mine. Turning, I notice I'm back in the hospital room, and when I bring my fingertips to my face, I feel tears. It was real.

I look at my daughter, her chest rising and falling slowly in rhythm. I press the call button and wait for a nurse to arrive. I place a gentle kiss on her forehead.

"I'll be right back, honey. I have to go see Zane. Mommy did something really bad and I have to go fix it." I say to her as if she were awake.

The door opens and a young nurse steps inside. I turn to her, "I'm gonna step out for a few seconds. I would appreciate it if you'd stay with my daughter. I know y'all are busy, but I would feel more comfortable if someone was in the room with her."

She looks from me to Rylee on the bed. Her eyes take in my daughter and her face softens. "Of course, ma'am. But, I can only stay for a few minutes. Please be quick."

"Thank you," I reply and quickly make my way out the door and down the hallway to the waiting room. I make it as far as the doorway and stand there. I take in the sight before me, Zane—he's sitting in one of the uncomfortable chairs, hunched over, his head in his hands. He looks miserable and I'm the cause.

I clear my throat and quietly call his name, "Zane."

His head immediately comes up, he stands, and quickly makes his way to me.

"Faith, is everything okay?" He asks worriedly.

"Yes, everything is okay. I . . . I need to talk to you," I tell him, feeling ashamed of my behavior. "Um, there's a nurse with Rylee and she told me she could only stay for a few minutes. Can you come back with me? We can talk there."

"Of course, baby," he tells me gently.

I turn and we make our way back to Rylee's room. When we enter, the nurse's eyes widen in surprise and admiration, but Zane's eyes are on me and only for me. Hers fill with disappointment when she realizes he's taken and she leaves, leaving us alone with Rylee.

"What's going on?" He asks me.

"I'm sorry," I say without hesitation. "I'm sorry I overreacted and for doubting your love. I should never have hurt you and I promise to make it up to you. I . . . you were right, Zane," I tell him. "I would've freaked out and shut you out completely. All this is hard to explain and understand, but some things in life are like that. If I had tried to explain my immediate feelings for Jake, I never would've had the time I had with him. And now—you're right. When I finally saw you, I felt that shock go through my body. I think that's what scared me the most. I had the same feeling with Jake. After his death, I convinced myself that was it for me. My forever was gone and I'd spend the rest of my life focusing on my daughters. I convinced myself I was gonna be alone. And then, *you* came along.

"I've grown up a lot since Jake," I tell him. "I'm not the same person I was back then. I had to change to continue his dream and ensure a good life for our girls. I've done things that many would disapprove of, but those things had to be done. I didn't tell you because I was also scared that you wouldn't accept me."

"What do you mean?" He asks me.

"Not right now, honey. I need some more time to put everything together into words—what I need to tell you. I have my reasons, and I hope you understand without knowing. I love you and I promise to tell you as soon as I can, but this isn't just about me but other people, too. Please, trust me."

I still haven't found the words to tell him just how much I've changed since the person he saw so many years ago. I know I'm in the wrong not letting him know, especially as he's just told me his history with Jake, but I need a little more time.

Zane stands up, bringing me with him. He holds me tight and I bury my face in his chest. I breathe him in and calm myself with his scent. His face is in my neck and we just hold each other. We've made it through our first "argument" and no one was hurt.

Now, we give each other strength and prepare ourselves to help my daughter.

"Momma," I hear whimpered from behind me. "Mommy."

Just hearing her voice makes my heart hurt for her. My beautiful daughter. I quickly make my way closer to her and I move my hand to touch her hair. She flinches and my heart breaks.

"Yes, baby girl," I say softly. "I'm here, love."

"Momma, it hurts," she tells me with pain in her eyes. "Mommy, he hurt me. I tried to fight but he was so strong . . . he kept hitting me over and over and yelling at me. He was so angry—he tore my dress and he touched me. I tried to fight him as best I could but it wasn't good enough—his fists and his hands were all over me." She breaks down and lets everything out. "It hurt so much. I fought so hard for myself, but he still hurt me. He kept telling me it was my fault, that it was time to pay up, and I couldn't stop him."

"Oh, baby . . . whatever happened," I say to her, "is *not* your fault. No one has the right to lay their hands on you in anger, no matter the reason. Who did this, Rylee? And where was Dean?" He was supposed to take care of my little girl. I had trusted him with her safety. Where was he?

"It was him." She shocks us with this revelation. "He did this to me. He lied to me and tricked me into going to the hotel—he told me it was just a party and he would take me home afterwards. So, we went and when he started drinking, I told him I wanted to go home. Instead, he took me to the room. When I refused him, he got angry—livid—and attacked me. He started hitting me and grabbing my dress to tear it off. There was so much anger and hate—he kept saying I owed him after all the effort he'd put into our relationship. That I'd embarrassed him so many times putting soccer as a priority and not him, and everything he had to put up with to be with me. He spent money on prom to butter me up and now I needed to pay up."

"That little fucker. When I get my hands on him, I'm gonna

fuckin' kill him," Zane says angrily. "A man never lays a hand on a woman and when she says "no," it means fuckin' "no." What he did to you makes him lower than shit, Rylee. Women are supposed to be cherished and protected, never hurt by our own hand. That little dipshit is a piece of scum and he'll pay."

"Please, Zane," she pleads. "Don't do anything. I don't want you getting in trouble. You need to be here for Momma."

"I'm not leaving, Rylee," Zane reassures her. "I'm here for you, Skylar, and your momma. I'm not going anywhere. But that boy needs to be taught a lesson he'll never forget."

"Rylee, one day you'll meet someone that will love you unconditionally. Someone you'll trust with your life. Until then, love, we're here for you. We'll do anything and everything in our power to help you," I tell her. "Now, I need to know everything. The police will be here soon. Please, I know this is hard, my love, but you need to tell me everything that boy did to you."

"Zane, honey, can you give us a minute, please?" I ask him, thinking it'll be easier for Rylee.

He nods in understanding and squeezes my shoulder before turning to leave.

"No, Zane." Rylee stops him at the door. "Um . . . can you please stay here with Momma? I—I'm okay with you being in here; you're part of our family and, well, everything will come out when the police get here. I want you here and Momma is gonna need you here. Please?"

"Rylee, I wouldn't be anywhere else," Zane tells her. "I'm always here for you. Always."

She looks at me. She takes a deep breath and begins reliving her nightmare.

I feel like a monster making her tell me, but I *need* to know. Halfway through, she grabs hold of my hand and my heart jumps; she's not afraid of me, to touch me, thank goodness. Rylee holds my hand, seeking strength, and Zane keeps a hand on me, giving me strength.

"I tried so hard, Momma. I fought as hard as I could, but he kept hitting me over and over. He grabbed my dress and ripped it, grabbing my breasts and hurting them. He laid his body over mine and moved his hand down there and inserted his fingers. He was so rough and it hurt. I started crying—I tried to buck him off and I swung and kicked, but I couldn't make him stop. I think he finally got tired and even angrier because he stood. I thought he had given up but I was wrong. He kicked my wrist and I heard a snap and the pain started to get even more overwhelming. I kept praying for it to end but it kept going on forever.

"I prayed, 'Please, God, help me and please don't let him hurt my legs.' I don't know what I'd do if I couldn't play anymore. Then, through the pain, I saw him aim at my legs. He knew where to hurt me.

"Before he made contact with his foot to snap my ankle, something happened . . . I saw Daddy," she says, shocking me and Zane, who tightens his grip on my shoulder. "I know it sounds crazy but I think Daddy helped me. Otherwise, I wouldn't have gotten away. One moment Dean was about to break me and the next he froze, and a vase appeared within reach. With all the strength I had left, I hit him, and somehow I was able to move and get away. While he had me, I was helpless and at his mercy. I thought I was gonna die. I knew I didn't want to and I prayed. And then, I saw *him*. I saw Daddy."

Now, I'm crying along with my daughter.

I look at my beautiful daughter and say, "You'll never feel like that again. You are a strong and beautiful young lady. You're alive, and I'm thankful for that. I can't lose you like I did your father. Losing you would kill me," I tell her through my tears. "You'll be okay, Rylee. You have all of us and we'll always be here for you. I'll do everything in my power to make sure that you never feel helpless again. Momma is gonna take care of this, baby. I promise. Now, the police are gonna come in here and ask for your statement. We'll be here for the whole time. I'm going to step out and make a call to Gunner. Zane is going to stay here with you. Is that okay?"

"It's okay. I know Zane won't hurt me and he won't let anyone get near me. I—I just don't want to be touched. Not yet," she tells us. "I just need a little bit of time."

"It's okay. I love you always and forever," I tell her before stepping outside the room. I make sure no one is able to hear and I call Gunner.

The phone rings and rings. It's late and I finally hear a gruff, "This better be fuckin' important."

"Gunner," I say into my phone. My tone must've alerted him because he immediately softens.

"Faith, everything okay?" He asks.

"No, Gunner. It's Rylee," I say, fighting angry tears. "We're at Memorial Hospital. You need to get down here ASAP. She's been hurt, Gunner. Real bad."

"I'm on my way," he tells me and I hear rustling as he puts his clothes on. "I'll be there in fifteen minutes if not sooner. I'm calling Damon. Is Zane there with you?"

"Yes, he's here. He's with her right now," I tell him. "Gunner, prepare yourself."

"I will, babe."

With that I hang up the phone and make my way back to my daughter. I walk in and see her staring into space.

"Rylee," I say to her. "I'm gonna let the nurses know that you're awake. Okay?"

She nods but says nothing. I press the button next to her bed and wait for the nurse. As we wait, Rylee, Zane, and I sit in silence. I sit in the chair next to her and Zane keeps back. We remain the same after the nurse leaves. Not until we hear the police outside do we move. I look at Zane and he at me. I turn to Rylee.

"Baby girl, they're here."

"I know, Momma. I'm ready," my brave little girl tells me.

∞∞

After the police leave and Rylee falls asleep, Gunner, Zeke, Damon, Jax, and Duke are in the room with us. They're furious and they want that boy's blood.

"That little fucker dared to put his hands on our little girl," Gunner says furiously.

"I'm ready to head out—all I need is the go-ahead," Duke

announces. He's ready to go get Dean and teach him a lesson, but we can't. Not yet.

"We can't. The police were just here and they're gonna handle it. Until then, our hands are tied," I tell them.

Zane is quietly observing our interaction and holding me.

"Do you really think they're gonna do anything?" Zeke asks. "Isn't his father friends with a judge?"

"Right now, I can only pray the system works. That boy hurt Rylee and there's concrete proof—there should be enough for them to try him and find him guilty. I'm leaving it in their hands and God help that boy if they fail," I tell everyone present.

And I'm serious. If Dean gets off, he will suffer. The punishment he'd receive from the law is child's play compared to what he'd suffer if it's left in our hands. Over the years, I've changed from that carefree girl I used to be. Now, no one messes with my family and goes unpunished. Not only do we have a name to uphold, but if I don't protect my family, who will?

Zane tightens his hold on me.

"Baby, if they don't do anything to him, I'll handle it. I promised I'd protect you and the girls, and that's what I'm gonna do."

I give his arm a squeeze to acknowledge his words, and I nod to the guys. Understanding me, they get up.

"We're gonna go and check some things out," Gunner says. "We'll have our phones on us, so let us know as soon as you get word from the police. We want this handled quickly so we can focus on our Rylee."

Zane and I cross the room to them.

"Thank y'all," Zane tells Gunner, taking the lead and Gunner follows. The guys recognize its meaning and the fact that he's doing that. They nod in acknowledgement and shake his hand in respect.

"Always, man," Gunner says. "Just take care of our girls; that's all we ask. They deserve all the happiness in the world. I may not be the man for that job, but I'll always be here for them. We all will."

"I understand," Zane answers him. "I've waited a long time to have this in my life and now that I do, I'll treasure them always. I'll protect them with my life that I can promise y'all."

They nod and turn to me.

"We'll touch base in a couple of hours if we don't hear from you," Gunner tells me.

They each give me a hug and a kiss on the forehead before heading out the door. I turn to Zane, he opens his arms, and I go to him. He wraps them around me and we hold each other. We stand there until I hear Rylee ask for me. He releases me and I make my way to my daughter. I give her some water and I sit in the chair next to her bed, holding her hand.

And I plan.

Several hours later, we get a phone call from the detective. Our biggest fear is a reality—Dean is out. His father called his friend and his lawyer, and now that little prick is out, scot-free. My daughter isn't going to get the justice she deserves because Dean's father has enough clout in this area and a judge in his pocket. Apparently, that puts him above the law. Neither the pictures taken of Rylee nor the fact that she's in the hospital and in pain will change the fact that Dean won't pay through the legal system. He'll face no jail time— only a slap on the hand and a "don't do that again." More like "don't get caught again."

Zane and I are furious. We agree not to say anything to Rylee just yet; there's nothing she can do and it'll only worry her.

"I knew this would happen," Zane says in the hallway outside Rylee's room.

I refuse to be more than a few feet away from Rylee, especially since that monster is out; I'm not risking leaving my daughter alone. He doesn't say anything else, just holds me tight as I shake from anger and silently plan my next move. I want to call in the team but I can't risk it just yet. Things need to be planned out and there can be no backlash for this to work.

"I want Dean to pay," I say. "I want him to suffer the same pain he put my daughter through. I want him to feel what it's like to feel helpless—to pray for your life. No man should ever lay his hands on a woman, much less my daughter."

"I know," Zane tells me. "That little shit deserves to be torn apart limb from limb. He'll get what's coming to him, I promise you."

"Zane, honey, we can't do anything rash," I tell him. "Rylee doesn't want you getting in trouble and I need you with me. You calm me and I need that so I can help her. We both need you."

"I won't do anything just yet."

"I'm holding you to that," I tell him. "I need to let the guys know what's going on and then we need to plan." He looks at me strangely. I can't tell him just yet, but I can give him hints. "We're in this together—you and me. I love you."

"I love you too," he replies without questions. "Go make your phone call and I'll keep watch over our girl."

I move to him and give him a peck on the lips before making my way to a more private area for my conversation with Gunner. I find a place and make the call. When he answers, all I say is five words.

"He's out. He's ours now."

Then, I hang up the phone. Gunner knows what that means. Now, it's time to get Rylee home and prepare. Like Zane said, that boy's getting' what's coming' to him.

It looks like my family life and my work life are finally going to collide.

Zane

That little fucker is out. I can't let Faith know just yet, but that little shit is going to bleed for hurting Rylee. She's not my daughter, but she's mine nonetheless. I'll protect my girls till the end of time.

It's time to let the ghost come out and play. For years, I worked hard to atone for all the horrible things I had to do for my country. Who knew one day those skills would be used for vengeance and to protect my family.

Life has a funny way of taking you full circle.

I've spent years working to erase and forget the ghost I used to be—now, I will embrace it.

Chapter 22

The next day, Rylee is discharged. It's time to take her home and get her settled. The next week is going to be a painful recovery, and Rylee's going to go insane not being able to play ball or go about her normal routine. As soon as she hears we're coming home, Josilyn immediately says she'll come over every day after practice to keep my baby girl company—she knows if she tries to skip class or practice, she'd get a talking to from all of us. I'm glad Rylee has made a best friend for life in her.

The forty-eight hours Rylee was in the hospital, Josilyn was there with her. We sent her home at night, but the next morning she was back. She felt guilty for leaving Rylee with Dean, but we quickly explained that she couldn't have known. No one could've known what that boy would do to Rylee. We trusted him, thinking him a good guy, but we couldn't have seen what was beneath his façade.

Right now, Skylar's in school, Rylee's resting and Zane's at home with her. So I make a quick run into work for a meeting with the guys. Arriving in the conference room, I'm surprised to see them all seated around the table, waiting for me and scarfing down Whataburger.

"Hey," I greet them. "She's home and resting. Zane's with her and Josilyn is coming over immediately after practice. Being on bed rest is killing Rylee—y'all know how she is."

"Just wait till she's feeling better but still unable to play due to doctor's orders," Gunner tells me.

Everyone knows our girl's love for soccer and how she's been practicing or playing with a soccer ball since the day her father gave her that first ball—a ball she has kept over the years and is now in a glass case in her room.

"Tell me about it," I reply. "She has her ball right next to her and I think she slept with it last night after we tucked her in."

"How is Skylar and what did she say when she finally saw Rylee?" Damon asks.

"She's doing well now. She was upset when she saw her the first time. We sat her down and explained to her that there are some really bad people in this world. People that sometimes hurt other people and that's what happened to Rylee. She was hurt by a very bad person and now needs our help getting better. I had to tell my daughter that before touching her sister, she had to ask Rylee's permission."

My voice quivers. I quickly compose myself and continue, "Y'all know what she said? With a serious face she told me, 'That person needs to pay, Momma. Don't worry, I'll take care of my sister,' before quickly running off to her room and returning with Alf. 'I'm gonna give her Alf until she gets better. He keeps me safe at night and he'll keep her safe too.'"

Everyone clears their throat. Alf was Jake's stuffed animal when he was a child and he kept it throughout the years. It was passed down to Rylee and when Skylar was born, Alf became her link to Jake. She's treasured that ugly thing, thinks it's the most precious thing in the world, and from the time she was handed that animal, she's never shared it with anyone. For her to give her sister Alf, even temporarily, shows how much love is shared between my girls.

"So, how are we approaching this?" Jax asks the question everyone is wondering.

"Well . . . there's one thing I want to discuss with y'all before anything else," I tell them nervously. Here goes. "I want to let Zane know what I really do at work . . . about us. While we were at the hospital . . . um . . . I discovered that Jake and Zane had met before and that Zane was . . . well, he was one of *those* soldiers."

I pause and take everyone's face in. They're silent, registering my words.

"What do you mean, he met Jake before?" Gunner asks after a little while. "We never served with him."

"Well, y'all remember the last time Jake was deployed and he was injured?" At their nods I continue, "Apparently, Zane was one of the men with him—a ghost attached to his company for a mission. Jake saved his life and when Jake was shot, Zane was the one that kept him from bleeding out until they were picked up."

"Fuckin' hell," I hear Gunner say. He turns to the guys. "I can't believe I didn't put two and two together. His eyes . . . it's those eyes Jake told us about. Zane's the one we always have an opening for in case he comes asking for a job—Jake's orders."

Even though I already know this, it shocks me I was never informed about it. Shoot, I'm amazed everyone is taking this in stride and not upset that Zane kept it a secret from all of us.

"What do you mean, the one he told y'all about?" I ask.

"One night when we were all together—it was that time we all flew in to see Jake after he got back. He was talking about his last mission. That one really did a number on him and he didn't want to burden you. He always tried to keep the job at work and away from home," he tells me. "He mentioned meeting a ghost and he swore us to secrecy. The 'ghost with purple eyes' he called him. We all thought he was crazy, but he swore up and down it was true. He said the ghost kept him together when he thought he was dying. Jake said that because of that, he would always have a place in our company if he ever needed it. Jake said he would one day come to us and we would accept him. After his death, I received a letter from the lawyer. The letter pissed me off and I put it aside, and never thought of it again until now. Understand that I wanted him to be wrong, Faith."

"What was in the letter?" I ask Gunner, curious to hear why Jake's last words would tick him off.

"Even though I only read it once, the words were burned into my memory. Jake knew about my feelings for you," he tells me with tortured eyes. "He knew that I loved you and now that he was gone, it was for me to help you until the ghost came to take over. He explained how he met the ghost and about extracting a promise from him to take care of you and Rylee if anything ever happened to him—that he trusted him to keep his word. He couldn't explain why, but he knew it was the right thing to do. He said one day I'd meet the love of my life, but she wouldn't be you. You were meant for someone else, someone that would come into your life after he was gone. I didn't want to believe him. To me, it was now my job to take care of you. In my mind *I* was gonna keep this company alive and

I'd wait for you until you healed. You threw all my plans out the window when you took up his dream. You loved him so much you put aside your career to ensure that his dream remained alive."

Hearing this, I'm stunned. Jake must've known something—he had to. But I wonder how? Is that why he came back changed from that last tour? He'd always shown me affection but after returning, it seemed like he couldn't get enough of me. Everything we did as a couple or family was documented on video or pictures. Those last months he was with us, we have more pictures and videos than we had all the years before. Could this be the reason for all those conversations we had—the ones I hated?

"Faith. Faith, are you okay?" Gunner asks me, bringing me out of my thoughts. At my nod his continues, "You mourned him for years, Faith, and I waited. Then, I went to Dubai. That's when you started to move on, and then Zane came along. Jake was right; you were never meant for me. I can't believe I didn't put this all together. Zane's eyes are fuckin' different and will weird you out if you aren't ready. They're purple, for goodness sake; when have you ever seen a person with purple eyes? He's the ghost Jake spoke about. He's the one that was supposed to come for you and Rylee, and he has."

My mind's in turmoil. Did my husband know something and didn't tell me? But how could he have known?

"What the fuck are trying to say?" Damon asks. "Are you saying Jake knew he was gonna die?"

I flinch at his words, but it's the same question I want to ask—a question I forgot to ask Jake.

"I don't know," Gunner replies. "I just know he changed after that last tour. It felt like he was trying to get as much of us as possible— he called more and he asked us all to visit him. He missed us, he said. I thought it was the mission, but maybe it was something else. All I know is that after getting back, Jake took out that huge life insurance policy on himself, saying he wanted to make sure y'all were taken care of." He looks at me. "And he started taking pictures of everything. That alone was strange because we all know that man hated taking pictures—Faith was constantly on his ass for it."

I nod. I remember thinking he was crazy when he told me he took out that lucrative policy. He wanted us set, was his only reply.

"I don't know either," I tell them. "I remember the last day we were together. He made me promise that if anything happened to him, I wouldn't give up. He said I needed to live again if anything went wrong with our plan. That I had to keep my heart open. He was more loving, and he came home at a reasonable hour from work, incurring the wrath of his battalion commander a few times. He didn't care—'My family always comes first,' he said."

"But how could he have known?" Zeke asks. "I mean, why didn't he say something to us? How could he—"

"Rylee says she saw him. When Dean was hurting her, she saw Jake," I say abruptly, interrupting Zeke. I don't mention my conversation with Jake, that's something that will remain private and a treasured memory.

"JAKE! JAKE!" Duke yells out loud, making us all jump. "Jake, man, if you're here, give us a sign."

I can't help but laugh at Duke's goofiness.

Suddenly Duke yells, "Ouch!"

We see some of his hair land on the table. Mouths wide open, we just stare.

"What the fuck, man, really?! You had to mess with the hair," Duke says out loud, making us all laugh; we know his hair is his source of vanity and most prized possession. I hear another "Ouch!" from Duke and then I feel a caress on my face.

I close my eyes and I feel Jake's hands on my face and his lips on mine for the barest touch.

"Bye, my love," I hear whispered before he leaves.

"Holy fuckin' shit!" I hear from the guys and I open my eyes.

"He was just here," Gunner says. "Well, that settles it, Zane's in," he tells us, pointing to the table. On the middle of the table is a purple rose—my favorite.

A couple hours later, I let myself into the house, trying not to make too much noise, I don't want to wake Rylee up if she's asleep. As I close the door, Zane meets me with a desperate kiss.

"You're not gonna believe what happened while you were gone," he tells me in a loud whisper, looking around the house as if searching for something, all the while holding me close.

"What happened, honey?" I ask him, knowing it has something to do with what happened at the office.

"It's gonna sound crazy, but I swear I felt a gust of wind go through the house and then flowers appeared in the bedrooms—outta thin fuckin' air! A purple rose on your pillow, a pink sunflower-looking flower on Skylar's, and a blue exotic-looking flower next to Rylee," he says. "Babe, I'm a little spooked here. Is it Jake? I hope it's him because I think he thanked me—he *spoke* to me, Faith! I heard a 'thank you' and I felt a pat on my back. Please, tell me it's him or we're gonna have problems. I'm not good with ghosts—you know, the spiritual kind—unless they're someone I know. Even then, ghosts tend to, um . . . scare me." His voice almost dwindles away on the last sentence.

"It is him, honey," I reply, smiling. My big alpha male is scared of the unknown. "He was at the office too. He left me a rose." I pull the rose out of my pink Louis Vuitton handbag. "He pulled Duke's precious hair, giving us a laugh. There's something going on here we can't explain, but I know he's here and he helped our girl get away. He's watching over us. It's okay, baby, I'll protect you."

"You better," he tells me seriously. "I can handle a lot of shit: spiders, snakes, rats, men shooting at me, fire, and anything that scares y'all, but I'm a baby when it comes to ghosts. I was traumatized by a movie Jackie let me watch when I was younger and ever since then, shit like this gives me the heebie-jeebies."

"We got you," I tell him, smiling. "The girls and I'll always protect you."

I bring his head down for a kiss before letting him go, and he gathers me in a tight hug. As we're holding each other, we feel a gust of wind swirl around us. I feel Zane tense up and then shiver as he pushes his face into my neck. I just smile. As I look to my right, I swear I can see a transparent Jake looking at us with a smile on his face. He blows me a kiss before disappearing, and my smile gets even bigger.

Jake's watching over us. Everything is going to be just fine.

Chapter 23

A week goes by. Zane is at the station. He's been scheduled to work the last few days almost nonstop, since there's a shortage of firefighters due to a crappy virus making the rounds at the firehouse. He wasn't happy about having to work, but I've kept him satisfied with constant phone updates.

Now, Julia's over, since the guys and I are in the kitchen making our plans for tonight. Yes, I still haven't told Zane about us, but with everything that's gone on, there's been no opportunity—I lie to myself.

Tonight, that boy and his father are getting their due.

Julia walks into the kitchen. "Make sure that little fucker pays for what he's done to our baby girl. I got plenty of money in savings so I can post bail for y'all if y'all end up in the pen-hole."

"Really, Julia," Gunner looks at her in astonishment. "If we get caught, then we're in the wrong business."

"Just letting y'all know I got the money and I'm sure Zane would help after getting over the heart attack of having his woman in jail," she says laughing. I give her a look and she laughs even harder. "Figured y'all needed a good laugh. I've done my job and now I'm headed up to my precious goddaughter's room to watch Disney princesses fall in love with their Prince Charmings."

She gives me a kiss on the cheek before leaving.

I turn to the guys. "Everything ready?"

At their "Yeahs" we gather our stuff and head out to the vehicles. Those monsters won't know what hit them.

Yeah, I got my mean face on. I'm a mother on a warpath. As they say, "Vengeance will be mine."

 ❦

I'm getting ready to take out the one and only guard on

Vanderson's payroll. I laugh to myself—Dean's father thinks he's so high and mighty that he needs protection; he's even posted a guard on his house. Psshh, that man's a fish in a little pond; he's going to have a huge wake-up if he ever ventures out of this small town.

Tonight, he's going to learn what it's like to go up against one of Phoenix's own. They're both going to regret ever messing with my family. I may be as sweet as pie, but if anyone hurts my family, I turn into a psycho bitch on steroids. I'll be your worst nightmare.

I quietly make my way to the guard where he's sitting in a chair. I am about to put him in a sleeper hold when I notice he's slumped over in his seat.

What in the world?!

"Gunner!" I say quietly but urgently into my mike. "The guard is out and it wasn't me. Do y'all have anything?"

"Hold your position," he tells me and I hear him communicate with the others on lookout. "Faith, no one has anything. We don't see anything on our cameras. Proceed with caution."

"Roger," I reply.

"Faith—" Gunner catches my attention.

"Yes?"

"Be careful and keep the communication feed open to all of us. We want our heads attached to our bodies, and Zane will go ape-shit crazy if anything happens to you," he informs me seriously.

"I will," I reply, smiling.

I carefully and quietly make my way into the house. In the foyer, I see their dog, and he isn't moving. I carefully check on him and notice that he's breathing deeply and very slowly. He's out. That's strange, but I continue, going up the stairs. I go into the Vanderson's room and notice his side of the bed is empty.

What the hell is going on? All our intel said he'd be here.

Not giving up, I head to Dean's room. Outside his door I hear muffled sounds.

Quietly and carefully, I open the door and slide inside. Dean's tied and gagged on his bed. His eyes open wide when he sees my head-to-toe-covered self in his room.

Well, this is going to be easy, I think to myself.

Then, I'm grabbed from behind. Before I can do any defensive maneuvers, I'm plastered face to foot against the wall, and I feel a hard body at my back. A hand covers my mouth—I can't move or make a sound. Whoever got the drop on me is freaking good and I want him on my team.

"Who the fuck are you and what the fuck are you doing here?" I hear growled in my ear. "I'm gonna let you go. If you make a sound or try anything, I'll fuckin' gut you. Got me?"

I nod and wait for him to ease his hold before turning around. The man has on an outfit similar to mine—black tactical op gear with a mask, like the ones you see in those warfare video games—but his is way better. He's completely covered up—I can't even see his eyes. He looks down at me and tilts his head slightly to the side. He suddenly jerks back and whispers quietly.

"Faith?"

I nod. I knew it was Zane from the moment he growled into my ear, so I relax and wait for the explosion that I know is to come. He surprises me with his next words.

"We're taking him down to the basement. I'll deal with you later, babe."

I follow him as he throws a now blindfolded Dean over his shoulder and heads down the stairs. I keep back a bit and let Gunner know Zane's in the house.

"The fuck you say!" Gunner exclaims. "We aren't reading anybody other than you and the residents. How the fuck is he doing it? He's like a fuckin' ghost!"

"I don't know how; I just know he's here and we're about to take care of business. He says he'll deal with me later. Whatever that means."

All I get in return is chuckles from all the guys.

At the bottom of the stairs I see two chairs and two bodies sitting on them. Both are tied and gagged. Dean is literally scared stiff and his father—well, that man is making a ruckus moving around in the chair. I feel like moving over there and tipping it over so he finally shuts up.

Zane moves to him and takes the gag off.

"Who are you? What do you want?" He asks after Zane warns him to be quiet. "Take anything you want; just don't hurt us." Tears are running down both their faces.

"Don't worry, I'm not gonna hurt your wife," Zane assures him. "I may be a killer, but I don't hurt women. Y'all on the other hand . . . well, I'm gonna fuck y'all up real good. I might even carve a little reminder into your bodies—a reminder not to fuck, or hit, anything that says no."

Vanderson and son look at me with pleading eyes. Ha—like I'm going to help them.

"You know what's ironic?" Zane asks them. "I gave years of my life fighting and killing horrible people overseas for my country. A friend of mine lost his life on his way to help one of his men. He gave everything to his country to keep her safe. And y'all know what?—it's here, at home, where his daughter is hurt so badly she's hospitalized for days and is still unable to move comfortably without pain. The little fucker that hurts her gets off without punishment because Daddy wouldn't let his reputation be ruined. Well, guess what? My girl may not be getting her legal justice, but where I come from, we take care of our own. I've learned enough in my life that I'll take care of this little problem. I'm gonna teach both of y'all a lesson today, one I hope you take to heart because I've no problem coming back and putting an end to your miserable lives. When it comes to family, I will kill in cold blood without remorse. I'll fuckin' enjoy it."

"Please don't hurt us," Vanderson pleads with Zane as he moves to remove Dean's gag.

As soon as it's off, Dean starts to cry louder. Wracking sobs come out of his body as he shakes in fear. I'm disgusted by both of them and instead of feeling bad for what's about to happen, I only feel pleasure. It may make me a terrible person, but this boy hurt my daughter. He wanted to rape her. I can't let that go.

"Y'all make me sick," I say out loud. At the sound of my female voice, both quiet down. "The girl your son hurt was helpless as she begged him to stop. Did your son stop? No, he didn't. He continued to hit her, kick her, he *touched* her, and made her bleed. My daughter will be scarred by your son's deeds. He didn't listen to her cries for mercy, just as I won't listen to yours. I was gonna come here and deal with y'all without letting y'all know my identity, but I've changed my mind. I want you to know I'm gonna take pleasure in your cries of pain—marvel as your blood flows from your face and body. Dean, you spilt my daughter's blood and now I'm gonna watch as yours falls. This may make me a bad person, but I've learned one thing in my years. If you don't take care of your family, then no one will. I wasn't there to protect her when she needed my help, but I'll make sure you pay. No one, and I mean *no one* fucks with my family and comes out unscathed."

"You're crazy!" Vanderson exclaims while his son continues to sob. "Sane people don't go around tying other people up in their homes. You're going to pay for this."

"Now that's where you're wrong," I say as I unsheathe my CRKT Ultima knife from my side. "Nothing is gonna happen to us when we leave here. After we get done with y'all, you're gonna forget you ever knew us. If we hear anything, even the slightest whisper, of you telling anyone about what will happen today, we'll come back and kill you in the worst and most hurtful way imaginable. After tonight, y'all will leave my family alone. All ties will be severed."

I move towards Dean's father but Zane stops me.

"I got this, love. I don't want you dirtying your hands with these fuckers. I'm proud of you, but let me do this. I *need* to do this for Jake, for myself, and for Rylee."

I understand where he's coming from. I step back and watch him put the gag back on both Vandersons. And then, he starts administering justice for our Rylee. He's setting the example—no one messes with our family without retribution.

Their muffled yells are music to my ears. Years ago, I never thought I'd be able to stomach watching two tied-up people get beaten within an inch of their lives, but now, I do. I watch and I feel a weight lift off my shoulders and a calmness spread through my body as their bones break and their blood spills.

Justice is served in my eyes.

After Zane stops, I move forward.

"Remember what I told y'all today. Y'all so much as breathe a word of this to anyone, including your wife, y'all are dead. Don't even think about it." I point at Dean's father. "I know everything you have ever done, and all of that will ruin you if it gets out. Before eliminating y'all, I'll make sure the world knows what scum of the Earth you are. The only reason y'all are breathing is because my daughter is now safe at home. Y'all are lucky she was able to get away. For that reason, y'all still exist—I do have a heart after all. Remember this night and learn from it."

Zane takes them back upstairs and lays their bleeding and broken bodies on Dean's bed. Our job here is finished. Zane takes my hand and together we walk out of the house and make our way home. Home to our girls.

Chapter 24

"Somebody better fuckin' explain to me why I just found *my* woman at that man's house decked out in op gear. Right. Fuckin'. Now!" Zane not-so-quietly yells in the living room of our house.

Wow—"our house"—I like how that sounds.

I come out of my musings to admire how delicious and hot Zane looks striding up and down the carpet. At the same time, I feel like a child; we're all, meaning the guys and me, sitting in a line across the couches like troublemakers in the principal's office.

Julia is sitting in one of the bean-bag chairs with a smirk on her face—that cow! She's having tons of fun watching Zane lose his head at my expense. She decided to join us when Zane led our little group directly into the living room as soon as we arrived, after inquiring about the girls.

"Zane, man, don't you think this is a conversation better had between the two of you? I'd feel more comfortable if y'all weren't airing out the dirty laundry in front of me. So, if you don't mind, I'm just gonna mosey on outta here."

Duke's announcement makes the others snicker as he stands up to make a quick escape, followed by Damon. I gasp at this betrayal while Julia laughs her ass off.

"Sit," Zane commands and everyone promptly obeys.

"What the heck happened to 'never leave a man behind' and 'we always have each other's backs,' huh?" I ask them.

"Well, let me put it this way," Damon informs me. "I want to live to see my next lay. I don't want to be torn limb from limb by this crazy fucker, so you're on your own, my darlin'."

"How dare y'all!" I gasp indignantly with a hand to my heart. "I would never—"

"Oh whatever, Faith," Julia gets out between gusts of laughter. "You know you'd be the first one out in their case. The only reason *I'm* still here is because I'm your best friend and best friends are always there to watch their besties get their asses chewed out and then laugh at them."

"You're such a cow," I tell her.

"I know, but you love me anyways," she replies.

"ENOUGH!" Zane roars, nostrils flaring. "Somebody better start fuckin' explaining why she was there by HERSELF!"

"Zane, baby—" I try to calm him down, but I fail.

"Don't 'baby' me, Faith, not now. I'm fuckin' pissed and I want an explanation. Right. Fuckin'. Now! I don't care who it's from, I just want to know why the fuck my woman put herself in danger and why y'all"—he points at Gunner, Damon, Zeke, Jax, and Duke— "let her."

"She did it for me, Zane," we hear from the entrance of the living room and as one, we all turn to see Rylee leaning in the doorway.

"Rylee," I say quickly, standing up to go to her, but Zane beats all of us to her. He picks her up and carries her to the couch, where Gunner gives up his seat to his goddaughter.

"What are you doing out of bed, Rylee?" Zane asks gently.

She just gives him a smile and starts to speak.

"Zane, I could hear you from my room and decided to come see what my Momma did now. Whatever she's done, it was for me and to make sure I'm safe. Once she's like that, there's no changing her." She turns to me and continues, "It's what you do, Momma. It's what you've done since Daddy died. Everyone gave up one thing or another to rally around us the day Daddy died." She looks at everyone sitting on the couches before focusing on Zane. "Please don't be angry, Zane."

"I'm not angry, Rylee," Zane tells her gently.

"Well, you could've fooled me with all the yelling that was coming out of your body."

We all chuckle at her words, and send up a thankful prayer to the Lord that she still has her spirit intact.

Zane smiles at her. "Sorry, Rylee. I didn't mean to scare ya. I'll keep it down next time. It's just your mother . . . well, your mother just . . . well, you know."

She laughs. "You didn't scare me, Zane. I was just wondering what Momma had done this time." At her words and my offended huff, everyone except me laughs.

Rylee turns to me. "You know I'm right, Momma. You used to drive Daddy up the wall at times with how overprotective of me you were from the very beginning. Remember when I started school and you were worried about the big kids pushing me around at break, and how you told me that it was okay to trip and 'accidentally' have my foot meet their shins or my fist their face—where do you think I got the advice for Skylar? There was also that time you bought me my first pocketknife and hid it in the secret compartment you made into my backpack—for protection you said—and I've always carried one. Except for that night," she finishes sadly, but then perks up. "Or when you convinced Uncle Duke to teach you how to grapple. 'You never know when you'll need to know how to fight from the ground, just in case we're attacked,' you explained to Daddy when he walked in to find Uncle Duke in a headlock close to passing out, because you *just had to know.* Or that time—"

"Okay, okay, we get it, Rylee," I interrupt before she can continue on with more stories of my finer moments.

"As I was saying, Zane," she says. "I wasn't scared. I'm not afraid of you or my uncles because I know y'all would lay down your lives to protect us."

At her words everyone lets out a sigh of relief. We feared Rylee would have a lasting fear of men or contact after Dean's attack, and we're happy to know she's comfortable and feels safe to come into a room where there's yelling coming from such a huge man, because let me tell you, my Zane isn't small.

"Zane, why don't you call me baby girl, like everyone else?" She asks him.

Zane looks at her in surprise for a moment before speaking. "Because that's what your father called you, Rylee. I don't want to overstep any boundaries or seem like I'm trying to replace him. I don't want to offend you."

"Well, don't be scared," Rylee informs him. "You're part of this family now, Zane. You love my crazy and wacky mother. You treat my little sister like a princess. I'm pretty sure you just did something illegal for me tonight. You're not my father, but you've fallen into the role of father-figure since the moment you met Skylar and me. You've taken on a responsibility that you didn't have to take up, but we're lucky that you did without any regret because you've made my momma happy again. You make her smile that smile she used to smile when Daddy was alive—back when we were a whole family.

"No one will ever replace Daddy because he was a man larger than life in my eyes and my hero—I was his little princess and Momma was his queen. But, he was taken from us too early and I know he's now in heaven, smiling down on us. Because you're here with us now and taking care of us. You treat Skylar like Daddy treated me and you look at her with eyes full of love. She never got to meet him and she never got to experience what it's like to be Daddy's little princess, but now she has you and for that, I'm forever grateful. Because you love my Momma, you love us, you put up with our crazy extended family, and because Momma is still breathing after you found her doing whatever crazy momma-bear thing you found her doing. Because of all that and because I love and respect you, when you feel comfortable, I want you to please call me by the nickname Daddy gave me."

"Okay, baby girl," Zane tells her, his voice thick with feeling.

Rylee looks at him.

"I won't ever be able to call you Dad or Father because that was all Daddy and I'm sorry," she says, "but I wouldn't mind introducing you as my stepfather and if Skylar ever decides to call you Daddy, Dad, or anything like that, I won't be upset. You deserve all that. I'm just sorry I can't do that for you—I was my Daddy's little princess and one half of his world, Zane. Please understand."

"That's okay, Rylee," he answers. "I understand and I'll be honored to have you as a stepdaughter."

"Okay." She clears her throat and gives him a hug. "Now it's time for you to deal with my Momma. Y'all should talk without an audience. Aunt Julia," she says, looking at her, "can you come with me to my room and give them space? I don't think they need you laughing at Momma's expense."

"You're no fun, girly," Julia pouts.

"Well," Gunner says, clearing his throat. "*We* are walking out of here now. Zane, it's always a pleasure and make sure to put your foot down, okay. Faith, darlin', we'll see you tomorrow or the next day." Zane gives him a look. "Night, baby girl, and you too, Crazy Julia."

After all the goodbyes, everyone files out, leaving Zane and me alone. Finally.

Well, here goes—

"Come here, Faith," Zane says, sitting on the love seat. I go to him and he sits me on his lap. "Alright, give it to me. Lay it on me while I'm nice and fuzzy from Rylee's words. Do it like a Band-Aid."

"Okay, honey." I pause and take a deep breath. "After Jake died, Rylee and I moved back stateside. With the money from Jake's life insurance and the money I'd earned playing ball, we were set for a comfortable life. I had my pregnancy to keep me going and I had Rylee, but it was still a very hard and dark time for me. Jake was no longer with me and I was—well lost. I went back to school for my master's, but that didn't make me feel any better, so I started helping Gunner with Phoenix when he needed it. The company was still new and trying to make a name for itself. I started out helping him with paperwork and doing regular secretarial stuff, and then it turned to more. Working there seemed to bring me a sense of peace. It calmed me. I felt closer to Jake's memory helping build his dream into a reality."

I pause and look at him. He smiles and nods in encouragement.

"Eventually, we started getting more and more job offers. Some of the jobs were people in need who couldn't afford the high fees of the more established security companies. I started meeting with clients and organizing assignments. We discovered I had a knack for being bossy and people listened to me after they realized I was serious and could get the job done. One thing led to another and I started taking more and more responsibility, until I basically took over the running of Phoenix. Of course, many thought I'd fail—

mainly the heads of other companies and other people here and there. They said, 'Women are weak, they have no place in this type of work,' but I proved them all wrong."

"How'd you do that?" He asks.

"I convinced the guys to train me. I already knew the basics of self-defense from having grown up with a military father and then being an Army Ranger's wife, but I wanted to know more. I wanted to know so that I wouldn't be a hypocrite—I wanted to know the job I was sending men out to do. I busted my butt off. There were times I couldn't move because my body hurt so much, but I didn't quit. I ended up going on some assignments when Carmen and Jacob could watch the girls; the less dangerous ones. People saw the effort and dedication I put into the company and word spread that I wasn't a pushover. It was enough for me to gain the respect necessary to be taken serious and things kinda went outta control from there. Jobs started coming to us from everywhere—word spread about the dedication and ability of the corporation. It seemed like overnight we were the new "it" company, the ones to hire, and we started recruiting more and more people. In the span of a few years, Phoenix has gone from small-time to being worldwide.

"Our main headquarters are here with me, where I meet with clients and look at all the jobs that come our way. I analyze and decide which ones we take on, and then I distribute them to the proper team. Jax, Damon, Duke, Zeke, and Gunner—they are located in different parts of the country and each is in charge of their own team. When I agree on a job, I hand it off to the team it fits the most or whoever is closest—depending on the situation. We also specialize in quick in-and-out jobs that are extremely dangerous and often not wanted by other companies. As opposed to when the team members were in the military, at Phoenix they get paid a tremendous amount of money."

"Why didn't I know this before? I mean, how could I've not known? I—I had a friend watching over you through the years and I never heard anything . . ."

"What I do within Phoenix isn't a secret," I tell him, "but it's also not public knowledge. If you're outside the business, then you couldn't have known. I go by F.C. Duval and I try to keep my picture out of the public eye. I figured only those that do business with us need to know."

"Or maybe he did it on purpose, that fucker," Zane says. "He'd do something like this as a joke and have a laugh when I finally discovered the truth. Why didn't you tell me before?"

"At first I couldn't tell you," I tell him. "I didn't know you and everything was so new. After . . . well, I was scared."

"What do you mean?"

"I was scared you would look at me differently. That you wouldn't understand or you'd be intimidated. When I retired and started working at Phoenix, many didn't understand. Then when I heard about you and Jake, I got scared."

"Why'd that scare you more?"

"Because," I reply, "you said you fell for the girl you heard so much about and met all those years ago. I'm no longer her, Zane. I've changed—there's no more athlete or carefree young girl with stars in her eyes. The ruthless business woman I've become differs greatly from the woman you see. It's not just about the money, but also the decisions I make, things I have to do, and the orders I give—they're not always "nice." When it comes to Phoenix, I'm not the sweet loving family woman you see and I show the world. I have another side to me that only a few encounter. The power I hold within the corporation can be threatening to some, and I was afraid you'd be intimidated or feel undermined. I've seen it happen before with Julia's marriage—her fame and success became a problem—and I didn't want that to happen to our relationship, especially since we had just begun. But mostly, I didn't know how to tell you, and I'm afraid you won't accept the person I am now."

"Faith." Zane looks me in the eyes. "I fell for your beauty and the emotions—the loyalty and love—you gave. I saw the look in Jake's eyes when he spoke about you and how he knew you were always there for him. When he thought he was dying, it was you he thought about and I wanted that. I'd just been betrayed by my best friend and I needed to know there was still loyalty, honor, and love out there. You represented all that and I wanted it. Now, I love the woman you've become. I got to know you and yes, you've changed, but everyone changes. It's how and why we change that matters."

"You really believe that?"

"Yes, Faith," Zane replies. "I believe that. You changed because you needed to survive. No matter how many people were there to help or how much money was at your disposal, your world was torn apart the moment Jake died—your dreams, your future were gone in a blink of an eye. Some people aren't strong enough and they fall apart, but you've fought hard to keep going and you've kept your family together. Not only that, but you didn't let Jake's dream die. You fought hard along with Gunner to make their dream a reality. How can I not love the woman capable of all this?"

"I don't know, Zane. I have baggage just like everyone else."

"Well, I do love you," Zane tells me. "And you're right; everyone has baggage, including me, but I love you. Everything about you. And it's my job to help you overcome any of your fears. I'd be a fuckin' fool to walk away from you just because some things aren't perfect. Perfect is overrated, if you ask me. I'd rather be fucked up with you than not have you in my life at all. I love you, Faith, and nothing is gonna change that. Like I told you that night at the club, I've got you now and I'm not letting you go."

"Are you okay with all this?" I wave my hand in a circle.

"Truth?" He asks. At my nod he continues. "I wish you were still playing because I've seen videos of you on the field and I've seen you play. I've seen how your face lights up and you're fuckin' incredible out there. It's cruel to keep that talent from the world, and I know it's what you love—your passion. But I'm not gonna demand you quit a company you've helped build. That would be me telling you I don't believe in you and that's not true. I respect and support you in anything you want to do. I'm your man and my job is to be here for you when you need me and to love you with all my heart."

"Thank you, honey," I hug him tight. "You're right, I do love playing and it's crossed my mind to go back at times, especially when I see Rylee play, but there's so much more to consider now."

"Faith, anything you decide, I'll support. If you remain the 'Boss Lady' at Phoenix, I'm behind you and if you ever decide to go back, I'll be your loudest fan. Well, the next loudest following Skylar because that girl sure as hell has a set of lungs on her."

We both laugh at his comment because it's true. Skylar is incredibly loud when she's cheering for her family and friends. She may be little, but she's fierce and loud.

"There are gonna be some changes around here," Zane tells me. At my raised eyebrows, he continues, "Tomorrow I'm talking to Gunner and I'm applying for a job. It's time for me to take the job offer Jake made sure was left open for me all these years."

"But you like being a fireman, Zane," I exclaim.

"Like, yes, but I don't love it. I needed to become a better man after the way I was living my life—I wasn't a very nice person. I felt my soul was dark and I wanted to become a man worthy of you. One you'd be proud to be with and know."

"Zane, I'd be proud of you regardless," I tell him.

"I know you would. But remember, to me you were larger than life when I first heard about you and then when I saw you, I knew I wasn't good enough for you being jaded as I was. Like I said, I felt my soul was blackened by a lot of the things I did—the way I behaved. I needed to accept myself. Every time I went through a fire, I felt my soul lighten and I grew to like myself. I could finally look at myself in the mirror and see a man worthy of a good woman. And as bad as it sounds, it gave me the adrenaline rush I missed from my days in the military."

"I'm with you in whatever you decide," I tell him. "If you want to go back into the military, because I know that is one life that's hard to leave, I'll support you wholeheartedly."

"No, Faith, I ain't going back to that. I've done my time and I'm happy here with you and the girls—I want to be able to spend time in your bed and not be gone all the time. I want to be able to say no when I want to, and I think Phoenix might be the place for me. That and I'll be able to see you at work and keep you out of trouble."

"Oh! Now the real reason comes out," I tease.

"Yeah, baby," he says, laughing with me. "I need to keep my eye on you and know how you are. And I have an 'in' with the boss."

"Well, I say you're hired."

"Babe, I have to talk to Gunner. I don't want people to say I fucked my way into a job," he teases.

"You're such a dork! But I love you anyways."

"Yeah, you love me and you're gonna be mine finally, Faith."

"Zane, I'm already yours."

"Not this way, love."

"What do you mean? What way?" I ask. He puts me aside and then he kneels in front of me on both knees.

"This isn't the way I was planning on asking but I think this is the right time to tell you that I want you to be my wife," he says, opening up a small black box. Inside I see one of the most beautiful rings I've ever seen, a Tolkowsky platinum engagement ring—my dream ring. "I'm kneeling on both knees for you, love, because you're a woman that deserves a man to grovel to even be in your presence, and I want you in my life forever. I want to live the rest of my life with you by my side. There will be times you'll want to kill me, but I promise to make every one of those times up to you. I promise I'll do my damnest to make you and the girls happy. I love you more than words can express—I love you with all my heart and soul. I'll spend every day for the rest of our lives loving you and working my ass off to make you smile. You, the girls, and our future children are my world—my most precious treasures. I'll protect y'all with my life. Marry me and make me the happiest and proudest man in the world. I love you, Faith. Always and forever."

With tears running down my face and no more secrets between us, I look at the man who's brought me back to living for myself. Before, I was a shell of myself—I existed only for my girls and Jake's dream. That one knock, so many years ago, on my door brought my world crashing down around me. My dreams, my hopes, my future with Jake disappeared in the blink of an eye. If it wasn't for Julia, my daughters, and Phoenix, I would have given up and gone into a dark, dark world. I loved Jake with all my heart—with all the love a young woman untried in the pain of life could give. I was so innocent, I thought I could plan my life, but I was wrong— so wrong.

Life had other plans for me. I was meant to change, to experience the loss of forever. Everything in life happens for a reason. You may never know immediately why but through time, the reason arises. Jake and I were meant to experience our forever for just a short amount of time, and I will always treasure our moments and memories. My life with Jake was an enchanting dream, similar to a fairy tale—he was my Prince Charming and our love was beautiful, but I took that life for granted. I assumed we had our whole lives together.

But now, I'll never assume, I'll never take anything for granted. Life can be short and it's meant to be cherished and treasured—every second, every moment. Now, I'll love harder. I'll love fiercer. And I will not be afraid—I *will* take a leap of faith because love is an amazing, wonderful, and precious gift. I've been blessed twice in one lifetime with the love of two strong, courageous and protective men. I have a second chance at love and I'm going to take it. I want to show my girls that love will always find a way. And, Zane is a man who accepts me for *me*—the woman I was, the woman I became, and the woman he will help me become.

"Yes, Zane. Yes. Yes. Yes," I tell him through tears and laughter. "I'll marry you and I'll always cherish our love. I'll show you every day of our lives how much I love you. You've shown me how to fully live again—thank you. I promise you that I'll always be your biggest supporter and I'll stand by your side. I love you, Zane. Always and forever."

"Yes, Faith," he tells me as he takes me in his arms and kisses me. "Forever, Faith. Forever, my love."

Zane

She said yes! She's going to be my wife, mine in every sense of the word—she's my woman, my queen, my treasure. My reason for being.

I'm going to give her the wedding of her dreams.

"Thank you, Jake," I silently say to him. I know he can't hear me, but I still need to thank him. "Thank you for believing in me, for being my friend, and for letting me take care of your treasures. I will love Faith and the girls with all my heart and soul. Always, my man."

I close my eyes and I hold my future wife in my arms.

Finally.

∝∽

Jake

I'm watching the woman I love in the arms of a good man. That old gypsy woman was right all those years ago. The ghost with the purple eyes now has my treasures and I couldn't be happier—I wasn't meant to be with them forever like I planned, but I know they'll be taken care of.

Zane is a good man and deserves the happiness and love he'll experience with my Faith.

Now, I just have to make sure that my girls and their siblings, along with our friends, find their own love and happiness. I may not be with them, but I will always watch over them.

Always.

Forever.

Epilogue

It's funny how life happens. It's during the times you're at your weakest that you find your strength. For me, that time was when I lost Jake. I thought my life had ended. How was I supposed to live without my other half? How was I supposed to survive without the man that showered me with love and affection from the first moment we met? His death almost killed me, but I survived and became a strong woman.

I became a woman strong enough to handle Zane. He drives me crazy and makes me want to punch him at times, but I love him nonetheless.

I'll always love Jake and he'll always be in our hearts, but now Zane is part of our lives and our family. With him life is different. Love is different. He's a cocky alpha male who I want to smother at times, but he makes me happy and he loves our girls. I couldn't ask for a better man to love me, cherish me, and support me in life. He's my partner, my love. And he accepts me.

I had to remember all this when he only gave me three months—*just three whole months* to plan my dream wedding. I freaked out and demanded more time. I almost threw a tantrum fit for the brattiest toddler, but he put an end to that in seconds. I remember Zane gently taking my face in between both his hands, cradling it and looking into my eyes.

"Babe, I've waited *years* to make you mine. It's three months with you planning our wedding, or I will. Just remember our shopping trip in Dallas and how successful I was at picking out dresses and shoes. Do you really want *me* to plan our wedding? Either way, in three months, you're gonna be mine in God's eyes."

After that little reminder, I got everyone—Carmen, Angélica, Momma, Jackie, Julia, and the girls on board—and three months later, I walked down the aisle on my Daddy's arm, dressed in my dream Pronovias lace wedding gown, to Zane. When Father

Federico announced to our family and friends: "I present to you Mr. and Mrs. Zane Alejandro Knight," a breeze passed through the church, twirling the purple rose petals Skylar had thrown out. They swirled around us magically, like in a movie, and we knew Jake was there with us.

I'm truly blessed.

The reception that followed was beautifully decorated in purple and charcoal gray colors. It was loud, fun, and everyone had a great time. As soon as possible, Zane and I made our escape, leaving the girls with Carmen and Jacob.

Our wedding night was amazing and beautiful. We spent all night worshiping each other's bodies and celebrating us. We finally belonged to each other in every way possible. That orgasmic wedding night is what got me into this predicament now.

✎∽

2 May 2014

"**O**w!" I moan loudly.

The contraction brings me out of my thoughts and back to reality. The reality that if Zane doesn't hurry his ass up, I'm going to give birth to our children in his *brand new* truck.

Yes, children.

Not only did Zane barge into my life, but he invaded my womb with his super-sperm and got me pregnant with twins!

"Honey, if you don't step on it, these little jellybeans are gonna come and they're gonna ruin the inside of your new toy. My grandma drives faster than what you're going!"

"Babe, I'm hurrying. You shoulda told me you've been in labor since *this morning!*"

"*EXCUSE ME?!* Are you blaming *me* for this? Oh hell, no! You do NOT want to start with me right now. I'll go off on your ass. Right. This. Second. Got me?" I practically shout at him.

Blaming me for this. Humph.

"I was trying to be considerate and allow you to watch your game, but now I see what being a considerate wife gets me—a husband who drives slower than molasses and blames me for being in labor with his children!"

"Okay, okay. I didn't mean for you to get all worked up. Thank you for letting me watch the game, but next time, just forget about it and let us go to the hospital. I hate seeing you in pain and honestly, I fear for my life. You look kinda scary right now, like you want to rip me apart."

"AAAAAAAAGGGGGHHHHHHH!"

This contraction hits hard and I grab on to the "oh shit" bar and lift my hips. I'm trying to do those breathing techniques they show you in Lamaze class, but it fucking hurts too much.

"Honey, right now, I want to rip your dick off and feed it to you. It's your fault I'm in such pain. If you didn't get so happy to see me all the time, I wouldn't be pregnant."

"Breathe, baby. Like this. He-he-whooooo, he-he-whooooo." Zane shows me, making the facial gestures you can't help but make when you do the Lamaze breathing, making me laugh. He looks ridiculous but he's trying to help. And he's smart, choosing to not defend his insatiable cock.

"Stop. You're making me laugh. Agh!" I groan, trying not to laugh.

"Yes! We're here."

He pulls up to the emergency room entrance and stops the truck. He doesn't even turn it off before jumping out and running to help me out. He picks me up and gets me out, but doesn't put me down; instead, he carries my *very heavily pregnant* body through the doors, ignoring the orderlies yelling at him to move the truck. He gets me to the front desk.

"My wife's about to give birth. She needs helps NOW! Or she's gonna kill me—she blames me, you see."

The poor nurses, seeing the distressed future father and my sweaty face with clenched teeth, get the idea and rush to help. I inform them I've been in labor since morning, but it didn't start getting painful until about thirty minutes ago. They get me into a delivery room and call to inform my doctor of my arrival.

I get changed into my hospital gown and get into bed. The real work is about to begin . . .

Half an hour later at 8:37 p.m. on May second, Zane Alejandro Knight II is born at six pounds, four ounces and measuring nineteen and a half inches. Ten minutes later, his younger brother, Jacob Orlando Knight, makes his entrance into this world weighing six pounds, two ounces and measuring nineteen and a quarter inches. Two very big boys—no wonder I was as big as a house.

"They're beautiful, Zane," I say in awe of my baby boys.

"No, they're not beautiful; they're handsome little men," Zane corrects me. "Thank you, Faith. Thank you for taking a chance on me, for making me the happiest man in this world. For giving me two beautiful daughters and for giving me my two boys. Thank you for loving me. I love you with all my heart always and forever."

Wiping tears off my cheeks—I'm blaming the hormones—I tearfully say, "It's me that's thankful, honey. You gave me a new life. You came into my life and didn't take no for an answer. You didn't let my fears conquer me and you made me fall in love again. You made me whole again. I love you, Zane. Always and forever."

"Forever, Faith, and always. Now, I'll be right back. I'm gonna go get the girls before they drive our parents crazy, and I'll bring Julia along since she so kindly let me be in the delivery room with you by myself."

We laugh. He hands me our sons and gives me a tender kiss on the lips. He kisses both their little heads and goes out to the waiting room to bring our daughters to meet their brothers and my best friend to be by my side.

I lay back with my little boys and start to feed them. It's awkward at first, but I make it work.

I'm a very lucky woman. I've been blessed to find love twice in a lifetime. The first time, our time was cut short. This time, no matter how long we have, I'll treasure every moment as if it's our last. I know how quickly life can change and I'm never taking anything for granted again. Every moment will be a precious memory.

No matter what life throws at you, you're given this life because you're strong enough to live it. You just have to have faith. All you can do is stand strong, live your life at its fullest, and take a leap of faith.

With Zane's love, I emerged like a butterfly from its cocoon and learned to truly live again—for my children, for my love, and for myself.

∞

This is the end of Faith and Zane's story—for now.
More stories will follow, each of a different couple.

Acknowledgements

Writing this story was a journey for me. For years, I thought about writing, but I didn't have the courage. I was embarrassed, and I was scared—what if I failed? It took years, but thanks to a supportive husband and a chance meeting by the pool, I decided to take a risk, and Faith and Zane's story emerged. I couldn't have done it without the encouragement and support of my family and some amazing friends.

To my husband: Thank you for believing in me from the very beginning. You've been on my case to write for years—"You read all the time, you should write—you'd be good." And now I'm listening. Thank you, love, for going out and buying my laptop when I started to jot down my ideas on your computer, and for encouraging me. Thank you for being understanding about the huge pile of clean and dirty laundry in the laundry room, the piles of dirty dishes in the sink, the pigs-in-a-blanket dinners, for putting the children to bed, and for falling asleep on the couch while I wrote so we could be together. But most of all, thank you for believing in me when I didn't believe in myself. I love you always and forever, my love.

To my two beautiful little monsters: Thank you for being patient and understanding when Mommy was on the couch "working." Thank you for not fighting me during bedtime, making it easy for Daddy to put you to bed, and taking the bribe—"I'll let you stay up until ten when Mommy finishes her book, I promise." And then struggling to stay up when Mommy finally did finish her story. Thank you, my babies—I love y'all always and forever with all my heart.

To my family: Thank you for your support, your words of advice, and for "liking" my author page on Facebook after I finally gathered the courage to tell y'all I had written a book. I apologize for keeping this a secret and I miss and love y'all very much.

To Brandi: That chance meeting by the pool last summer has changed my life. My husband has believed in me for years, but you . . . you pushed me to actually put those voices going on in my head into print. Thank you for showing me that it's possible to dream and follow your dreams and for answering my *many* questions. I know this makes you feel weird because you don't see yourself at her level, but you're my Colleen—she's your inspiration and you're mine.

To Anne: Thank you for taking time out of your incredibly busy schedule for me. Thank you for accepting to give my story a try when I Facebook messaged asking for your help, for giving me a lesson on blog etiquette, and for answering every question I've thrown your way. We've never met in person, but you're one of the people whose support and encouragement has made this journey possible. Thank you for rallying the troops, helping me, and giving me a chance.

To Cassy: Thank you for taking a chance and saying yes to creating my book cover when I messaged you out of the blue with only Brandace's name as a reference. Thank you for telling me to ask all the questions I wanted and for answering them. My book cover is beautiful and I *love* it!

To the awesome beta readers: Christabella, Krystyn, and Kiarra—thank you for answering the beta reader request on Goodreads. Lisa, Carrie, Joanna—thank you for offering your help when I needed more beta readers. And Heidi—oh dear sweet Heidi—you've listened to every freak out session, read every version of this story, and no matter how many times I called and messaged, you were there. Thank y'all for taking time out of your busy schedules and for slaughtering me nicely with your feedback. Y'all are freaking awesome and amazing and I am very grateful.

To my editor: Champagne Book Editing, thank you for making my story so much more readable. When I sent you the file it was filled with typos and you've made them go away.

To my formatter: Tami, you squeezed me into your schedule to fit my deadline. You went back and forth with me with all my questions and changes, and even when I sent you a *long* list of specifics, you didn't complain. Instead, you went above and beyond making the inside of my book beautiful. Thank you so much.

To Debra: Thank you for the amazing cover reveal and exposure. When I told you I was new to all this, you sent me detailed instructions for everything. Thank you.

To Kimie, Kimmy, and Sharee: Thank you for pimping me out and within hours of Facebook messaging me, shocking me speechless.

To Christina, Cybill, Dympna, and Amy: Thank you for reaching out to me, posting my teasers (my crappy first attempts…LOL), pimping me out, participating in the cover reveal, and overall for being freaking awesome to me. Thank you!

To Alicia: Thank you for taking the time to make sure *Leap of Faith* was "perfect." I know this genre isn't your preference and you might've skipped several scenes, but your willingness to read my story (when I needed a new pair of eyes and I was having a small panic moment) means the world to me.

To anyone who will read my book: Thank you. Hate it, like it, love it . . . thank you for taking a chance on me. I'm forever grateful. <3

About the Author

ML is currently stationed overseas with her very supportive and loving husband and two beautiful little monsters. When she's not writing down her "ideas," she can be found trying to catch up on piles of laundry and house work or with her Kindle in hand hiding in her bathroom. Her obsessions are Luke Bryan, coffee, dark chocolate, the color purple, wild berry Skittles and romance novels—the happily ever after kind, of course.

After years of comments from her husband to write and a chance meeting by the city pool that involved a "Fan Girl" moment, ML decided to take a leap of faith into the amazing and exciting world of writing.

She can be found at the following social media and would love to hear from you. <3

Facebook: https://www.facebook.com/MLRodriguezbooks
Twitter: https://twitter.com/MLRodriguez09
Goodreads:
https://www.goodreads.com/author/show/13853543.ML_Rodriguez

Printed in Great Britain
by Amazon